D0912358

THE BARBARIAN OF THEROS

THE BARBARIAN OF THEROS

SKHARR DEATHEATER™ SERIES BOOK 05

MICHAEL ANDERLE

his lean form. Despite the good fortune that had enabled him to become a member of the council, there was no getting the street rat out of him. The instinct to collect and store as much food, coin, and material wealth as he could had served him well.

Fakos looked a little like Micah's sister, although she lacked the innate grace Sera possessed. She was a warrior, no doubt about that, and a fighter to her core. Micah disliked having to deal with the woman. Her violent, sadistic streak made her difficult to control, although Taurin was even more impossible due to his sheer bull-headedness. Leading his clan had given him the kind of attitude she had come to expect from lords and ladies.

Perhaps that was exactly what he was among his kin.

"Otan has already arrived," Fakos announced. "My guards are making sure he won't try anything in this room."

The man in question was another lowly creature who most of the smaller businesses relied on for protection and loans when the guards and the banks refused to help them. He liked to speak about how he helped the helpless, but she had been present to watch him squeeze the life out of those who owed him. The fact that it was sometimes a literal squeezing showed exactly how terrible he was at his job. What sensible businessman would kill those who owed him instead of collecting the coin owed?

It would soon be time for her to depose him from his position, but not quite yet.

A moment later, the fat man pushed through the doors with two guards to escort him. The other three in the room reached quickly for their weapons. There was no trust between the group, and any sign of hostility generally meant that bodies would inevitably fill the sewers.

Micah was the only one who made no attempt to arm herself. It was easy to see that neither of the guards was armed and their presence was merely meant as a show of force to those in attendance.

If violence was the idea, she would have both men strangled

with the innards of their corpulent employer before they could reveal whatever hidden weapons they might have brought in with them.

"Have no fear, my friends," Otan rumbled and gestured to the men at his back to close the doors behind them. "I fear we have greater worries to consider than each other. As I am sure you are aware, trouble returns to this city in the form of a barbarian who caused us a great deal of damage and lost coin. I would see what you have in mind to deal with him."

Deal with him? She didn't like the sound of that. As much trouble as the barbarian could cause unintentionally, she had a feeling he could inflict considerably more damage if he put his mind to it. The man had a talent for destruction.

"We can't allow him to encourage anyone in the city to think that we are weakened," Taurin responded, his tone almost a growl, and shook his head. "If you think the gentry are above trying to take our positions for themselves given the opportunity, I'll have you know how wrong you are."

The dwarf made a point. Micah traced her fingers over her chin and listened carefully to the others as they made their arguments. The lords and ladies of the city portrayed airs of elegance and talked of honor and respect, but they were as money-grubbing as the lowest of thieves. The fact was that they wouldn't think twice about participating in criminal activity if they felt they would not be caught doing so.

Takos appeared to nod slowly in agreement with the rest of the group, but she had a better idea of what the barbarian was capable of and had no intention to commit her people to the job without assurances being made. Micah had a feeling that the first assurance she would seek was that her people were not those who stood toe-to-toe with Skharr.

If she had to guess, the woman would volunteer the services of a couple of her men carrying crossbows and nothing more if that was what the group decided. Tera would not take any sides with it. They had been killed, brought back, and killed again, hundreds of times during the period they had been trapped in there with it. All that was left were husks enslaved to the demon who stared at him, ready to attack.

It was appealing, he decided. Demons were more starved for fun than he was, generally speaking, especially when they were trapped inside a mountain with no way to escape.

The fire flickered in the corner and a figure formed from it. It wasn't even remotely human in shape. Tentacles of flame flickered out from the original fire and surged toward him. They stopped short like they were merely feeling him out, unsure of what he had planned.

He smiled, tilted his head, and watched as the form of a wolf extended from the flames. The eyes of the husks lit up and they started to close on him as well.

Violence would probably be fun too. Unfortunately, what he wanted would bring the whole mountain range down with him.

Most assuredly, he couldn't have that.

His presence grew. The three minds within him coalesced in the face of the threat, drove forward against the flames, and pushed them back into the wall. The whole room shuddered and shook as stroke after stroke from the demon was thrust back relentlessly.

The retreating flames sucked the fire from the husks and all of them flopped, suddenly lifeless, with nothing to hold them in place.

It stopped its attack and sagged against the wall, which allowed him to relax his control of the room.

There would always be a price to pay for displaying himself like that. He looked down and grimaced at his robes. They were in tattered shreds and hung around him like he had grown three sizes and torn the fabric.

The cloak itself was beyond repair, having already been in a threadbare state to begin with.

"Youzzzzzz...." The fire spoke while it continued to retreat from his gaze. "What...are you doing here...Quazzzeeellllllll? Have you come to harass me for fun?"

He sighed and shook his head. "Please. That is more the pastime of my asshole of a cousin, Janus. Our fun comes in different forms and different sizes. We won't enjoy making you suffer but will enjoy what happens when you are released."

The being's flame flickered and shifted from a bright red to yellow, then green. Demons were flighty, the type that didn't subscribe to what was taken as writ outside their home realm, but he could feel the confusion in the one who stood before him.

It was destructive by nature but didn't know what to make of the creature who stood before it.

"Creatures."

"What?"

"We're not only one creature. We hold the same shape but there isn't only one of us. You need to stop thinking of yourself as only yourself. Don't bother believing that you think for me."

"My apologies. I didn't mean it that way. Would you mind having this conversation when we don't have any company?"

"Yes, but it is something to keep in mind."

If the demon wasn't confused before, it was now

"Why are you still here?" Quazel asked and took a step toward the flames. "We assumed your kind weren't fond of this realm. It's a little too cold for your tastes, yes?"

"The mage...who summoned me...closed the chamber once... I was through," the demon admitted. "He did not want...to risk me possessing him...and taking him with me."

"A fair assessment. We've seen what your kind do to humans you take back and might have underestimated the mind behind bringing you here. Had we known, we might have helped him —before he ran face-first into an annoying barbarian, of course."

"What....do you want...of me?"

11

The fire began to grow again and the small smile on his features disappeared.

There was no need to antagonize it.

"We'll get to that," Quazel whispered and waved his hand toward the door of the chamber that had been sealed. "What we need to know is what you want of us."

The rocks began to dissolve and created a path for him to approach the lich's chambers.

"Virgins have always...been my price..."

He smirked and shook his head. "Of course. We never did understand why you'd want virgins. Maybe we never will. We would want folk with more skill and experience ourselves. Call it a personal preference."

CHAPTER TWO

Horse was probably happy to be back.

Hell, Skharr found that being out of the confined spaces of the city was more of a blessing than he thought it would be. Heavens forbid that he become more and more civilized as time passed—something that seemed highly unlikely with the buildings bearing down on him. Still, as he headed out to the paddock where he'd sent Horse to live out his twilight years the first time, he could feel his shoulders miraculously unclench.

"Don't you worry, old'un," Skharr whispered and patted the stallion on the neck. "I won't leave you here, not if you don't want it. I think you'll always have a corner in this place, though. A nice stable with enough apples and a brood of mares to keep you company."

Horse snorted and tossed his mane, which made Skharr laugh.

"Yes, I suppose isolation can be a boon to some, but then you've always had me with you."

He didn't expect an answer but Horse nickered anyway.

"What am I if not company?"

They were already close to Sera's property beyond the city gates, and it was very different than what most farms were. There were fields to be tended but large swathes were measured out into paddocks, where various kinds of livestock browsed the thick green grass. They were mostly horses—and from the size of them, war horses—but a few of the areas held cows instead, with a handful of mules and donkeys mixed in.

Sera appeared to make a point of diversifying her holdings and made sure they were all fat and happy, although the steers would probably not last quite so long in their life of plenty.

The barbarian patted Horse on the neck again. "It isn't too different from what you and I had in mind back in the day. Before that rabid shit showed up and bought us out, yes? Well, maybe more in the way of creature comforts, but I guess that comes when you're much richer, yes?"

The stallion had nothing to say to that, of course. It was a comfortable location to spend a few days, but Skharr could understand how it was the kind of haven that would drive something more accustomed to war into madness. Peacetime was appreciated in short increments, but it wasn't something he would ever be accustomed to. Perhaps the same applied to his four-legged brother.

"Skharr!"

He heard her coming, of course—a young woman with flowing, golden curls and a bright smile. She looked different than how he remembered her. He noticed that her figure was a little fuller and she was less gaunt, with fewer rings around her eyes.

She looked like a woman now, confident and unafraid.

"Ingaret," he replied and let a smile touch his face. "Country life suits you well."

"I think it agrees with me," she commented, flicked her hair to the side, and approached Horse with a calm demeanor.

There weren't many who the beast allowed to approach him

so offhandedly, but he remembered Ingaret, leaned into her hand, and nickered softly.

"We were terrified when you ran away," she scolded and scratched the pale white streak on his forehead. "I thought you had been attacked and ran away to stay alive. There have been reports of wolves in the area from the other farmers."

"When did you find out that he'd come after us?" Skharr asked.

"When Sera returned. We told her the bad news and she laughed and said Horse had caught up to the caravan a few days after you'd left the city. We were happy to hear that you were alive, you big oaf."

The barbarian could only assume that she spoke of Horse and not himself.

"Sera sent word that she wanted to speak to me over the midday meal," he said once she and Horse had finished their affectionate reunion.

"She will return momentarily." Ingaret motioned for him to follow and clicked her tongue so Horse would do the same. "She said she had business in the city for the morning but she would return for the midday meal and that we were to expect you as well."

Within minutes, Skharr could hear the sounds of a horse approaching while Ingaret found him something to drink. It felt a little odd to be served but she had gone about it without him so much as asking for help.

The guild captain seemed to be in her full armor as she approached, although pieces were pulled off by a couple of the servants who followed her to a small veranda he had been led to.

"It is nice to see you again, Skharr," Sera called, pulled a pin from her hair, and let it flow freely down her back as she approached. "I've heard you've been busy since we parted ways."

"I am a mercenary," he admitted and tested one of the wooden chairs before he sat gingerly. "I take work to attack and defend using my particular skills with weaponry in exchange for coin."

"So I've heard. You brought my brother to power, then killed an elder god by the sound of it, all in the few months since I left you. Oh, and two more dungeons. Most don't run one in a lifetime. How many is that for you now in total?"

"Was I supposed to keep count?"

She sat across from him and grinned as she settled and waited for a few servants to approach with warm food that had been prepared for them.

"Yes. Yes, you were."

The warrior narrowed his eyes. She seemed comfortable being waited on. It wasn't something she had revealed about herself when they traveled through the wilderness and it made it difficult to know which part of her was the real one.

"The emperor's sister, sitting and making small talk with a barbarian," Skharr commented, picked up one of the sweetmeats, and tasted it carefully. "I don't suppose the kid so much as sent you a message?"

"He is my half-brother," Sera corrected him. "And given that my mother was disowned decades ago, I doubt he would even know we existed. Well, no, there would have been folk in his court who kept track of all the bastards in case one suddenly demanded that they be recognized as a son or daughter of the emperor."

"So he would know about you?"

"Yes. But I think he would see me as a threat to his power rather than a loving sister. Besides, I've never spent much time with him. I didn't even know he existed for most of my early life, honestly."

Skharr nodded and looked at the small feast set out for them. He wanted to say he wasn't hungry but that was a lie. He had learned long before that food was never a given, and when it was provided in large quantities, it was to be eaten in large quantities.

The best part was that she seemed to agree and piled her plate almost as high as his from the dishes that had been set for them.

"Why would he think of you as a threat?" he asked. "It isn't as though you have a desire to take the throne for yourself, is it?"

The guild captain tilted her head. "Is that my friend Skharr asking or is it the barbarian who brought an emperor to power?"

He could understand her concern—not only for herself but for her sister as well. It was no secret that he had played a major part in bringing the emperor to power, and folk could be forgiven for assuming that he still acted on the new emperor's orders to root out any possible threats to his reign.

"Your friend Skharr, always," he replied softly and shook his head. "Your half-brother seems a decent man, but I am well aware that the gratitude of an emperor has a short half-life. I had no intention to be a part of his government, although he did try to convince me otherwise."

She smiled, took a bite from a chunk of yellow cheese, and followed it with a small piece of apple. "In that case, my answer is no. I am quite content with the life I've built for myself here. Although my sister might have certain aspirations, I doubt she is a threat to his reign either."

"Besides, he'll know better than to try to anger you. I told him, as I beat him into a proper fighter, that you taught me my skills with the blade. He would have to send a godsbedammed army... an army he now commands." Skharr scowled and shook his head. "My apologies if that comes to bite you in the ass and feel free to call on me to help you out of any trouble I might have inadvertently caused."

"I might take you up on that." Sera laughed. "Is it true that you fought a dragon?"

"Fought?"

"Yes. That is what the official story is, of course."

"Of course it is. No, what happened was more along the lines of running desperately away from a dragon."

"In fairness, I can see why they would leave that part out of the tales and ballads being sung. There is no need to portray the new emperor as anything but a mighty warrior with a dead dragon propped behind his throne."

"He'll need a fucking army for that as well."

"A sound point." She leaned back in her seat, most of the food gone from her plate, and released a loud belch that was decidedly unladylike.

She laughed when she saw Skharr's raised eyebrows.

"Do not pretend surprise. You know I might play the lady but am a soldier to my core. That includes eating, drinking, singing, and belching as loudly as possible."

"You left out the copious amount of fucking in exchange for coin."

"I could do with a little of that as well."

The barbarian grinned. "I think Horse could do with some of it too. I hoped he might find himself a home here while I remain in the city. Being closed in a stable is not the life for him. Should he choose to travel with me when I leave again, I'll take him and spare your people the trouble of worrying for his safety."

Sera took a sip from the iced wine and smiled. "I think that could be arranged. His stable is still waiting for him and Ingaret will insist on spoiling him with apples."

"Someone has to."

Once he was assured that Horse was comfortable and enjoying his new quarters, Skharr began his long walk on the road to the city. His easy strides kept him ahead of those who followed—travelers, mostly, who were anxious to reach the gates but also might wish to talk.

He had already been through the gates many times and was easily recognized by the guards. This meant no delay when he slipped through, although a few of them still watched him carefully as he navigated the traffic that streamed through the gates in the afternoon.

A few more caravans had arrived, which suggested there would probably be work for him at the guild the next day if he was interested.

Like Horse, he was not made for a life of peace and plenty. The chances were that he would end up dead in a ditch somewhere or failing that, would return to his people once he'd had his fill.

The Swilling Mermaid was easy enough to find with its massive wooden carving of a gorgeous woman, her breasts on full display and her lower half that of a fish. Skharr avoided most of the folks who headed in and out by entering carefully through the stables.

Most of the hands knew him well enough from his frequent visits to Horse and had no questions when he simply moved to the entrance of the Inn and strode up the steps.

Of course, his usual room was already taken and the innkeeper told him he was meant for finer accommodations anyway. The Lord's Room was generally kept free for those who could afford it and would only settle for the finest of accommodations, and even though Skharr fell in the former category, he was not among the latter.

Still, the down-filled mattress was more comfortable than those stuffed with straw and an elegant bronze bathtub could be filled with warm, scented water. It had been a few times, even though he hadn't asked for it.

He had always been taught that luxuries had a habit of weakening a warrior, but as he moved up a little in the city, he discovered there was little issue with enjoying the luxuries he could afford while he was there.

It was easy enough to justify this with the reminder that he would have more than enough time to suffer once he was on the road again.

A small carafe of wine had been set out for him, and Skharr

took the liberty of filling a bronze goblet with the contents and taking a sip.

"Hmm," he grunted and studied it with interest. It was finer than what was usually served in the Mermaid. Either that meant the innkeeper had saved his finest casks for whoever was housed in the Lord's Room or the man was better stocked than before.

The barbarian decided he would ask and find out what was happening.

The common room was already awash with activity. It was still an hour from what was generally recognized as the peak time when most of the folk descended on the establishment for their evening meal. This inevitably meant that things would probably only get worse from this point forward.

"This is why I prefer the wilderness," Skharr reminded himself when he saw that almost every table was full and more than a handful of patrons enjoyed their food or drink while still on their feet. "There is far too much noise in civilized places."

That wasn't true of the richer regions of the city, of course, but he wasn't quite that wealthy yet.

Still, the numbers in the room were something of a surprise. They seemed to be drawn from the higher classes as well, with men and women who wore finer flax and silk robes calling for spiced wine and the thick lamb chops that were served along with the inn's famous fish stew.

They weren't the only curious changes in evidence either. Skharr noted that the innkeeper—still behind his counter— looked different as well. His chin, which was generally covered in thick gray bristle, was cleanly shaven. All his clothes were in bright colors, and he wore a glossy leather belt with a thick silver clasp to hold his trousers in place.

The barbarian's eyebrows lowered as he approached the man, who was carefully issuing orders to the young men and women serving food and drink while he kept track of the coin paid for everything.

"I'll need to hire a godsbedammed coin counter," the man grumbled as Skharr approached. "Nora! Nora, keep your eye on the folk near the door. They haven't paid for their last round of drinks."

The warrior stopped, leaned his arm on the counter, and turned his gaze on the rest of the common room. "Business is booming."

The innkeeper didn't see him for a few moments.

"Aye, and keeping up with it will be the death of me." He brushed a few strands of hair from his face as he looked at the red-headed giant of a barbarian who stood across from him. "And you, of course. You'll be the death of me as well."

"I always thought that to be the case," he admitted. "But what exactly have I done?"

"All this is your doing, whether you meant it or not." He pointed an accusing finger at him. "I don't know whether to thank you or curse you for what is happening."

Skharr studied the room again and raised an eyebrow as his gaze returned to the grizzled innkeeper.

"I am still unsure as to how I am the cause of this."

"Folk learned that the Barbarian of Theros sleeps under my roof." The innkeeper returned his attention to counting the coins that came in a steady stream while he continued to speak. "And that you were currently under my roof. Your efforts to kill a dragon and throne an emperor have not gone unnoticed, and miserable idiots that they are, they all have decided they must have some of what draws the mighty barbarian here."

"It's the fish soup." Skharr nodded firmly. "And the fact that you allow me to beat the troublemakers in exchange for considerations regarding my room and food."

"Aye, I told them that meself but none would listen. They demanded finer food and drink and were willing to pay. Then more started to arrive. I think the lords and ladies find this inn as an attractive, dangerous option for adventure."

"It's a passing fancy," he said reassuringly. "And besides, that probably does mean less fighting, yes? Which…cannot be a good thing for me."

The innkeeper's laughter was practically mirthless as he shook his head. "I wish that were the case. No, not less fighting. Perhaps even more. See?"

Skharr tilted his head and narrowed his eyes at three young men who all looked and dressed as though they were numbered among the gentry of the city. They already acted belligerent and complained loudly about the lack of seats in the room.

"Watch," the innkeeper muttered, and counted the coins hurriedly, and pushed those that he'd tallied into a small leather purse. He unlocked a chest and put the purse inside, then locked it. "Ever since it became known as an establishment you frequent when you are in Verenvan, some of those who wish to make names for themselves come in to cause trouble. Many now come simply to see what they consider idiots are doing and hope someone decides to fight them."

"Have they caused you too much trouble?"

"Not as much as I have feared yet, but I cannot shake the feeling that it will only be a matter of time. That said, they have been a problem for my serving staff—mostly the young women in my employ."

The barbarian narrowed his eyes and studied the three as they called for drinks. They appeared to be at least partially inebriated already.

"I haven't been in a fight in a while," he admitted and cracked his neck.

"Other than the other night when you had just arrived?" the innkeeper asked, his head tilted.

"That was almost a week ago now," he retorted, rolled his shoulders gently, and took a deep breath. The whole room smelled of thick fish stew mixed with the lamb chops and fresh bread being baked. It was hard to make anything else out. "And that wasn't much of a fight to begin with. I barely worked the muscles in my right arm before the dandy fainted from sheer fright."

The older man tilted his head and narrowed his eyes at him before he extended his hand. "Do you have a gold piece on you?"

Skharr nodded. "Aye. Why?"

"I expect there to be damage. Although if you don't cause too much of it, I'll pay you a gold coin and your room and board will be free."

"That beautiful room you provided for me?"

"It is all I had available. If the truth be told, it was not available when you arrived but that changed when you removed the previous occupant."

It sounded like the beginning of an interesting story, but Skharr had focused his attention on the trio who now started to harass one of the young women carrying platters of food.

It was time to make sure they didn't cause any trouble. He had no inclination to tolerate their nonsense in the only inn in town where he had a mind to spend his evenings. They could find another establishment in the port to have their teeth forcibly removed.

Another of the young women was accosted when she passed them. The larger of the three reached for the back of her dress, yanked on it, and almost pulled her over as he fumbled for what lay beneath.

She evaded the touch deftly and pulled away as the men laughed.

"I'll make it three nights for free if that man needs to be carried out by his comrades," the innkeeper stated angrily.

"Is that your daughter?"

"Aye. But don't kill them."

"Have one for the road ready for me." Skharr nodded, pushed up from the counter, and sucked in another deep breath. This time, he barely noticed the aromas.

"The road is but fifteen paces away."

"I'll be thirsty before the fight ends. Why wait?"

The innkeeper smirked, retrieved a heavy mug, and filled it with the crisp ale the Mermaid was known for before he slid it across the counter for him.

His heart thumped noticeably faster and his fingers practically tingled with anticipation as he watched the three attempt to harass one of the other groups, hoping to drive them out so their table could be claimed.

The young woman who narrowly escaped an unwelcome fondling by the group returned to the counter with an empty tray, her gaze fixed on her father.

"It's about time you hired someone to keep these animals under control," she snapped and pushed a few errant brown curls from her freckled face before she turned to see what her father was nodding at. "Oh…Sir Skharr."

"No sirs here," he rumbled and took a long sip of his ale without looking at her. "Might I help you take a few more beers to the table?"

The way was clear. His fingers ran over the shredded wood that stood in his path and opened an entry from the room where the demon had been trapped into where a certain lich had sustained himself for decades.

Staying alive that long while keeping a monster like a demon at bay when already summoned was impressive enough that Quazel began to feel a little guilty over leaving the mage to summon the demon alone. He'd assumed it would end in utter and complete failure and the demon would rip through the mountain in a revenge-laden rampage—fun for all—before he took the mage to the nether realms to suffer for his idiocy.

But no. He'd managed to remain in place and stall until

someone came along for the demon to possess. It hadn't gone well in the end, but he'd had a solid plan. With a little more support, it might have worked.

It was enough to earn the man a second chance—or lich, rather. It would make no real difference to the ultimate end, but humans tended to get tetchy when they were misrepresented.

He entered a small hallway that brought him to the center of the dungeon, the very pinnacle of where all the power was focused. It remained untouched for now, but that would change in a few moments.

There were signs of a fight here and there—a fallen Black Knight whose armor remained and a few more undead who had been summoned to the lich's defense.

A few more were sprawled on the floor as he approached the staircase leading to the throne, where the lich had seated himself for decades. He saw no sign of a fight at the top, although the creature's remains were clearly visible at the base.

"It was rather unfortunate for him," Quazel whispered and shook his head. "If only he'd had a little help."

"We left him here so he wouldn't have any. The bastard was too stubborn to die the old-fashioned way."

His second voice made a good point. Quazel closed his eyes and felt the power from the pyramid that permeated the room begin to soak into him. It filled him with a pale white light when he placed his hands inside the pile of dust.

There was still an aura of power in that detritus. It wouldn't have surprised Quazel if a few cultures around the world could find a use for the disgusting substance.

Calmly, he whispered a few words and felt the light seep out of him through his hands and into the pile to draw the fragments of the lich together again.

Most of the light in his body slipped out and coursed through the aberration he was bringing back from whatever hellhole he'd ended up in. He straightened and brushed the remaining dust particles that remained on his hand onto his tattered robe.

"Do you think he'll be happy to be back?"

"Do you think we care?" He raised his hand over the lich growing before him. "Come together and meet your coalescence of power, the mighty Wolfgod Togroz. It is time you became what you intended. And may Chaos reign once more."

The inn was too godsbedammed full. They'd been told it was a quiet establishment, the kind that was only noisy and exuberant when there was a fight to be had or a particularly good fiddler was present, ready to rouse the locals.

It seemed as though too many had heard of it and now, they needed to clear a table for them to settle around. Sure, a few of the folks were still eating their meals, but those who had finished and had chosen to remain could find themselves somewhere else to drink.

Callos scowled and tried to find a table where the group in possession of it appeared pleasant, full, and contented enough that they would have no interest in being embroiled in a fight when asked to relinquish it.

The young waitress was making the rounds again, and he stretched his hand to take one of the beers she had on her tray and maybe a little more if it was on offer. He could hear his comrades laughing as he reached out to her and came up a little short of her dress as she closed on them from behind.

"Here are yer drinks," she called, and Callos tried again to reach back for her.

Instead of the soft, pliable, willing flesh of a woman beneath the thin fabric, however, something decidedly unwomanly met his hands. He stretched a little farther and wondered if he'd accidentally grasped a table instead. Whatever he'd taken hold of, it was moving closer.

He looked up at a tree of a man who stood over him as the young waitress retreated.

"Those jewels belong to me," the giant rumbled, reached down, and removed his hand from his groin.

CHAPTER THREE

At first, the encounter seemed interesting rather than intimidating. Callos thought the man only looked taller, but as all three of them stood in front of him, he began to feel that they faced something that was decidedly not human.

Perhaps half-orc, but he'd never seen any with a head of ginger hair. Not only that, they generally had tusks jutting from their bottom lip, no matter what part orc they were.

This one, his somewhat startled brain insisted, was pure human and easily one of the largest he'd ever seen. It didn't help that the slab of meat and muscle still held his hand in an iron grasp.

"Try that again, you godsbedammed maggot-brained slime-sucker, and I'll break your spine so you can learn to pleasure yourself with your tongue," the barbarian said coldly and twisted his hand gently before he released it slowly.

"I didn't mean to grab your bollocks if that's what you mean," Callos replied and tried to jut his chin out in defiance. He didn't want to go against the man on his own but losing face in front of his cronies wasn't an option

"That is clear enough." The giant placed a hand on his

shoulder and the gesture emphasized the very obvious difference between their sizes. "You won't grasp anyone's anything from this point forward. In fact, you have two choices on how to leave here."

"You can't make us walk out of here," Mirka snapped and took a step forward.

Yes, they did have an advantage in numbers, but it still didn't make the ringleader feel any better about their chances.

"I never said that was one of the options." The hulking ginger monster grinned at the idea, which only made Callos feel worse about their chances, but he brought his fist up and hoped to land a clean blow to end the fight in a single surprise strike. Their opponent was big and slow and faced three men who divided his attention. It would only take one clean strike for him to go down.

Not the craziest thing ever to happen, he reassured himself.

If they wanted to start the fight, he wouldn't stop them. He had ached to crush a few skulls after a week of tedious peace, and he'd given them the chance to back away, walk away, and find another inn to drink in—hopefully where the women were more experienced and wouldn't tolerate their offensive harassment.

Skharr grinned, watched the fist that arced toward his face, and leaned his jaw into the blow.

It was hard enough to make his head and jaw ache somewhat, but the man fell back and clutched his hand in agony, and the sight brought enough satisfaction to make it worth the pain.

The other two lunged quickly, hoping to catch him unawares, but there would be no more free punches, not while he was still standing and more or less conscious.

He caught the fist of the one to his right while he stepped away from the other. With a deft twist, he drove the man's fist into his own face before he caught him by the back of the head and pounded it onto a nearby table. The impact upset a handful of drinks and spilled a little of the liquid but didn't topple the mugs.

There was no chance they would leave it at that, of course, and Skharr needed to end the fight quickly before things escalated beyond what he was able to put a stop to.

The one with golden hair who had managed to land a blow early had recovered and he and his friend both surged toward him. They took him by the waist and dragged him over the table to upend the drinks this time. One punch landed hard in his ribs and made it difficult to breathe for a second as he was on his back on the table and with what felt like a fork digging into his back.

The barbarian twisted himself on the hard surface, hammered his right foot into the closest man's jaw, and knocked it and a few teeth out of place before he grasped the first man by his hair and yanked hard enough to pull a few strands out as they both fell heavily.

Skharr straddled his adversary, held him by the throat, and landed a hammer fist into his nose. "A taste of your own medicine, you idiot spawn of Janus' hairy armpit."

A satisfying crunch, a spurt of blood, and a whined cry of pain from his opponent was enough to tell him that he would probably not put up much more of a fight.

Still, there were prizes to be earned and he didn't want him to walk out of the inn under the power of his own two feet.

Another powerful punch dropped the man's head back and blood seeped from his mouth and nose as his eyes closed. A hasty glance assured Skharr that they weren't likely to open again for a while.

The barbarian paused for a moment and noted the silence that had fallen over the Mermaid's common room as if all those present weren't sure what to do next.

Suddenly, a voice broke the silence.

"The fucker spilled my drink!"

He knew there was no chance that one of the fallen would be blamed for the spilled drink and it was confirmed by the hard impact of a mug into the back of his skull. The blow spilled beer and shards down his back.

A collective roar erupted among those who were aching for a brawl, and Skharr forced himself to his feet. He staggered a little but regained his balance and stared at the four men and two women seated around the table he'd fallen on.

"It's like that, is it?" he asked, rolled his shoulders, and readied himself as two lunged at him and tried to beat him back with their fists. "Well, come on then, or are you waiting to finish sucking on your mother's dugs?"

The barbarian absorbed the first blow and grinned as he jerked his whole body forward so his temple crunched into the attacker's nose. The other fist missed and the momentum of the man's swing made him stumble away to knock over one of the smaller tables and spill their drinks while those at the first table rushed at Skharr.

"This is a godsbedammed fucking brawl!" he roared before he was shoved back to upend another table and drag two of his assailants with him.

Sera hadn't thought that things would escalate so quickly. She didn't expect Skharr to live a peaceful life when he had other options available but she had thought he might attempt it while he was in the city—and had suggested it on more than one occasion.

It would never be the rule, of course. Fights tended to find the bastard wherever he went.

Then again, it wasn't like he avoided them and if the sounds that issued from the Mermaid were what she thought they were, he had found himself a decent fight.

Shouts, along with breaking glass, wood, and bone were clearly audible outside, enough to distract her from the vulgar sign the inn was famous for. It wasn't the kind of establishment where she generally spent her time, but she intended to find him, even if it meant throwing a couple of punches of her own.

The guild captain pulled the door open and paused before she stepped inside as a body bounced off the door frame and sprawled across the entrance, groaning softly.

She shook her head, stepped over the fallen man, and looked around.

Half of the common room had descended into chaos. Tables were overturned and dozens of men and women threw punches, protected by the excessive drink in their bodies which kept their fighting spirits up and numbed them to pain.

The other half was backing away but seemed to make no effort to stop the fight. In fact, it appeared as though more than a few cheered a couple of the fighters on.

Skharr was easy to locate in the chaos. Fighters had gathered around him and tried to contain the barbarian and bring him down, but they had very little success. She smirked when he caught one of them across the cheek with the back of his hand. Even against five, he held himself back and toyed with them, although he took a great deal of punishment as a reward for keeping himself in check.

Despite his restraint, the blow was enough to spin the victim into a nearby chair, which broke in the fall.

Instead of wading in to help, Sera approached the counter behind which the owner of the establishment stood calmly, cleaned a couple of mugs, and set them out to be filled by the staff.

"Aren't you going to help your friend?" the man asked when he noticed her.

"How did you know—"

"I've seen the two of you together before. I have an eye for faces and I won't forget yours. Now, will you help him?"

She inspected the melee and saw the manic grin on Skharr's face as he wrestled three of the brawlers to the floor, which brought another group of five down as well.

"Against this crew?" She shook her head, took one of the full mugs, and sniffed it cautiously before she sipped. "He would likely be upset with me if I tried to stop it. I suppose he'll pay for all the damage caused?"

"I asked him to start the fight," the innkeeper muttered with a shrug. "One of the men there tried to put his hands on my daughter and I would not have any of it. I told Skharr to try to avoid killing anyone but to make sure they would not be able to leave under their own power."

The guild captain nodded and sipped slowly, her focus on the brawl. Of all the things folk would be able to picture in Skharr, self-control was likely not among them, but she had seen differently during her time around him. He was the type who could kill a man with a single blow in the right place, but he was toying with those around him to make the fight last longer so he could enjoy it more.

That was something he would do.

Except something was wrong. Sera put her mug down and narrowed her eyes as she studied the crowd around her and tried to determine what exactly was happening. The fighting appeared to be winding down. Skharr was still one of the few on his feet and he breathed heavily and looked bruised and battered. Blood seeped from his mouth as he held off a couple of his opponents.

But one of the men wasn't attacking. He appeared to circle the barbarian, looking for an opening that would catch him unawares.

The flash of reflected light caught her eye, and before the reality of the situation had fully registered, she was already reaching for her sword. The familiar hilt filled her palm and she drew it in a single, smooth motion.

The sound of steel sliding over leather caught the would-be assassin's attention. His gaze flicked to her and the sword in her hand before he lunged at Skharr from the side and thrust the dagger in his hand toward his ribs.

"Skharr, look out!"

The smile vanished from the barbarian's face as he turned his attention to the new threat. He realized the danger he was in barely in time, twisted his body, and jerked his elbow onto the man's wrist.

The knife struck flesh low in his hip but still deep enough for the blade to stick. The barbarian swung his hand powerfully into the assassin's jaw and the man staggered and fell.

Gone was the fun-loving Skharr who was only in it to make the fight last as long as possible. Sera saw something in his eyes— something manic and terrifying as he advanced on the man who tried to back away while still on the floor.

"Where are you going you pus-filled fucking troll's dick skin?" he roared, caught the assassin's skull in both hands, and lifted him smoothly. "I've a mind to rip your godsbedammed heart out and shove it so quickly down your fucking throat that it beats you to death for me."

She looked away as he dragged his assailant to a nearby table and pounded his skull into the wood before he dropped him. The hapless man wasn't old but he lacked the build of a fighter. It seemed ridiculous that he had been sent to try to find a way to kill a man who had problems understanding the concept of mortality.

Stopping the barbarian now would be an effort in futility, and the assassin's screams of pain echoed through the room and made her wince with each sound of fist beating flesh into submission.

As impossible as it seemed, the assassin was still alive. Blood ran from cuts on his cheeks and over his eyes, which had begun to swell closed, but he pushed onto his hands and knees and flailed at a world he was now almost blind to. Skharr stepped forward and kicked him hard in the gut. The man collapsed and curled in a ball.

The warrior paused for a moment, looked at the dagger jutting from his hip, and touched the handle before he focused on the rest of the room.

"Anyone else?" he asked, his hand still on the knife. He seemed unsure if he should pull it out yet. "Are there any others with knives hidden and ready to try to turn a simple brawl between folk into an assassination?"

None of the others looked like they were in the mood to try to take the giant on. Sera imagined that after seeing that he had been toying with them before, they weren't in the mood to face him when he had every intention of beating their skulls in or worse.

A few even began to right the tables and chairs that had been knocked over and picked up the platters, flagons, and mugs from the ground. It would take a fair amount of effort to clean the whole common room, but she had a feeling they would pitch in with that as well.

Skharr hefted the assassin by the arms, dragged him to the door, and flung him out like he was a hunk of dead meat.

Sera sheathed her weapon slowly as he approached the counter, still inspecting the wound in his side.

"How likely do you think it is that the blade might be poisoned?" he asked and wiped some sweat and blood from his cheek with his sleeve.

"Not very," Sera told him as she dropped to her haunches to inspect the weapon. "If it had been poisoned, he would have hoped to swipe you somewhere he could reach easily to let the poison in without engaging you directly. Without...well, letting you beat him to a pulp."

He nodded and smiled as the innkeeper offered him a towel to clean himself with. "Or it could be he didn't know how to handle a poisoned blade. He wasn't much of a fighter."

She shook her head and picked another towel up before she drew the knife deftly from his hip.

"Fuck!' Skharr hissed and looked at the wound as she pressed the towel to it. "Well?"

She raised the knife to look more closely at it. It hadn't gone in too deep and had stopped at his hip bone and left most of the blade without any blood on it.

"There is no sign of poison on it," she said, her head tilted in concentration. "I don't think they would have contracted a poisoner to kill you. Not again."

Skharr nodded and held the towel to his hip to staunch the bleeding. There were a few bruises that needed tending to as well, but Sera had a feeling he would see them all tended to once he had a drink and something to eat.

"How's Horse doing?" he asked as the innkeeper brought him another drink.

"Horse?"

"Aye. Horse."

"Can I get you something to eat?" the innkeeper asked. "I think they have food piling up in the kitchen since the fight started, so it's best if I get some coin out of it."

"I thought you said—"

"You're lucky I don't charge you for all the damage you caused. So, food?"

Skharr nodded and turned his attention to Sera again.

"Horse is…settling in nicely," she replied as she took another sip of the chilled ale. "Ingaret is spoiling him with apples and my horse master says a few mares are willing to meet with him again. The mares want colts and it isn't my desire to keep any from them."

He nodded. "Good."

"Does that mean that you'll remain in the city? Because if not, I might have work for you later in the week—assuming your wounds heal."

"I'll be fine." Skharr growled and shook his head. "And Horse is more than capable of spending time without me as long as there's something to get me out of this fucking city."

"Peace and plenty do not agree with you?"

"They never have."

"I'll send you a message then. When you've healed."

Sera pushed up from her seat and felt both men's gazes following her as she strode to the door. She had a mind to ask the assassin a few questions about who had paid him to attack Skharr.

When she reached the exit, however, he was already gone. Given his condition, she assumed his cronies had carried him off to report his failure.

"I doubt that'll play out well for you," she muttered and kept her hand on her blade. The man would likely not last the night.

Darkness had fallen. They had warned him that Skharr was a beast of a man who would require considerable cunning to kill. The fight that broke out felt like the perfect moment where good fortune and opportunity came together.

Yarin had always been a lucky fucker. Everyone who knew him said it and he'd never doubted it until the woman had suddenly appeared with her sword and shouted a warning when his blade would have cut into the giant's spine and severed it.

Instead, he'd caught his hip—and a beating.

Blood seeped from what felt like a dozen wounds.

It was probably only a few, though—a couple of cuts around his eyes that he knew of. His ribs were broken but his stomach hurt the worst. The beast had hammered two strikes into his

CHAPTER FOUR

"I thought you killed the dragon."

Skharr looked up from the bandage on his side. It was sloppy work done by himself, but there wasn't exactly a line of folk who wanted to make sure he was well enough to fight.

That was probably his fault. But the amulet he wore was already working to heal the wound and it itched fiercely.

The rest of the bruises had begun to turn from purple to a sickly yellow, which indicated that they were also in the process of healing. It would be a few days at least until he was in full fighting form, and they would be an ache-filled, painful few days.

"Skharr? Are you still in this world?"

He nodded slowly. "Sorry."

"I heard that an attempt was made on your life," Pennar said and inspected the bandage. "One can only hope they continue to mistake your heart for your hip, eh?"

He couldn't help but agree with that.

"But why are you here looking for work?" the guildmaster asked and looked at the papers set out in front of him on his desk. "My position here does provide me with a few benefits, one of which is knowledge, and I happen to know you are a rich man. And now you've killed a dragon and collected its hoard as well?"

The barbarian shook his head. "They honestly spread the story about how we killed a dragon, did they?"

"Do you have a mind to contradict them?"

"Well, the dragon is still alive as far as I can tell." Skharr took one of the contracts from the table, only to have it snatched from his hands by the man opposite him. "The way I saw it, dozens of men were killed, horses were eaten, and we managed to sneak past it and hide. It isn't the stuff of legends and ballads, I know, but in the end, what is?"

Pennar laughed. "I have seen and heard enough bullshit tales to know when one smells of it, but a few of your tales that I know to be true... well, they do make a man wonder about certain things. But you should know that even if you do not have the hoard yourself, there will be many who think you do. It's something to keep in mind."

"Well...shit." Skharr tried to keep the grimace of disgust off his face but wasn't entirely sure he was successful.

"On the other hand, I do have at least seven different requests from the good ladies up the hill for your services." The man drew a handful of scrolls from under his desk. "You were asked for specifically, of course, and they await your convenience."

He cradled one of the bruises on the side of his skull and shook his head slowly. "I'd rather not. That is not the kind of attention I seek this day."

"Rich women wanting your body?"

"That would be acceptable. But there are always...complications. And the richer they are, the more complex their demands turn out to be. I have to fight my way into their beds and then there are suitors and husbands left upset who I have no mind to deal with. The last one had me poisoned, you know?"

"But...you did murder him in the end, yes? At his wedding."

Skharr smirked and nodded. "True."

"One of them even insisted that her measurements be sent with an artist's depiction of what you could expect."

"An artist's depiction?"

Pennar opened one of the scrolls and withdrew a small piece of parchment that portrayed a young woman with bright red hair curled on cushions and wearing absolutely nothing.

"By Theros' balls," the man whispered. "They should find a name for that mountain range."

The barbarian couldn't help but nod in agreement. "I'll call them the Twin Peaks of Perfection."

"Oh, right." The guildmaster took an instinctive step back and swallowed. "My apologies. I forgot."

Skharr narrowed his eyes at the man in confusion. "What for? I've no idea how Theros feels about his balls or their invocation, no matter how holy. But a woman of such proportions would likely have his attention as well."

"Shouldn't you be offended?"

"Because you called on his balls?" The barbarian shrugged and felt a twinge of pain in his shoulders. "If he has a problem with what you have to say, he can tell you himself. I'd rather not have his voice in my ear again. And if the woman is offended by an accurate assessment, maybe an artist's depiction should not have been sent."

"Hold…you've spoken to him?"

"Too often. The last time, he was angered over what occurred between me and one of his closest followers. It would appear that he thinks of me as a bad influence."

"And?"

"What is there to say?" Skharr sighed. "I am a DeathEater. If he wishes to be annoyed when I follow my nature, I cannot stop him. And if he had an issue with his paladin, he should have told her himself."

"Her?"

Skharr paused, held a hand up, and closed his eyes. Maybe a

few mugs of ale with his morning meal had not been the wisest choice.

"This information remains between you and me, understand?"

The guildmaster raised his hands. "Say no more."

"Have you any other work for me? Something that does not involve the rich, powerful, and bored of this city?"

"Rumors of problems for the most part." Pennar waved his hand at the stack of papers on his desk. "There have been reports of outlaws near Yortun on the coast and problems with a group of Orcs taking over some farmland. That is the kind of problem that has crossed my desk more often of late. A group of mercenaries traveled that way a week ago. There were some problems here in the city with thieves. There is a bounty out on a few killers who were rumored to haunt the Wetland Barrow section of the city."

"Nothing major then?" Skharr asked. "I could check on the blade I am having built. I'll need a script for the blacksmith to draw from my account with the guild. Is that possible?"

"I can arrange for it to be possible. You commissioned work from the AnvilForged clan, yes? They are well-regarded by the guilds, so any writ you have with them will be honored." Pennar reached into one of his drawers and withdrew a piece of blank parchment. "It's enchanted so any bank mage will know the hands of the signatories. It should prevent a pickpocket from being able to relieve you of your coin."

He took the blank parchment and inspected it carefully before he tucked it into his coin pouch. "Much appreciated, Pennar."

"I'll always look forward to our conversations, DeathEater."

The barbarian bowed his head slightly and turned to move to the door of the Guild Hall before he paused. "Should anyone ask for me, you know where I am housed, yes?"

"The Mermaid."

"Of course."

track of him. Those who had wanted him dead perhaps wanted to know if he planned an attempt to exact retribution.

Skharr doubted that he would. A message had been sent with the man who had made the attempt and hopefully, those who had a mind to see him dead would know how poorly that would end for them if they tried again. Still, he had learned from an early age never to bet on the humans being intelligent—not that any of the other races were much better.

As casually as he could, he stopped in the middle of the abandoned street and watched two figures approach him. Both were heavyset and larger around the shoulders than most—the kind that usually resulted from laboring for hours over a blacksmith's anvil or cutting wood in the forest.

These, however, looked like neither blacksmith nor woodsman. One was larger than the other—larger even than he was, which made him wonder if he was a half-orc or something similar. There weren't many of those in the world any longer and certainly not in this region, but he could soon see the tusks protruding from under his bottom lip.

He was certainly not a full-blooded human, that much was certain. Skharr inched backward and watched the two continue toward him in the narrow street. It seemed highly unlikely that they weren't waiting for him, and if he had to guess, he would have put coin down on these two being who the children had warned of his impending arrival.

"Out of the way," he stated sharply. He could see no weapons aside from the knife he'd secured on his belt and a small club the human carried. The other didn't appear to need any weapons. He clenched his fists and seemed more than ready for a fight.

It soon became clear that they wouldn't move out of the way. The barbarian took a deep breath. If he wasn't still aching from the night before, he would have welcomed a little gentle exercise in the form of a brawl in the middle of the street. As things stood, though, he would need to find another way through it than a blind charge into the two of them.

The human moved first and tied his thick brown curls back behind his head before he darted forward. He aimed a kick at Skharr's right leg and swung his club toward his head. It was an opening attack and not designed to deliver a killing blow. The barbarian sidestepped the first strike and leaned to the side to avoid the second. He watched the half-orc circle him in an attempt to corner him on the street.

"You might have wanted to bring more help in," Skharr commented, rolled his shoulders, and let a small smile touch his features. "Stopping me from running away might have been a wise move too if you had any fucking brains between you."

Neither answered. They were both professionals and not the kind to be incited by much of anything.

The warrior put them a step above what he had seen at the Mermaid, which meant something else was happening as well. Neither carried the weapons to kill him, for one thing. Admittedly, the orc could probably do so with his hands and the club would do the job eventually, but a professional team would attack with daggers to finish the fight quickly and efficiently. The longer it took, the higher the chance that their prey would run or that someone would come along and interrupt the fight by calling the guards.

The half-orc attacked next. He surged forward with a rumbled roar as he powered into Skharr and drove him back into a nearby wall. The breath rushed from the barbarian's lungs but he still pushed his elbows into the half-orc's back with all the strength he had in him.

A loud thud resulted and he gained the few inches he needed to push himself out from the massive attacker's grasp. Unfortunately, he careened directly into the path of the club that arced toward his head.

"By Janus' hairy vermin-crusted ballsack," he bellowed and

dragged in a breath. It had only been a glancing blow but he still saw stars and staggered back a few steps instead of being able to press his advantage. The big assailant was a little slower and while he was impressively strong, Skharr knew he could work around him. The man with the club, however, knew to wait for that, cutting his avenues to flank them, and making sure that there was nowhere for him to be except in the path of the hulking mass of a half-orc.

Something different was needed. He had to find another more expedient way to end the encounter. Attacking the human seemed like the only option. If he could get him out of the way quickly, it would make it easier to navigate the narrow streets with only the half-orc to worry about.

He could feel that the cut on his side had opened again. The amulet he wore took time to effect full healing and the wound seeped blood into his bandage and down his trousers. He grimaced and accepted that he had to ignore it for now and worry about it later when this was over.

"Let me guess," he goaded, hoping to rile the man into an attack. "Your father was a fucking butt-ugly goblin half-breed and your mother a scrawny-assed troglodyte. I guess that makes you a godsbedammed brainless bag of bones and shit."

His ploy failed and when the half-orc attacked again, he inched toward one of the walls and waited until the last moment before he flung himself to the side. His large assailant barreled past him and into the wall and gouged a chunk of it out with his tusks. The barbarian rolled over his shoulder and the motion triggered a shockwave of pain to sear through his body as he pushed to his feet. He paused and waited as the human rushed forward, swinging his club.

Skharr darted to the side and grinned when the club dug into the wall as well. It wasn't deep enough that it stuck but it was sufficient to buy him a moment. In this instance, a moment was all he needed. He lunged forward and ducked under another wild strike as he crashed into the man and drove him backward.

"How much fucking coin am I worth?" he roared, grasped the man's wrist, and twisted him to keep him between himself and the half-orc. "Who is the godsbedammed goblin-spawned ass-fucker paying to have me killed?"

"Do you honestly think either of us will talk?" the human asked and pushed against the tight grasp on his arm. "Veron, get the fuck up!"

A flicker of motion caught the barbarian's eye a moment before the man in his grasp stiffened and his eyes widened as he looked at his chest.

Skharr turned quickly to look in the direction the movement had come from. He narrowed his eyes and swept his gaze across the face of the building until he was rewarded with a shifting motion that indicated a presence looking down on them.

A hooded figure stood in a nearby window and held a crossbow with no arrow in the slot. With another small and almost imperceptible movement, the figure was gone. The barbarian lowered his gaze to where a crossbow bolt protruded from his assailant's back. The man's body sagged in his grasp.

"No! Lauto!"

He looked up from the dead man in his arms a moment before the mountain of half-orc collided with him to drive both him and the body into the wall. The attacker wrapped his arms around them and the full power of the creature caught him by surprise.

Creature certainly felt like the right term for what he now experienced. The assassin roared in a language the warrior couldn't understand. It sounded like an actual language, though, and he decided it must be orcish.

He had little time to consider that further as even with a man impaled on a crossbow bolt between them, the half-orc squeezed hard enough that the barbarian found it hard to breathe.

"Fucking…godsbedammed maggot-riddled troll turd," he yelled, although it was hard to hear himself through the bellows from Veron.

It didn't seem right, but he was left without any other options and before he could waste time trying to find one, he lashed out and thrust his arm between the half-orc and his wounded comrade to deliver a powerful strike to his attacker's groin.

Veron gasped, stumbled back, and clutched his painful nether regions. Skharr dropped to his knees, sucked in a deep breath, and regained his composure as he watched the half-orc lean against the wall, the rage still in his eyes.

"Why are you looking at me like that?" he asked. "It's not like I killed him."

His words only seemed to enrage his assailant more and he pushed his massive bulk clear of the wall.

"I'll fucking kill you!"

"Stop talking about it and get it done then, you lump of lard and pig shit." Skharr snarled a challenge, yanked the bolt from Lauto's body, and readied himself as the half-orc rushed toward him again.

He needed to stop talking in the middle of a fight, he thought inconsequentially.

A rock-like fist collided with the side of his skull and he fell back. The world spun around him and made it difficult to focus on much of anything except the half-orc, who surged into another attack with murder in his eyes. The barbarian didn't think. He simply thrust the bolt out and buried it into his assassin's shoulder and pushed as hard as he could to force him back.

It wouldn't be enough to kill him but it would level the field somewhat.

Veron jumped clear and shook his head as Skharr straightened, drew a deep breath, and tried to clear his head.

The half-orc made no effort to attack again.

Instead, he stared at his wound, suddenly unsteady on his feet.

"It wasn't that bad," Skharr rumbled and took a deep breath. "Shake it off, you overgrown fucking butt-faced idiot and let's have a proper fight."

Veron didn't seem to hear the goading and with an odd expression on his face, he touched the bolt and tried to pull it out as he dropped to his knees.

The warrior stepped closer and narrowed his eyes as he approached. "Veron? Blood doesn't make your stomach roil, does it? That would be a terrible thing for a hired blade such as yourself."

The half-orc didn't answer and instead, sagged against the wall as if he'd lost all the considerable power he had in him to remain upright.

"You cannot possibly die from a shoulder wound," Skharr protested and tried to think of some explanation that would stop his mind from reaching the only unwelcome conclusion. "Did I miss something? I have never heard that orcs were vulnerable to shoulder wounds?"

"Poison," Veron whispered. "A poisoned bolt...supposed to kill you, not...not Lauto."

He scowled and glanced at the dead man in the street with them. "And not you either, I assume. It explains why the crossbowman only took the one shot." It brought no satisfaction to know that his instincts were right.

"Yorrugg frog...poison is...not plentiful," the half-orc admitted and his head lolled forward.

That was common knowledge and certainly beyond dispute, but what it lacked in availability it more than made up for in efficacy. The fact that Veron was still able to speak at all with it coursing through his system was a testimony to the power he possessed. Even so, it would act quickly, turn his whole body numb, and render him unable to breathe.

Overall, it wasn't the most unpleasant way to die because it was relatively painless and extremely rapid. He could recall a handful of generals famous for taking it to end their lives after a humiliating defeat.

The sounds of boots on the cobbles drew his attention away from the dying half-orc and in moments, a group of guards crowded the street, their weapons pointed at him. He raised his hands and winced when his body protested.

"They attacked me," he said and pointed at the two assassins. "And a third with a crossbow, but I don't think you'll find him."

One of the guards approached and examined the corpses before he looked at the barbarian. "You are Skharr, yes?"

"Aye." He nodded. "And I'd have a care with the bolt in that one's shoulder. It is laced with deadly poison."

The captain moved closer and gestured for the others to lower their weapons.

"We will take note of it," he said and pulled the visor of his helm up. "Did you see where the crossbowman went?"

Skharr narrowed his eyes. "No. Hold a moment—someone believes a barbarian, now?"

"No." The captain grunted what might have been a chuckle and motioned for his men to take care of the bodies. "But we do trust the word of the Barbarian of Theros. Will that be all?"

He couldn't shake the annoyance that the fact that he had been attacked was less important than his reputation of being associated with a local deity. Then again, the fact that they believed him was the important part and the reasoning was less so. It had earned him a respite from endless questions and suspicions so he ought to simply be grateful.

"No," he answered and shrugged. "But it is a start."

"Of course, sir."

"I'm no knight."

The captain studied him in silence for a moment, then nodded. "Of course, sir."

CHAPTER FIVE

I t certainly looked familiar and caught his attention immediately.

Skharr approached the glass case that was positioned in the center of the forge, narrowed his eyes, and examined the pieces that had been put together.

They were all about his size and the leather straps hadn't been adjusted to fit anyone else. In fact, the dummy wearing it had been enlarged to fit the size of the armor that seemed to have been left intact.

"It is fine work, yes?"

He turned and shifted his gaze when he didn't notice anyone at eye-level. With a smile at his foolishness, he remembered where he was and looked down at the smaller, stockier stature of the dwarf who stood beside him.

"I thought so," Skharr answered and straightened his back so he wouldn't focus his full gaze on the dwarf. He knew how they disliked it when it seemed like folk were adjusting to their presence. "You're leaving the armor on display like this?"

"Aye. The armor of the mighty Barbarian of Theros, survivor of the Tower, is a prized possession." AnvilForge crossed his arms

It was interesting to note that all the stories were wrong.

"There is a new evil arisen in the Dungeon of M'Lemnoch near the Belvish Mountains," Janus told them and waved his spear over the pond so they could see what he was speaking of. "A magus lich has been brought into my realm. I will not have it, nor will I have my tight-assed, judgmental brother spout endlessly about the glory after already having one of his own destroy another lich. This one is significantly more powerful. Use the opportunity, my servants, to disperse the knowledge to those who fight in my name."

Tristan nodded and hoped feverishly that he remembered every word that was spoken.

"The follower or followers who help to destroy the creature will be rewarded," Janus continued, waved his spear again, and brought up the image of the rewards he had in mind. "Gold, silver, treasures enough to spin the mind, as well as my highest esteem. The same will be given, of course, to the priest who sent them on their path."

They all exchanged hasty looks. There was no denying that each one had become the high priest of Janus for personal, greed-touched reasons. It was encouraged and expected.

"Go now, my servants. See to it that my word is heard and my mightiest warriors are assembled."

Janus raised the horn to his lips and blew a powerful blast, loud enough that Tristan covered his ears and closed his eyes.

In the next moment, he was in his bed. It was comfortable and warm compared to the cold that made rising from sleep difficult.

Not many demanded that a high priest rise before he preferred to, and he found there weren't many who minded that he worked from his bed on the colder days.

Today, however, would demand more presence from him.

He pushed the heavy blankets aside, shivered as he climbed out of the bed, and rang the small silver bell placed beside his bed to enable him to call his attendants.

A small clutch of servants rushed in, their eyes wide when they realized that the high priest was awake at such an early hour.

"Assemble the council!" Tristan shouted, pulled his bedwear off, and gestured for his robes. "We must meet at once."

"Of course, my lord," one of them said and bowed deeply while the others rushed to help him dress. "What should I tell them is the reason for this haste?"

"I have heard the word of the Lord High God Janus in my dreams," he responded sharply. "Go now and do not tarry."

CHAPTER SIX

Teros hated being up this early. Something about the chill of the morning air made him feel sick, for some reason. He wasn't even sure what caused it, but it didn't change the fact that he would be miserable for the whole day.

But with the news spreading that Janus had sent word out, it meant that every guildmaster available was called in to hear the great word of the mighty god of warriors.

"There are too many gods," he muttered belligerently and read the message that had been sent. "But when one starts shouting about goblins, we need to get our asses up and ready for a fucking fight. He probably expects us to be thankful, the bastard."

"Guildmaster?"

He shook his head and waved his attendant's worries aside. By this point in his life, he had dealt with the words of deities for long enough to realize that if one of them was interested in dealing with his blasphemy, they would likely have done so already.

Then again, Janus was known for being particularly capricious about those who spoke ill of him but he still didn't care. The gods were full of shit anyway, and if they wanted to make his life more fucking difficult than it was already, they would have to work hard at it.

"Send the word out," Teros said finally and handed the message to his attendant. "Janus promises great reward and godly benefits to those who can kill the magus lich in the Dungeon of... oh, gods, I won't pronounce that. Go on. Spread the word."

"Of course, Guildmaster."

Another word from the gods was certainly enough to stir things to a new level of anticipation.

It had been a while since the divinities had been involved. Volia shook her head and settled into her seat to sign the contracts that would have all the god's followers rushing to attack the nearest dungeon. Very few were in a position to attack the one named but it would spark interest in the tradition anyway.

"How many of these have been sent out?" Tamara asked and picked the contracts up, her expression curious.

"All the guildmasters have been given word—from Rouran, to the Imperial City, to Verenvan," the other woman replied, pulled some of the hair from her face, and winced when she saw a few gray strands. "Unlike the other Guild Halls, we need to send word out that there is a contract to all the guilds."

"Not all the guilds."

She looked up and nodded. "The word is that the Theros guild is not to be included. I don't know why and I don't care. Let the gods resolve their differences. I won't be part of that."

Pennar folded his arms and looked around the groups that had been assembled. He didn't like the Janus priests, who took after their patron god. All of them were arrogant, pious brats who decided when and where they needed to get their way without consulting anyone else.

They were making a proper mess of the entire affair and he would be expected to sort it all out.

"Why in all the fucking hells is the Theros guild being excluded?"

He scowled again and tried not to look up from the papers he needed to send out.

"Eh, Guildmaster, I was talking to you."

"I know. I was not listening," he snapped. "Intentionally."

"But if you know, should we not know as well?" The mercenary planted his fist on the desk. "They send those Janus bastards out for all the wealth and glory of a god-sponsored dungeon hunt while we are left to patrol for orcs and escort caravans."

"If you have a problem with Janus, you can take it up with the god himself," he replied. "But if you place your hand on my desk again, your problem will be with me, boy."

His word still carried enough weight that the man backed quickly away from the desk.

"My apologies. But—"

"We could always change our creed," another mercenary pointed out. "If Theros will not glorify us with the mission, Janus would be more than willing."

"There's safety in numbers too. The word has been sent out across the continent and the last I heard, they were hoping to gather a small army to attack the dungeon."

Pennar hated to think it but they did have a point. Hundreds would gather on the word of their god, and if there was ever a time to assault a dungeon, it was now. All they needed to do was abandon their loyalty to Theros and transfer it to Janus instead.

He had a feeling the idea would occur to more than a few of Theros' mercenaries. No one wanted to be excluded from such a mission.

The hour was growing a little later than he preferred. Skharr could see the sun climbing higher in the sky and noted that it was four hours from midday at the most.

He generally liked to have his morning meal as early as possible to avoid feeling heavy when the heat of the day was at its worst, but things had certainly changed.

The inn was permanently too godsbedammed full. Every meal brought in dozens of customers, all hoping for something. He wasn't entirely sure what they were looking for, but he wouldn't insist that any of them be sent away. It was good for business for the Mermaid,

Still, it was unsettling to think that so many people knew where he was at all times, especially when folk were trying to kill him.

This meant it was better to have his morning meal once the initial rush had left. Unfortunately, it required that he spend a few boring mornings in his room. The baths helped, of course, but their novelty soon faded.

Eventually, however, he did need to go downstairs and he could immediately tell that the common room was not quite as empty as he'd hoped. Most of those who had come for the morning meal were gone, but a few remained and all turned when he appeared in the doorway.

At least a few were familiar faces. Sera and her right-hand man, Regor, were seated at one of the tables, and she immediately waved him over when she saw him.

"You've risen rather late, haven't you DeathEater?" she stated as he sat across from them. "Are you enjoying a little peace and quiet before the fun starts again?"

"What do you mean?" he asked as the innkeeper's daughter approached with a mug of something frothy and cool. He would have to learn their names eventually but for the life of him, he couldn't remember if they'd already told him and he'd merely forgotten.

"We heard there was another attempt on your life yesterday," Regor explained. "This time involving a poisoned arrow and two dead men."

"One dead man," Skharr corrected. "The other was a half-orc."

"There aren't too many of those in the city," Sera noted. "But there is a growing number out in the Wetlands. Refugees from the wars come in from all over, and that would be the area where it's easiest for them to establish themselves without having to go through the gates."

Skharr nodded and sipped from the mug of stout provided to him. "Neither was willing to confess why they tried to kill me or who was paying for them. But I did discover that there were three of them and one survived. I caught sight of a crossbowman in a window. Whoever he was, he didn't bother to remain after he fired the one bolt."

"I heard that part as well," Regor replied. "And that the poison used was…uncommon."

"Yorrugg toad poison," he confirmed. "All told, I would say Verenvan is becoming a little too dangerous for me. If you happen to have work beyond the walls, I would welcome it."

"Do you think you'll be safer beyond the walls?" Sera asked and bit a chunk from a sausage before she replaced it on her platter.

"At least I'll know who is trying to kill me. I can look them in the eyes while I fight them instead of waiting for a dagger in the back."

The two guild mercenaries exchanged a glance before the man chuckled.

"I told you that he would be interested," Regor said.

"Interested in what?"

"Nothing," Sera replied.

"But you did say you had some work for me later in the week. This is later."

"That contract has been removed," she all but growled and shook her head.

"Why?" Skharr asked as a platter arrived for him as well. "Your folk are generally reliable enough to deal with any problems you might encounter. More so than the other mercenary groups, yes?"

"A problem developed," she said with a scowl. "A large reward has been promised to whoever purges a dungeon near the Belvish Mountains. Just our luck, it is precisely in the path of where our contract was to take us. Well, closer to the coast but in that general direction."

"South?" Skharr asked. "I thought that was where the goblins still held sway."

"It is," Regor interjected. "The Empire has been dealing with the fuckers rising up from time to time. They breed fast, so every time a pocket is eliminated, another tribe comes along and takes over the territory. This time, however, something has the Lord High God Janus' temples in a fit and all their warriors are off chasing gold, glory, and god-given gifts."

"And not always in that order," Sera muttered as the barbarian dug into the food provided for him. "I blame you for that."

"Me?" he asked around a bite of fresh bread and cheese.

"With all the rumors of your success, those who fight for Janus want to eclipse you and gain greater glory than what you've achieved. Of course, the promise of riches and gifts from a god might drive them as well, but it is mostly to outpace the stories with your name on them."

"He's an ass," Skharr argued, bit off a mouthful of sausage, and sipped his stout. "Any gifts he gives will surely bite the hands and asses of those who accept them."

"Maybe not," Regor countered. "It would appear that Janus is in a rage about whatever is in that dungeon, and he insists that only those fighting in his name be allowed to partake in the contract."

He raised an eyebrow and shook his head. "Like I said. He's an ass through and through."

Sera smirked. "Indeed. I have seen most of my men abandoning their oath to Theros in order to find a place in the groups headed to the dungeon. And I am not the only one. Most of the lower gentry houses are losing guards to the promise. It is fairly chaotic how many seem to be willing to face a dungeon that has been ordered purged by a god."

"Are you two going?" Skharr dipped some of the bread into the thick fish soup.

"Janus isn't my god." She scoffed. "Although I wonder if there will be anything to worry about since warriors from all over the empire appear to be assembling. I'm surprised they haven't gathered generals to lead the assault yet. It's like the priests are stirring them all up into a fury for the glory alone, never mind whatever rewards await them."

"What they have promised is…well, substantial," Regor admitted. "Honestly, the rewards alone would be enough for you to have the bards singing about you no matter what."

"Dungeons without a purpose end with folk dead for no purpose," Skharr muttered. "Janus is never a good reason for me. Someone else is welcome to the glory and the gold. I only hope they survive long enough to spend it."

"What about the godly gifts?" Sera asked, took a few chunks of lamb from Skharr's plate, and ate them slowly.

"I'm not sure what I'd want from the fucker," he muttered and glared at her for stealing his food. "Unless he was willing to help enchant my ax—but no. I think not. I'd not want the stink of him on the blade made for my people."

"Well, I am looking for a new crew willing to take on the other contract," the guild captain said, leaned back in her seat, and grinned as she popped another mouthful of his lamb into her mouth. "I don't suppose you would be interested?"

"Of course," Skharr replied and pulled the platter a little closer to avoid any further thievery. "You always were good for a tussle or three."

She smirked. "Barbarians."

"You can't help but love us," he retorted.

"The last I heard, you've had more than enough loving," she snorted. "How many times have you been to the hills of the royal section of the city?"

"None," he admitted. "I've already had two attempts on my life. Putting myself between lovers, suitors, and jealous husbands will result in strife that will span years. I don't need more ire to send more killers after me over a night of passion."

"What of the waitress?"

"What of her?" he asked. "She told me she appreciated me giving her the piece of the mug I used to break some fool's head with the other night."

"I thought she was interested in giving you something else. Wet too."

Skharr shook his head and Regor snickered. "No. But I might need to find myself a willing wench eventually."

"Barbarians will always know if they need a good wench." The man chortled.

"DeathEaters tend to need the wenches," he admitted. "The question is only how selective we happen to be. The longer since a woman's touch, the lower our standards."

"I thought barbarians wenched every night," Sera interjected. "Is that the term? Wenched?"

He tilted his head. "I don't think so. And only when we are youngsters. As we grow older, we grow more selective. We learn that not every night with a willing woman is worth the effort. After too many drinks, you all too often find what you thought to be a good dream turned into a nightmare waiting for you come the rising of the sun."

His companions both joined his laughter at the idea.

"You look younger than when I met you," the guild captain commented and leaned forward again. "I suppose all the beauty sleep is having an effect."

"Maybe." He didn't want to enter that conversation yet. "But my memories of troubled mornings remain, no matter how wondrous the sleep."

CHAPTER SEVEN

D ozens of the creatures rushed into the corridor.

In all honesty, Faroll had hoped there would be hundreds—or expected there to be hundreds, at the very least. Many of the troglodytes pushed through the center of the hallway armed with crude spears with flint heads and tried to swarm over them. They were foul-smelling creatures and lacked eyes completely, which appeared to be replaced by massive jaws that could open like a snake's. None wore a single article of clothing and they relied on the soft, leathery skin that covered their bodies for defense.

It proved to be a poor decision on their part. Faroll drove forward and used his tower shield to push the creatures back as Halman picked them off with his bow. Coral took her time and attacked them cautiously, but they had discovered that she had a little difficulty containing her power. It was best if she didn't cast one of her fireballs into the narrow hallway.

He rushed forward and swept his blade into a swipe that cleaved the monsters left and right. Their ranks were decimated by his attack but they still surged into his path as if they attempted to stop the group with their numbers alone.

The tactic might have worked had they assaulted a lesser team, but not in this case. He and his companions knew how to keep them at a distance and he allowed his comrades to clear the ground in front of him.

In the end, the sword was only used to deal with those that remained after the rest were killed.

"You died in the name of the Lord High God Janus," Coral whispered, dropped to one knee, and said a blessing over the dead monsters. "Know that your deaths glorify his name forever."

Faroll tried to not roll his eyes. He had never been one to subscribe to the worship of the deities. He lived in a world where he couldn't doubt the existence of Janus but in the end, what exactly made him a god? By all accounts, he was merely a man imbued with magic that allowed him to live almost forever.

Perhaps that was all that it took to make a god.

"I assumed this would be far more...challenging," Halman whispered as he retrieved his arrows from the bodies of the fallen. "When they said Janus needed our services, I thought there would be some kind of...well, power behind these creatures. They appear to be a little more than a few tribes gathered together for warmth."

Faroll didn't like to admit it but the archer was right. Fighting mindless, mightless, blind creatures held no real challenge for them.

"We will clear this dungeon as commanded," Coral snapped to the ten-man team once she'd finished her prayers. "The fact that Janus saw fit to command us to do this in his name is indicative of our power, not of the lack thereof in the creatures about us."

"True," he whispered. "Maybe it would be challenging to others who are incapable of fighting hordes of troglodytes."

He grasped his sword a little tighter. It was a good sign, he decided. Maybe Janus would see fit to use them more in the future—if they needed to fight once this was over. With the riches that were promised, the option would remain for them to live a life of ease, basking in the knowledge and fame of what they had accomplished.

Of course, they would not include the part of how the mighty quest had been nothing more than fighting through a few tribes of unarmored savages. He would allow the bards to write whatever they pleased on the subject.

The hallway came to an end at a massive stone door that was already open as if waiting for them, although the signs of the tribes living in the area ceased immediately.

"There are tunnels above us," Coral told them and pointed with her staff to the ceiling, where tunnels could be seen snaking into the mountain above them. This was likely where the troglodytes had come from and not the massive chamber that opened before them.

"This is an odd place," Faroll whispered, rolled his shoulders, and adjusted his hold on his shield. "I don't suppose you could raise more light for us?"

The cleric did as requested and lifted her staff so they could see the chamber in the white light that issued from the tip.

"If we weren't in the bottom of a dungeon, I would say this was a palace," Halman whispered. "We might consider taking notes. If the coin from this venture flows as promised, we might be able to fund our own palaces and I would want one like this."

"The high ceilings are certainly interesting," Faroll responded. "I would like a few more windows, however. Stained glass would allow the sunlight to pour through. A little more light would not go amiss."

As if waiting for the comment, the sound of stone grinding on stone suddenly filled the chamber. He looked back as the massive stone doors at the entrance closed slowly and a flame began to encircle the entire room and illuminate the statues that surrounded them.

In white light, oddly enough, they had looked quite harmless, merely bits and pieces from an artistic mind and a skilled hand.

When the fire cast light on them, however, they grew considerably more ominous. The flickering of the flames caused them to look torn and misshapen and leering glares and terrifying grins manifested on the faces that should have had no expressions at all.

Even worse, he could hear something now too. A low, rumble of laughter echoed to fill the room and their gazes were drawn to the massive granite throne on the far side. A figure was seated there, one that had remained so motionless that they hadn't even considered that something was waiting for them.

Faroll tightened his hold on his shield and grimaced as the laughter grew louder and the sound became more focused. At first, it sounded like it came from the flames but it was clearly issuing from the creature atop the throne.

"Visitors!" The word seemed to rumble through the room. The figure stood from his throne and straightened to what appeared to be over seven feet tall. The staff he carried was almost as tall with two fist-sized rubies at the crest. Initially, it looked like the gemstones were merely reflecting the light but as Faroll studied it more carefully, he realized that the light emanated from them.

"The magus lich," Coral warned them and drew a deep breath as the light from her staff began to grow. "We were warned that it would be in this place."

He nodded. It was true that they had been warned about it but he'd hoped that, like most liches, its power would have dissipated already, which would leave them with the simple task of destroying its phylactery. That didn't appear to be the case.

"I see Janus has sent his weakest to test me first." The lich began to descend the steps slowly. He moved stiffly, but the same fire that filled the room was visible in his eyes as well and the blaze had begun to flicker oddly. It appeared as if tails flared and moved through the tongues of flame.

"Your evil is no match for the power of the almighty Lord

High God Janus," Coral stated, struck the end of her staff on the floor, and unleashed a wave of power on impact. There was no way to tell if her attempt to intimidate the creature would be effective, but it certainly did wonders for the morale of the group around her.

The lich had power of his own and it was not lacking either.

Faroll hefted his sword, took a deep breath, and struck his shield with it loudly as he took a step forward to meet the gaze of the creature in front of them.

"We are not afraid of a mindless monster!" he roared. It was difficult to look the being in the eye. It made him feel like the fire would spread into him but he held his ground and steeled himself for the battle to come.

"You should be."

The words were simply spoken but the weight of them caught him in his chest and his courage began to wane. This wasn't helped by the fact that his troop looked hastily around the room when they heard stone grinding over stone again.

No doors opened this time, although Faroll wished more doors would open and the troglodytes would rush through and attack them. The alternative was that the statues were slowly coming to life and drawing the weapons they carried on their backs or collecting the spears that had been carved with them.

"Coral!" he shouted and gestured for the troop to gather around him. They were in for a real fight now, and he had a feeling that the cleric's magical ability would be their mightiest weapon against the living stone.

Swords would have little power against them. Shields might do better, both to wield as weapons and to protect. His team-mates quickly realized the same and stepped forward to protect their cleric as she summoned as much power as she could hold in herself before she launched a bolt of lightning across the room to the closest of the monsters.

The whole room lit up for one glorious moment and Faroll's

ears were left ringing at the crack that echoed through the space. The stone monster she had targeted exploded into a thousand smaller chunks of rock that scattered across the floor, gouged pieces out of those statues that were close to it, and chipped the marble pillars.

A cheer rose from the group. It appeared that her lack of control over her power might be the difference in this fight and give them a chance at victory.

In the next moment, their hope disappeared. The statues surged forward to attack with impossible speed and drove into the group like they were a thin wall of ice. Faroll readied himself as the closest one attacked him and seemed to brush off a strike from his sword before it swung a club into his shield.

His arm broke with the impact and before he could utter a pained cry, a nearby pillar pounded into his back and he fell heavily.

The blow knocked the breath from his lungs and he knew it would be painful to breathe in. He would do so eventually, but it would take a moment. Holding himself back was delaying the inevitable, but he couldn't bring himself to make the attempt.

All he could do was watch as the stone creatures barreled into the lines of his comrades. A few were battered by their weapons while others were simply crushed underfoot and utterly destroyed.

It was painful to watch but as he sucked in a deep breath and tried to stand, every broken bone in his body screeched in agony and Faroll sagged with a deep groan. His face twisted in pain, he reached to where his sword had fallen.

"We'll have to make the monsters a little more powerful in the future," said a chilling voice not far from where he lay. "Either that or we'll have to fight these plebian annoyances on a daily basis. This is the second group that has traipsed in here with no idea what they are facing."

Second? Plebian annoyances? For a moment, the irritation at

being called such was enough to overcome the pain in his body and he managed to turn and see who had spoken.

The lich walked calmly to the massacre it was empowering.

Another higher-pitched voice spoke from the same mouth. "I do enjoy these quick and easy fights. They think they have all the power in the fight and are inevitably at a disadvantage against me. In fairness, however, it has been a little too long since I've had humans to play with."

The laughter that issued from the lich was painful to his ears but it wasn't quite as painful as everything else that was happening in his body. For some reason, he seemed entranced by the creature that continued to walk toward the fight. It appeared to be talking to itself, which seemed like an odd thing for a lich to do.

Confining their life force was normal, but a hint of insanity? That was a step too far.

He pushed up and tried to crawl to where the fight was all but over. Most of their troop was dead and had been discarded in a mangled pile of limbs. He couldn't distinguish even one of his comrades from the other, but the fight wasn't over yet.

Three more of the statues were left in pieces and Coral dove to the left after her attack to avoid a powerful strike from one of the monsters. She rolled over her shoulder and regained her feet and without a second's pause, fired another bolt of lightning at the nearest of the statues to destroy it like she had the others.

He might have thought she had control of the fight if there weren't a dozen more of the stone enemies remaining. Many others remained standing as though they were real statues, and the cleric looked tired to the point of exhaustion. If the rest of the group had managed to put in an effort, she might have had a chance, but it didn't look like she had another attack in her.

Unfortunately, it seemed the lich felt the same. With a flick of his wrist, the remaining statues froze in their tracks and he watched her as she panted for breath, barely able to hold onto her staff or even remain upright.

"A fine effort," the lich said. "But futile. What have you accomplished in the end?"

Coral had no answer for him. She couldn't draw more power for another lightning strike. Instead, she cried out and swung the staff to try to strike at his head.

It was another fine but futile effort, The lich caught the weapon, yanked it from her hands, and flung it aside. A hint of smoke rose from his hand when he touched the sanctified weapon.

"Not that long ago," the first voice intoned as the entity grasped her neck and lifted her struggling form off the floor. "You fought that barbarian."

"I can only hope to speak to him again in our future."

"On that one thing we can agree."

"May the light…of Janus…illuminate the path of those who die in his name," Coral cried suddenly in a choked voice. Her eyes lost their focus and a blue light began to emanate from them.

The lich's hand moved faster than Faroll could think and he looked away hastily, although he still heard the cleric's head tumble to the floor with a wet splat.

He tried not to move or to make any sound to draw attention to the fact that he was still alive. Any hope that he would survive this place had been crushed but he didn't have it in him to fight any longer. He also didn't have it in him to run. But if he managed to play dead, they might forget him and ignore him and he would manage something.

Something. Anything.

The statues began to walk to where they had originally stood, their work done and nothing left in the room to kill, and the lich moved toward his throne.

"You think I forgot about you, yes?"

A chill traced up Faroll's spine when he heard the high-pitched voice as the heavy footsteps approached him.

"You are not quite as dead as you seem yet. But you will be."

The footsteps began to recede and move away and his heart almost gave him away when it pounded desperately inside his damaged chest. The fires began to go out and the doors remained closed, leaving him no avenue of escape.

But he was alive, he reminded himself a little desperately. Alive was all that mattered.

Darkness filled the chamber. It seemed to permeate through him and made it seem impossible that anything like light could have ever existed in his memory. And in that darkness, something moved.

The light taps of bare footsteps drew closer. Clawed fingers grasped his shoulder and dragged him from his position. A groan of pain escaped his lips as something dull and painful pressed into the side of his neck, hard enough to cut into his throat.

He couldn't see anything, but the roughness of the hold on his shoulder receded. The pain was gone. Hopefully, the cleric's final prayer had been heard.

CHAPTER EIGHT

"I t's not the same. I'm asking you to join me this time."

Skharr appreciated that they'd put a stool out for him to sit with Horse. He assumed Ingaret had something to do with that. She shared a special connection with the beast and he had deduced that she spent time out in the pasture with Horse whenever she had a mind to.

His coat shone more than usual and he had a little more roundness in the belly than before. It wasn't the worst thing and merely meant he was enjoying his time away from the road.

The stallion nickered softly, nudged him, and almost toppled him off of the stool.

"I understand," he whispered, regained his balance carefully, and gazed at the rest of the pasture. More horses were out in the paddocks enjoying the sun and fields of luscious green grass, which created a serene vista. This was the type of setting where he imagined a princess would want to spend her time when she wasn't traveling the land, looking for monsters to kill.

He placed his hand on Horse's neck, tugged his mane, and leaned his head on the beast's shoulder. The animal turned slightly to nibble at the hem of his shirt.

"They've been spoiling you with apples here, I see. But if you want to join me on this trip south, it likely wouldn't be too tough of a trip for you. I've always liked traveling south. It's always felt like going downhill and there shouldn't be too many problems. There aren't many bandits in the area as they tend to avoid the goblin tribes. We might have to fight a few of those goblin tribes, of course, but they aren't as bold as they used to be—or so I've heard."

Horse tossed his mane and whipped Skharr in the face with it.

"I wouldn't say that trouble finds me wherever I go. With that said, it's not an inaccurate statement. At least lately. Maybe I should turn mercenary again and join an army. Ironically, it would be a more peaceful way to live, although we would make considerably less money—which means fewer apples for you."

The snort was all he needed to hear on that subject.

"So, do you think you'll join me?" the barbarian asked. "I could always find another horse in a less comfortable state to travel with me."

That time, Horse did knock him off the stool and Skharr laughed, pushed up slowly, and removed a few pieces of straw from his hair.

"Fair enough. We'll leave tomorrow and you will carry most of the load. It won't be more than what you have carried before, I don't think. If we fight goblins, I'll want to bring armor."

The stallion seemed content with that, and he appeased him with a few more apples until the idea of him taking another horse on the trip was gone from his mind.

Ingaret appeared on her way out to the paddocks. She carried a bucket of grains and oats for the various horses to where Horse generally ate.

"Skharr!" she called and waved to him as she entered before she closed the gate carefully again. "Are you missing Horse already?"

"Yes. I was also telling him that we will help Sera with her contract. I suggested taking another horse but he didn't appreciate it much."

"I thought you wouldn't travel around much anymore." She filled a small elevated eating bowl with grains for the stallion.

"It was a possibility, but with Sera needing help in the field and too many folk in the city with my name on their lips who aren't the kind who wish me well… It seems best to spend time away from the daggers they wish planted in my chest."

Ingaret smiled and shook her head. "I suppose it is. You and Horse will both be missed, of course. I've spent time out here in the fields with him and I think he enjoys having his coat brushed. You might want to take some time for that while you are on the road."

He nodded. "I think I will."

"I do enjoy working with you, of course."

Skharr tilted his head and inspected the amulets that had been set out for him. "Why?"

"Well, not many adventurers have the coin required for my services, and those who do tend to need something standard." The mage retrieved a few bits and bobs for him to inspect as well. "They want cheap items that will protect them from magical attacks and the like. It pays for my food well enough, I suppose. A few of the lordlings also want my help with their marital issues and I even had one in here who asked me for something that would help him divine the intentions of his enemies."

"Is that so?" He raised an eyebrow. "Were you able to help him?"

"I realized that he had no magical skill of his own so I handed him an amulet that alerted him to poison in his food and told him it would warn him when someone was attempting to murder him. I haven't heard from him since, of course, which means it either worked or it didn't."

"A dead man cannot complain about the failure of his magical trinkets," Skharr agreed. "But I imagine that dealing with such trivialities can prove boring, no matter how much they pay."

"I've enjoyed a few different pursuits, but there is a certain pleasure that comes from applying my skills for the benefit of those who can make good use of them."

Skharr liked to believe that was something of a compliment.

"Will you go to join the other mercenaries on their way to that dungeon I've heard so much about?" the mage asked curiously. "I have you to thank for the business that has come to my door for the last few months, and all those who prepared themselves to raid a dungeon wanted to know what kind of items you chose to take when you did so."

"I will not join them. I'm helping a friend as most of her men have left her to journey on the path to that same place. It should prove less dangerous."

"Might I ask why you are stocking up on my goods then?"

The barbarian simply shrugged and picked up a small black rock with a couple of gemstones stuck inside. "Consider it planning from the pit of my stomach."

The mage nodded, drew his long black hair back, and tied it deftly. "I see. I have continued the work that allows for one to be warned of an enemy's plans—should I ever have a similar customer—and some progress has been made. An amulet that will warn the wearer of impending danger to their life has been the best of my efforts thus far. It will vibrate if you are wearing it when your life is in danger."

He picked up a small necklace that was strung through what looked like a small coin about the size of Skharr's thumb with a griffin's head stamped on the front. The beast's eyes were made of a pair of red crystals that flickered when he looked at them.

"It will vibrate when I am in danger."

"When your life is in danger. I've tried it and it won't prevent you from stubbing your toe and whatnot. Only dangers that threaten your life activate it."

That sounded oddly subjective but Skharr nodded and indicated that he would buy it.

"Wonderful. I assume you will take the usual selection of magic and poison dampeners to protect you as well." He pushed a few more familiar trinkets closer to those the barbarian had already selected. "If I may offer another suggestion, there is an item that I have been developing from a few of those you brought me."

He narrowed his eyes as the man pushed a small, stained coin made of copper on one side and wood on the other.

"What does it do?"

"It's difficult to explain the process without going into the details of how the human body works, but what I discovered is that it is able to heal the human body—and, to some lesser extent, dwarves, elves, and orcs."

"I already have an amulet for that," he pointed out and pulled the original one he'd purchased from under his shirt. "It works wonders."

"Yes, but this one is unique as it only works if the wearer has some kind of alcohol in their bodies. It works by…well, it infuses any ale, beer, wine, or spirit consumed and present in your blood with mild healing properties that expel poisons and even help to seal and heal wounds. It isn't as effective as I would like yet but if you have a mind to try it, I would be happy to sell it."

That certainly sounded interesting. Skharr inclined his head and leaned in a little closer. He noticed an inscription of Guidar, supposedly the god of festivities and celebration, but he knew him better as the patron deity to those who indulged excessively in a variety of destructive vices.

His sigil on such an amulet seemed appropriate.

"I'll take that one as well."

"Twenty-five gold pieces should cover them all, I think."

The barbarian narrowed his eyes. "All others think I have coin to drown in after surviving a dragon and have hoped to relieve me of as much of it as they can. Your prices are surprisingly reasonable."

The mage laughed and shook his head. "Well, I could say you are the finest example of the quality of my wares to those who wish to buy them. I cannot have you dying and putting a curse on what I produce and sell."

"I somehow doubt that is the truth."

"I might be a mage but I am a businessman as well. Like it or not, you are exceedingly good for my reputation. Never let it be said that Sarin does not care for those who do him a good turn."

Sarin. That was the man's name. The warrior wondered if he needed to keep some paper on his body at all times so he didn't forget everyone's names. Or maybe there was a magical amulet for that as well.

There were better ways to test an amulet of quality, Skharr told himself. Running head-first into a lion's den was one or maybe trying to hug a troll while it was sleeping, but he decided that using it to test his food was another sound way to check the efficacy of his new purchase.

Then again, if there was no vibration in the medallion, he would either find out that it wasn't working if he started to feel the effects of the poison, or nothing would happen and he would have to wait for an opportunity for another test.

The small tavern was conveniently located on his route to the Mermaid and his errands had left him too hungry to wait. Part of him wondered if his lodgings wouldn't be safer, but as he hadn't seen anyone following him, he decided he could take the risk. It was unlikely that anyone would be quick enough to poison his meal if he ordered immediately and he'd never eaten there before so they would likely not expect him to.

Still, despite his reasoning, he held his spoon a little tighter, took a deep breath, and finally tasted the soup.

It was rich, flavorful, and filling, the kind of meal that required a little work to make but didn't cost much in the way of coin—a worker's meal.

The amulet did not react so he had to assume there was no hint of poison in it. He dipped some of the dark bread that had been provided into the soup, tasted that as well, and narrowed his eyes. Yet again, he had to accept the absence of poison. He shook his head. This was what came from worrying about living in the godsbedammed city. Worrying about death by under-handed means was not something he enjoyed. It wasn't some-thing he ever wanted to grow accustomed to either.

Assuming he didn't die first, of course.

He took another mouthful followed by a third with a little of the dried meat and cheese that had come with the bread this time —which only served to enrich the meal a little more. It wasn't quite to the standard of the meals at the Mermaid—especially lately—but it was certainly a good, filling meal.

Better yet, it probably had no poison in it.

He paused and tilted his head as he lifted the bowl to his mouth to clean the dregs. A thin wall separated the booths and he was able to easily hear a conversation on the other side of where he sat. The voice was all too familiar, one he had hoped he wouldn't have to hear for a long time, yet there it was to annoy the hell out of him.

A fight was probably not the best thing to involve himself in. Not with folk trying to kill him and looking for the first oppor-tunity to do so, but he wouldn't make himself too easy to find in the city.

That said, the voice was one that generally made his fists itch for a fight.

"Is that the truth?"

"I do not lie. I've beaten the man in single combat already. I'm sure any stories about him killing a dragon are utter lies. Either that or it was already half-dead and all he had to do was plant a spear to finish the work."

Endel narrowed his eyes and sipped his mug of ale. He had heard similar things in the past. Hells, he had said similar things in the past himself and almost every time had ended poorly for him. A thought occurred to him that Skharr, like the Lady of the Mirrors, seemed to appear every time his name was spoken with foul intent.

He'd learned his lesson. Even the free drinks that were offered by those who hated the man were no longer worth the trouble that followed him every time, as the Barbarian of Theros found him somehow and it ended with Endel needing to visit a physician.

It was odd to watch others make the same mistake. This was the first time, in his experience, and he wanted to see if his comrade would face a similarly poor fate as he had.

Connar laughed and took another long draught from his drink. "I tell you, the man is a little larger than you might expect but as long as you avoid being intimidated by it, he'll crumple with the first good blow you land."

That could have been true for all he knew. Unfortunately, he had never been in a position to land the first blow. He'd seen a friend land one but it hadn't crumpled Skharr. In fact, the giant had seemed to enjoy it.

"That is not how it happens," Endel said, brushed away some brown hair that had fallen into his eyes, and shook his head.

"And how would you know that?"

"Because I've come to blows with the man—more than once, as a matter of fact."

"Did you win those fights,?"

"No. I don't think they qualified as fights, to be honest. They ended rather poorly for me on every occasion."

"Hah!" Connar tossed his hair back. "I should have known you would defend that shit's honor. Let you fuck him in the ass, did he? All so someone would spread the stories that have made him rich well beyond what he deser—"

The braggart's words were loudly interrupted and Endel wasn't at all surprised when a fist drove through the thin wooden partition between the booths. It grasped Connar by the collar of his shirt and dragged him through the hole, making it larger when he passed through it.

"Interesting," he whispered and took another sip of his drink. "It does happen to others. How bizarre."

It was less miserable when it happened to others, he realized. It was rather hilarious.

The sounds of a scuffle came from the other side, although he could only see flickers of movement. Connar shouted something but was quickly cut off when a fist collided with his face.

After another two punches, his friend's voice stopped and a moment later, Endel raised his eyebrows as the man was shoved through the hole, bruised, battered, and bloodied. He slumped over the table, muttered something incoherent, and exhaled a long, horrific snore through his broken nose.

All he could think to do was take a sip from his flagon and study his unconscious friend. Had he appeared so weak, frail, and idiotic after the beatings he had taken?

Finally, Connar groaned, propped himself on his elbows, and looked back to see half of himself still hanging through the broken partition. He groaned again and tried feebly to drag himself through.

"That happened to me as well, oddly enough," Endel said and patted him on the back of the head. "And now you have a story that rings of the truth."

The man had no answer for him aside from another moan as he tried to pull himself free again.

Skharr inspected the bruises forming on his fist as he rose from his seat. Thankfully, nothing had been spilled in the scuffle and he was able to finish his meal calmly and quickly before he stood and walked to where he could see a young waitress telling the owner of the establishment what had happened.

Before either of them could say a word, he placed two silvers and a gold piece on the counter.

"My apologies," Skharr said calmly and nodded his head toward the broken section of the wall.

The gold piece was more than twice what it would cost to replace the wooden paneling, but the tavern keeper nodded quickly and pocketed the coins in the blink of an eye.

"I am sure the fucker deserved what he got," the man said simply and tugged his beard idly.

The barbarian nodded. He didn't need to say anything further as he turned and strode toward the door of the establishment, feeling the gazes of the score or so patrons who were still in their seats following him to the door.

Before he could reach the latch, however, heavy, armored boots marched to the entrance of the building. He already knew what was waiting for him outside but he had to pull the door open anyway and looked into the eyes of a handful of guards who had been summoned to deal with the situation.

Or, more accurately, to deal with him.

The captain stepped forward, straightened visibly, and squared his shoulders in an attempt to not appear too small compared to the barbarian he faced.

"I thought we would find you again," the captain snapped and took a step back so he didn't have to strain his neck to look at

Skharr. "But not so soon. I would have assumed you would try to stay away from trouble after our last encounter. I suppose you are the monster who was beating an innocent patron."

"Name?" he asked.

"What?"

"Name. Yours."

"Captain Yur Sarkaan, of the Verenvan City Guard."

"Captain Sarkaan?" The tavern owner rushed out and tried to step between Skharr and the other guards. "Yes, yes, good captain. I am afraid that you were called over a simple misunderstanding."

A couple of the officials circled them and headed into the tavern when the captain motioned for them to move.

"A misunderstanding, you say?"

"Aye. A simple misunderstanding between folk. There was something of a scuffle, but it was quickly resolved with only one injured party and frankly, he deserved it with the way he was acting. I doubt he will have any complaint about how he was treated after bothering the rest of my patrons."

Skharr inclined his head and watched the man curiously. It appeared his gold was enough to buy a certain loyalty from him.

The two guards exited quickly. One of them looked a little red in the face like he had been laughing at what he saw inside.

"The man appears to be...well-stuck," the guardsman said after a few attempts while the other guard snickered and interrupted him.

"Stuck?" Sarkaan asked and raised an eyebrow.

"Yes."

Both were fighting back paroxysms of laughter.

"Well unstick him!" the captain hissed. "Do it!"

They rushed in before they could break out laughing again.

"Pull him hard," Skharr called before they were out of earshot. "By the belt. Or open the hole wider."

Sarkaan scowled deeply and tried to ignore the sound of laughter coming from inside the tavern.

"Do you need me?" he asked. "I have business to attend to."

"Business?"

The barbarian nodded. "Important."

"You have nothing to hold him on," the tavern owner pointed out. "Yes? Or you would have clapped him in irons already."

The guard captain tugged gently at the leather strap that held his helm in place. He had begun to sweat.

"No, you are not being held," he stated finally and narrowed his eyes at Skharr. "You are still resting your head at the Mermaid, yes?"

He nodded and moved past the man. If the guards wanted to find him, he had a feeling there would be too many who would be able to track him down.

All they needed to do was slip a few coppers to the children on the streets of the city. It wasn't a comforting thought.

"What think you, barbarian?"

Skharr lifted the bow, studied it closely, and inspected the craftsmanship. Most of the bows made by his people were made of the horns, bones, and tendons of the larger creatures that lived in the mountains where his folk resided. They were large and tough for any but the strongest arms to draw, but that proved to be wise as they needed the strongest and best shots on the mountainsides.

He thought he had the knowledge in his mind on how to build a proper bow—the kind any DeathEater would be proud to carry into battle—yet the one he held was magnitudes finer than anything he had ever built himself. A few of the older masters might have been able to best it but not by much.

"It is fine work," he muttered and ran his fingers over the taut bowstring. "What materials were used?"

"Simple yew wood for the outside there." Throk patted the external section of the bow. "It's usually used in the longbows the count wants for those who can shoot them. I reinforced the back with troll ribs. Those are exceedingly difficult to acquire. The string is made from the sinew of the same troll whose ribs are on the back. It's expensive but I think you'll find it is worth the coin."

He presented Skharr with three arrows and directed his attention to a wooden dummy some twenty yards away that had been fitted with a hauberk and padded armor as well.

The barbarian narrowed his eyes and tested the string again before he drew the arrow back slowly. His back burned from the effort and he took a deep breath before he released it. He nocked the second arrow in quick succession, drew, and fired, and followed it almost instantly with the third.

All three hammered into the dummy and the third struck with enough power to knock it over despite the heavy bags of sand that had been placed to hold it firm.

"I've included two dozen arrows with the price of the bow," Throk told him as they walked closer to inspect the damage done by the arrows. "You know how to make your own arrows, of course, but you'll want the shafts to be stronger to take the power of the bow or they might break before you fire them."

"There are more than two hundred pounds in the draw weight," Skharr replied and retrieved the first of the arrows that had buried itself almost halfway, enough that the tip protruded out the other side.

"Aye. Two hundred and thirty, I would have said. Enough, with your strength, to cut clear through a man and into a second behind him if neither are wearing armor, so you should take extra care or you'll kill someone you weren't aiming for. It still wouldn't cut through the plate some knights and paladins wear but not much can."

The barbarian nodded and inspected the shafts of the arrows. "I'll take them. Added to the price of the armor too."

"A hundred and twenty gold coins for everything." Throk nodded. "I've already contacted your bank for the payment and they await your signature."

He nodded. The dwarf had a keen mind for the work and had anticipated that he would need weapons and armor for his latest venture.

Although, when he started working on the weapons and armor, he had also assumed that the barbarian would head to the dungeon with the Janus acolytes. Skharr could guess as much by the quality of the materials, but they were still the type of armor and weapons he would want to have on hand in a fight.

Sera had a tendency to send him into the thick of things, after all. Or he simply ran directly into the thick of things whether she was there or not.

"They've started packaging everything for you to take with you." The dwarf took the bow from his hand, unstrung it deftly, and handed it to one of the assistants from the forge. "We are always glad to work with you, DeathEater. I am sure my kin in the mountains will be tickled to hear that I have been working with one of yours out here in the city."

Skharr nodded and still felt a burn in his back. The draw was a good forty pounds more than even the heaviest bow he had drawn before. It would take time before he was used to the weight.

Then again, being able to shoot two men with one arrow did seem like something to aspire to.

"Would you like to carry it all with you?" Throk asked once all the packages were readied for him and his signature was applied to the parchment that would verify that it was his signature and not a forgery. "We could have it delivered to the Mermaid, should you prefer."

The question reminded him that yet another person knew

where he laid his head at night. It was only a matter of time until someone attempted to murder him in his sleep.

"Have it delivered," he answered. "I have a few more stops to make."

The dwarf bowed deeply at the waist. "Of course. I look forward to your next visit, DeathEater."

Skharr nodded and patted the haft of the unfinished ax. "I'll return to take you to your proper home, have no fear."

He had a feeling that the men who worked with weapons their whole lives could understand the concept of speaking to them or even thinking of them as friends or members of the family.

After a few minutes on the street, he lowered his head and tried not to think about the way folk appeared to watch him everywhere he went. Perhaps they didn't like the idea of barbarians wandering among them. Or maybe a few had heard of him. He knew he was fairly easy to recognize as there weren't too many DeathEaters in the region.

He couldn't allow himself to forget those who likely wanted to slip a dagger between his ribs at the earliest opportunity. They were being paid to, of course. Folk who resorted to killing in a city for a living were those who were truly desperate. Knifing folk on the street in the open was the kind of thing called for by those who had little compunction for the death of those they sent out to do the killing.

In the moments before the attack, Skharr could almost feel them converge on him. Five of them tried to use the cover of the crowd but seemed to have forgotten that folk tended to stay away from him, especially on the street.

They reached their target at about the same time, a little shocked that things hadn't quite gone according to plan, and immediately decided their idea to catch him by surprise required that they all attack together.

While their skills were a far cry from the professionals Skharr had dealt with the last time, there were enough of them to pose significant risk.

Significant enough that the amulet he wore around his neck had been vibrating like a tiny earthquake against his chest. It was the only warning he'd had of their approach until they began to rush toward him.

He already had his knife in hand and watched for the two who had chosen to attack him from behind. Instead of immediately turning on them, he flipped the dagger so he could hold it by the blade and tossed it as hard as he could into the three who rushed in from the front.

It buried itself to the hilt in the neck of the man in the middle and he fell back and threw the other two off balance. The barbarian whipped around and caught a hand that tried to drive a dagger through his ribs. The blade sliced his arm but it was barely a scratch and he thrust the blade away and pointed it instead at the second man who tried to attack from what had been his left when he had faced away.

The knife drove hard into the assassin's shoulder. Skharr caught both by the neck and twisted them as hard as he could.

The other two tried to attack while his back was turned. Both assassins he held collided with the one closest to him and he felt a searing pain across his arm again when the thrust caught him as he spun out of its path.

"By Janus' hairy butt crack—enough," he muttered belligerently, caught the man by the collar before he could back away, and jerked his head forward. He smirked at the decisive crunch of a broken nose. "Stupid fucking scum-sucker."

Before the assassin could recover, the warrior swept his legs out from under him and, still with a hand on his collar, drove him hard into the cobbles.

It was at an angle he hadn't planned for and he heard a loud crack. The man went limp in his hand, his neck twisted at an odd angle.

He turned to face the other three and expected them all to surge into the attack in the hopes that they could upend him with their combined mass, strength, and momentum. Surprisingly, no assault seemed imminent.

One of them was curled on the cobbles, holding a dagger buried in his stomach while he groaned pitifully. He was beyond recovery as blood already seeped from his mouth as well as the wound, but Skharr couldn't remember when he had delivered the blow. Perhaps he had accidentally received the fatal wound when he had tossed them into each other.

The other two tried hastily to disappear into the crowd that slowly gathered to watch the fight. The courage that had filled them when they attacked as a fivesome vanished quickly now that three of their number had fallen.

"Poison?" Skharr asked as he grasped the dying man by the collar.

"No," he whispered in reply as his body grew limp and his eyes lost focus.

In fairness, the amulet had ceased vibrating, which indicated that the danger had passed, but he chose to be extra cautious. He already knew his enemies had no issues acquiring rare and expensive poisons to kill him with.

"Did you see that? How does something that big move so fucking quickly?"

Sarn shook his head. He wouldn't bother with the hypotheticals of how the giant had been able to intercept the five of them in a matter of seconds. Admittedly, one of the others had been killed by his weapon, but he wouldn't tell anyone that was how it had happened.

Skharr had been the one to kill them all and that would be that.

He hadn't even met the other four assassins before that day. All they had been told was to knife the fucker in the street. The coin would be the same for the five of them, so if a couple were killed during the fight, it meant there would be more coin split between the survivors.

Now, there were two survivors.

Three, if they counted their target as well.

"How does anything move that fast?"

The would-be assassin scowled at his comrade when the boy dropped to his haunches and covered his face with his blood-soaked hands.

Perhaps sending boys to deal with the barbarian had been a mistake. It was clear that their target was not the witless brute they had been told he was, and they would need to discuss how the next attempt would be made. Otherwise, they would surely find themselves in a bloodbath.

A strangled cry from his comrade made Sarn suddenly feel angry. If the boy was going to cry, he would have to beat the tears out of him. The godsbedammed child shouldn't have been out and killing folk if he couldn't take it.

He turned to see the youth fall back with a black dagger stuck in his throat, which elicited another gargled moan as his voice clogged with blood.

Before he could even shout his surprise, something struck him in the throat as well. It wasn't thrown but carried by a figure in black robes and leathers.

"At this rate, it would be safer to kill the fools who send fools instead of the fools who were sent," the figure muttered before he thrust the knife hard into his chest.

Things did not look encouraging. Sera had spent years putting together a team she trusted. To do this, she had diligently scoured the mercenary groups for those who were both skilled and the type folk liked to work with.

Most of those had already left for what they perceived to be the greener pastures of a dungeon that needed to be cleansed, which left her with the dregs. A few of her regulars were still there, of course, but she didn't feel comfortable with a group she'd never worked with before.

Still, the die was cast and she had to be ready to head out from the Guild Hall in the morning.

"I'm the one she'll be looking to!" a voice shouted from her group. "Sera Ferat will make it known that I am the one she will name as her second in command come the time to march. You watch and see."

The man was tall and handsome with the look of a knight from his bearing to his weapons and armor—a heater shield, light plate, and hauberk, as well as an arming sword and a dagger carried at his hip. He even insisted on being called Sir Denith.

"You don't know what you're saying," Regor mumbled.

"What did you say?" the man snapped and strode to where Regor was still seated, tending to his stock of medical supplies. "Why don't you speak louder so all can hear you instead of mumbling like a fool?"

He raised an eyebrow. "I said you don't know what you speak of. If you need help hearing, I can write it down for you. Assuming you know how to read."

Denith growled something Sera didn't catch, grasped the other man by the collar of his shirt, and tried to drag him to his feet. She had already moved her hand to reach for the sword at her side before she realized it wasn't needed.

It was a little odd that the man hadn't realized the peril he had placed himself in before Skharr stepped in behind him. The barbarian could move without making a sound despite his size when he wanted to.

The self-proclaimed knight's head snapped around but a huge

fist hammered across his jaw and he fell without so much as a whimper.

"Is anyone else thinking of causing trouble?" the warrior asked and looked around the group, his eyes narrowed and body taut and ready to fight.

Sera scowled at the additional bandages over his body as he led Horse in slowly behind him. She knew better than to ask but it looked like he had been in a few more fights since she had last seen him.

"No? Then get back to work," he continued and patted Regor on the shoulder by way of greeting. "If the godsbedammed preening mirror-fucker wakes before we leave and can tear himself away from his perfect reflection, he'll dig latrines for the first few days. If he doesn't, we'll leave him behind."

She honestly couldn't have said it better herself and a small smirk touched her lips.

"I guess that makes you my second-in-command," she said as he inspected the packages on Horse's back.

"I thought Regor was your second."

"He's the medic. He will always be needed as a trusted advisor, but it seems you know how to keep the newcomers in line should they step out of it."

"Should you need any of them rendered unconscious, you need only tell me."

CHAPTER NINE

He could feel the man's furious gaze on him.

Skharr doubted that he would ever be on even remotely friendly terms with a person like Denith. The butthole was overbearing and abrasive while he considered himself a powerful and charismatic leader of men. The fact that he insisted on being called Sir Denith during their first day on the road was annoying to the point where none of the group offered to help with the chore of digging latrines.

The barbarian had met many like him before. The man thought that if it wasn't for his interference, he would be a leader and respected in the party and so focused all his anger and hatred on him. He also made sure it was known through the constant glares as he continued his digging.

The fact that he'd already needed to correct him to keep the latrines away from their source of water was enough to make Skharr watch him to make sure he didn't do shoddy work on purpose. He would dig the latrines for the next few days at least and he would have to develop a few skills in the not-so-subtle art.

Of course, it was on the warrior to make sure that the food

was ready as well, and the idea that he was only able to work as long as he didn't need to supervise the latrine digger did not endear the rest of the men to the self-proclaimed knight.

Skharr hoped the bad tempers would fade sooner rather than later. Having something like that simmering had a way of souring the spirit of the whole group, a feeling that would likely end with Denith and others dead.

He would need to settle things quickly. Something would hopefully happen soon to bring resolution.

"I remember that you can make magic out of mundane ingredients," Sera commented as she sat next to him near the fire. "I can only hope that your abilities remain intact despite so much time spent having others cook for you."

"The skills of the cook are reliant on the ingredients they have on hand," Skharr replied. "Our ingredients will dwindle, given where you want us to travel to. There is little worth eating in goblin lands unless you are particularly strong of stomach."

"Not eating the goblins themselves, surely?"

"They can strip almost any land they come across of all the food and never plant anything to grow in its place," he explained. "I've seen them make soup from the bark of trees. I suppose that would be the kind of creature you become when you have to make your living from the rock deep under the mountains."

"So you say we might have to resort to eating goblins?"

"Provided we can't scavenge anything from the groups we find," Skharr countered. "They do tend to collect anything they can and carry it to wherever their tribe has settled. But in the mountains, where there is less to gather, we have resorted to certain…extremes."

Sera made a face. "I doubt even you could make that taste good."

"It tastes a little like pork—a hint of bitterness and very lean, but very similar to pork. And if you salt and dry it, the bitterness is gone."

"I've been on my share of battlefields. I am aware of the desperation that can touch those who have been left without proper food, sometimes for months at a time." She shrugged. "I don't know why the concept of eating the dead still shocks me."

"It's a natural reaction for a civilized person." He nodded and tipped the spice mix he had been preparing into the pot that simmered over the fire. "No matter how uncivilized we become, there is a moment of introspection when we have to decide what lengths we will go to for survival."

"That sounds oddly philosophical, coming from you."

"I could recite the works of the great minds such as Sorante, Trelor, and Voranis."

"Can you truly?"

"No, but wouldn't it be hilarious if I did?"

Sera did laugh then and shook her head as the rest of the group began to gather for the meal that was being prepared. Even Denith took his place among the rest, having washed the dirt and sweat that accumulated from the digging. Skharr had a feeling he hadn't heard the last of the man's complaints, however.

He was still nursing the bruise on his jaw that would keep him timid for the moment. It wouldn't last but the silence was at least a welcome change, aside from the hungry slurps and grunts from the group as they ate their fill.

Warm meals were a luxury that wouldn't last more than a few days out of the city but for the moment, they could enjoy the fresh ingredients that would go bad soon and so had to be consumed quickly.

After that, it would mostly be dried meat, mushrooms, and way bread. These were filling but not the kind of food that made their stomachs rumble and mouths water.

As the week progressed, Denith's attitude grew more amenable toward the others in the group. He even went about his chores without the endless complaints that generally accompanied digging latrines. At that point, Skharr decided that it was probably for the best to alternate the chores.

The group began to settle into the rhythm of their journey and the barbarian grew more comfortable with them, although he assumed that Sera was not the type to trust easily. Regor was like her and avoided the newcomers in favor of those he had traveled with before. This left him as the coordinator of their little troop and he shouldered the responsibility to keep the men moving and in good spirits.

The coastal road was mostly in good repair for the first half of the week, as it was the road used to a variety of shipyards in the region. Most of the caravans leaving Verenvan usually ended up at one of them.

But once the roads led south, there was a distinct difference in their quality. They clung a little closer to the coast where the elements eroded almost anything made by the hands of men. Little to no effective repairs were carried out in the isolated towns and smaller cities in the region.

It wasn't entirely surprising, of course. The repairs only went where the coin still flowed.

"It will take three days to reach Creanda," Sera announced as they began to settle in for the evening. "We'll have to increase our pace if we want to maintain that schedule, and from there, we can resupply and continue our journey. It will be mostly fish but still, it's better than scrounging in these fucking forests for roots and berries, eh, Skharr?"

She looked around for the barbarian, who was on the other side of the camp, working on the packs that Horse carried.

"I heard you," he rumbled as she approached. "But I have an odd feeling and I think I should look into it before we travel farther."

"That feeling wouldn't be the need to get out of your fair share of the work of setting up camp, would it?" She leaned on Horse's side and watched him as he pulled the heavy bow he had been practicing with out from where it had been packed. "You're taking your bow?"

"I'll scout ahead," he replied and slung it over his shoulder. "Suppose I should find myself a deer with no means to kill it?"

"I remember the last time you scouted ahead and what you found was certainly not deer."

"You did promise me a little violence if I came along. Yet here I am, doing your work for you."

Sera smirked and shook her head. "Of course. Be careful out there."

"Naturally." Skharr slung the bow and quiver over his shoulder and hooked his ax onto his belt. "Horse, stay here with her. And if I find trouble I am unable to handle, you come and help me, yes?"

The stallion snorted.

"I think that means no," she stated.

He smirked. "I didn't know you spoke his tongue."

"Derision is a universal language."

That was true enough and he had no answer.

Soon, he grew a little more accustomed to moving on his own through the thick forests. The shipyards were making great inroads into clearing the land of the trees but for the moment, all was as it had been for the past few thousand years.

It was a warm night, pleasant for traveling alone.

When the sun came up and there was no sign of the barbarian, Sera fought the urge to send a search party after him. She wasn't his mother and Skharr was more than capable of taking care of himself in any adverse situation.

And if there was something in the wilderness that could kill him, she didn't want to send her men out to find it. The chances were that she would lose a few of them, if not all, if they went out to search for him when he didn't want to be found.

"There's something ahead in the road, boss," Regor shouted and turned his horse to face her from the front of the group. "Someone, to be more precise."

She nudged her horse forward. Much to her amusement, she had begun to talk to him like Skharr did with Horse, but it didn't quite feel like a conversation as much as it did when she talked to the stallion.

Perhaps most horses weren't used to being spoken to like Horse was. Holding a two-way conversation with folk who weren't used to conversing was probably something that needed to be learned.

"Let's see what we have facing us now, Cody," she whispered and patted the gelding on the neck as they approached where it appeared the road had been blocked.

It was an odd sight, of course. A tree had been felled to create a barrier across the road but instead of hiding, it looked like the bandits had positioned themselves around it as if to take advantage of anyone who might arrive. Of course, the fact that they had set themselves up in plain view was interesting and an immediate warning to take another path.

It seemed they didn't have any horses to stop those who tried to run away either. That much was enough to tell her that the group they faced were not the most skilled or even the most experienced in the business of robbing travelers of their livelihood.

If she were to guess, these were locals—woodsmen, fishers, and even farmers who were in need of a little extra coin and decided to expand their endeavors. It had probably seemed like a good opportunity when most other bandits had left the region to find themselves coin in the dungeon.

In the end, with most of the better-quality guards having taken the same route, she had a feeling the untried robbers would have found a decent amount of coin had anyone but she and her men passed through their area of the woods.

The men appeared to be confident enough despite the heavily armed group that advanced on their position. Sera assumed it had something to do with their large numbers—easily twice as many as she had in her small team—although if Skharr had been present, their group would have appeared a little more intimidating. Perhaps they would have considered hiding and letting them pass.

Then again, she doubted that they had too many brains between them. None wore any armor and a few carried spears as well as a handful of wood axes, but the rest held seaxes and daggers, the weapons of those who likely couldn't afford any better.

"We'll need the tax for this road," the leader said and stood on the fallen trunk so he would look taller.

"You don't bear the count's sigil," Sera replied with her hand resting calmly on her sword hilt. "Clear the way and we might pay you for the trouble of lifting the tree from our path."

"You'll pay more than that." The bandit hopped off his perch to reveal that he was almost a foot shorter than the rest of his group. "Count ha'en't been on these roads for years, so we have more claim to it than he. You'll hand over your weapons, horses, and all your supplies and we'll let you leave with your lives."

The guild captain scowled and nudged her horse forward ahead of the rest of the group. The bandits hadn't brought any archers unless a few were hidden in the trees. Then again, the whole group should have been hiding in the trees. The only possible way that they would be able to make any coin from their endeavor was to intimidate anyone they encountered with their numbers.

"You'll need to find another group to try to intimidate with your bravado," she called and grasped her sword hilt, ready to draw it at the slightest provocation. "All those who remain on this road will die. Those who clear it before we pass will live."

"The first battle of our trip and the barbarian is not even present," Denith grumbled behind her.

Sera couldn't help but agree with the sentiment, but she didn't want to think that they relied on Skharr for their safety on the road. If he wasn't present, they would be able to handle the gods-bedammed idiots on their own.

The leader took a step forward and leered at her with a sickening smirk. "I would be willing to let the rest of your lads leave with their clothes as long as you discard yours and give yourself over for the use of myself and me boys. We might even leave you enough food to reach the nearest village provided you make us all happy."

On that comment alone, she drew her sword, ready to cut the man's head off and let the others come and claim what they appeared to want. Before her blade cleared its scabbard, however, the little man grunted and gaped at his abdomen.

A hole had appeared to release blood and expose his viscera to the air. Sera paused, flicked her sword to the right and away from her horse, and tried to determine what had caused the wound.

Her eyebrows raised when a second man fell clutching an arrow that had buried itself in his stomach.

She hadn't even heard the song of a bowstring anywhere nearby, but there was only one kind of bow that could perform that kind of feat. Unless there was another DeathEater in their region, she had to assume Skharr was the archer.

"Is there anything else you would like to say?" she asked and flicked her sword from side to side to loosen her wrist. "Or any other comments on what you might demand from your regular passerby or traveler on this road?"

They appeared to have nothing more to say. The group seemed more interested in finding out where the arrow had come from.

It took them a few moments to see the hulking mountain of a barbarian who slid out of the shadows cast by trees, another arrow nocked and ready to fire into the group.

"The woman asked you a question, you maggot-brained spawn of Janus' sweaty armpit," Skharr roared and held the arrow pointed at the nearest of the bandits until the man backed away. Calmly, he shifted his aim to the next.

Soon, it appeared as though they were all busy backing away from the warrior to avoid being the next one to be shot.

The guild captain thought that her second in command would be content to scare the group off after having killed only a couple of them. She was surprised, therefore, when he loosed another arrow and pinned one of the bandits to the tree trunk that blocked the road.

"I heard what you said, Denith!" the barbarian called and Sera grinned when the man's face turned pale as he drew away from the group. The bandits felt as though they had no other option and rushed forward with a collective cry, intent on at least dying a violent death instead of being hunted like wild animals. More than a few rethought their position rather quickly, however, when they saw Skharr raise his bow with another arrow in it.

Threatening a group would only lead to violence, but the barbarian had a way about him that made each one feel threatened in a very individual manner.

She could hear the twang of bowstrings from the rest of her team as they started to join the skirmish.

Another one of the bandits was punched off his feet when an arrow caught him in the chest. Sera expected to see it emerge on the other side to penetrate the man behind. When it didn't, she assumed it had caught on his ribs, which prevented it from going through all the way. She spurred her horse forward and swung her sword, ready to catch the bandits as Skharr rushed toward them.

Another one almost backed into Cody in his effort to get as

far away from the rampaging barbarian as he could. She stopped him immediately, lopped his head off with a graceful swipe of her blade, and followed it quickly with a rapid cutback that sent another one to his knees, clutching his throat.

Skharr held three arrows in his drawing hand and two in his bow hand as he loosed another two in quick succession. They streaked into the group and felled their targets as she slid from her saddle and moved beside him. A single skilled swing of her blade sliced into one of the men who attempted to attack from the side and opened his stomach neatly as the warrior let another arrow fly.

It was odd to see him straining that much with the bow and it slowed him somewhat. A thin film of sweat covered his forehead.

"It isn't your regular bow, I take it?" she asked and deftly parried another strike, slashed the man's throat, and kicked him into the path of his comrades. Around them, the rest of her mercenaries had entered the fray as well.

"It's a heavier draw," Skharr admitted and strained visibly to launch more arrows at his chosen targets. "It is certainly more of a strain than I am used to."

"I can see that." Sera didn't want to admit that the small reminder that he was vaguely human was unsettling. At the same time, the fact that he was still able to fire the bow despite how much he had to work to draw it was annoying.

She knew how to shoot a bow and had on occasion in the past, but the heavier the draw, the more her aim inevitably suffered and that would not make things easier to deal with, not with him around.

The guild captain moved back slightly as Skharr fired the last of his arrows and dropped his bow. He immediately became even deadlier with an ax and a dagger in hand and rushed into the group that was being driven back by her men.

"Do you think our boys are safe in there?" Regor asked as he shouldered his recurve bow and watched the barbarian lunge into two of the brigands. His ax cleaved deeply into the first one's chest and he slashed another open at the belly with his dagger.

"Why do you ask?"

"Well, give him a moment to wind his blood rage down. The man clearly heard something he didn't like from them, and he'll take his rage out on the fuckers for a while yet."

He had a point. A few of her mercenaries were already withdrawing from the fight, reluctant to be caught in the vortex of death and destruction that Skharr had become.

"He'll probably bitch unmercifully if we don't leave enough of them for him to kill," she agreed. "Pull back. When half are dead, any of you who has a taste for it, feel free."

"What about you?"

"I'll stay here and kill everyone who gets around you. I'll not risk annoying the DeathEater."

As if they'd had the same thought, her men retreated from the attack and moved into defensive positions where they cut down those bandits who tried to escape Skharr's wrath. He had worked himself into a frenzy she hadn't seen before, and it was genuinely terrifying to watch even from a safe distance.

It would be something else altogether to be in the path of his weapons when he was in that kind of fury. The armor he wore brushed off most of the attempted damage dealt by the unfortunates and allowed him almost free reign to terrorize them as he saw fit.

The only real combat the rest of them saw were those few who decided to run from the fight. Regor and the other two archers in her group made a point to fell them with precise arrows, and those who found themselves in the path of the other mercenaries were quickly cut down as well.

Sera winced when one of Regor's arrows sailed a little too close to the barbarian, although he didn't so much as look back when he heard it whistle past his ear.

"You stick me and I'll feed you your own fucking arrow!" he roared and she put her hand on Regor's arm to lower his bow.

"I would suggest," she said, "that you avoid hitting the large barbarian on a rampage."

The unfortunate brigands might have had better luck with other caravans and travelers. In this case, they had made their own charnel house.

Finally, Skharr stood alone and drew deep breaths as he looked at the carnage he had created. He was covered in the blood of the fallen as he wiped the red from his weapons.

Sera approached him carefully, not wanting to be accidentally cut down if the barbarian was still in a bloodletting mood.

"I assume you had a fruitful scouting trip then?" she asked as he wiped some of the blood from his face.

"I think so. I happened upon their camp and followed them to the road, where I saw them trying to…well, I saw them stopping you."

That explained the rage she'd seen in him. She doubted there was much she could say about the man himself that would anger him, but he did seem like the type who would attack if he heard insults offered to his friends.

"I don't suppose you needed to kill all of them?" Sera questioned and tossed him a cloth to clean himself with.

"I didn't," he replied. "Some were intelligent enough to make their escape while the rest sacrificed their lives. Chasing them through the woods might be the best for the surrounding lands, but I doubt we have the time for it. All we can do is hope they learned their lesson and continue on our journey."

"They didn't make it far." She pointed to the bodies the others had managed to kill as he collected the arrows he'd loosed.

The scene was a sobering reminder of what the man was capable of when he had a mind to kill.

"You heard the man!" Sera shouted. "We'll find a way to move this tree from the road and keep moving!"

"What of the bodies?" Regor asked as he retrieved his arrows as well.

"Take what you like from them but I doubt you'll find much. Aside from that, leave them as carrion. They don't deserve a proper burial."

There was no argument there. The barbarian looked uncharacteristically winded after the fight but still managed to put his back into helping them move the log from the road to make it passable again, despite the dozens of potholes.

"Did you get any sleep last night?" Sera asked while he loaded all his items on Horse's back once they were properly cleaned.

"I might have. Why do you ask?"

"You look a little more exhausted than I am used to seeing you."

He scowled at her, but it didn't appear to hold any malice as he pushed a few of the packs to balance the weight.

"The godsbedammed bow is heavier than I'm used to. I'll have to practice with it."

"Of course." She nodded, mounted quickly, and patted Cody on the neck. "See, this is why you were gelded. Keep your balls and you'll drive yourself half to death simply to prove your worth."

It was a little unfair, she supposed, but the barbarian needed to hear it anyway.

CHAPTER TEN

"**F**ucking ass. You need to keep moving or I'll find another donkey to carry my possessions across the world."

It was an empty threat and the donkey knew it. They had been together forever—or so it seemed—and they weren't about to part ways over a little spat. The beast was simply in the mood for something to eat and he could yell and shout as much as he wanted to but in the end, it would eat its fill of the thick, luscious grass around them and that was that.

He would need to find something else to do in the meantime. The old man sighed and tugged his beard irritably before he shook his head and took an old wooden pipe from his pocket. With methodical care, he packed a little fragrant leaf inside and lit it using a piece of flint and the steel of his knife.

"Heavens know why I chose you for a companion," he muttered and took a moment to groom his mustache with his fingers when he heard boots on the sand around him.

The open landscape made it difficult to approach anyone without them being aware and even if that failed him, he still had ears.

Those were sharp enough to hear the heavy boots of the men still trying to follow him.

"Why won't they ever listen?" he whispered, drove his staff into the sandy ground, and buried it almost halfway. Thankfully, an oasis like this had been fought over often, which meant there were numerous bodies for him to choose from.

Not that many were needed. The brigands who approached him from behind were the desperate kind and if they hadn't smelt so offensive, he might have given them a hint of warning before all five were bogged down.

"What the devils?"

"The ground! It's… It's moving!"

Cries for help did not interest him. Perhaps his sister would have a heart and teach the marauders the errors of their ways, although he frankly thought all her stories about forgiveness were crap that even bulls would be ashamed to drop.

She insisted on the truth of them, however. The old man found no use for such things and the screams of terror turned into gargled moans until silence reigned again.

When he looked back, his gaze traced only sand that no longer held his footsteps, nor those of the men who had pursued him. It was an unsettling feeling but one he had grown used to in his many, many years wandering the earth.

"Janus was always better at finding the right folk for the right task," Theros said softly and shook his head. "For myself, I always found the wrong man or the wrong task. It's annoying, honestly, as I generally have to perform those tasks myself with no help from the rest of my siblings. Don't you think it a little unfair, Veidar?"

The donkey still had nothing to say to him and munched placidly on the patches of grass that grew in the small oasis.

Respite from the unbearable heat of the desert was certainly welcome. The dry air made it so even the slightest shade was enough to cool him a little. He filled his waterskin at the small pool that seeped from under the ground.

With that safely strung on his belt, he wet a small rag and draped it over his head as he worked to prepare himself food for the midday meal. He might as well since the godsbedammed donkey was already enjoying his. A rough blanket would suffice for his picnic and he set out a hunk of dried meat, cheese, bread, and a few dried fruits and nuts. He could take a moment to enjoy in comparative comfort before he inevitably needed to continue through the godsbedammed desert.

A loud crackle filled the air accompanied by the scent of ozone as he looked up from his humble meal. Dark clouds formed in front of him and parted at the sound of lightning. A figure stepped into the desert through the vaporous gap. He was easily ten feet tall and clad in armor of silver and gold with jet-black hair flowing from his shoulders. He held a silver spear in one hand and a massive horn in the other.

Theros returned his attention to his meal and popped a dried apricot into his mouth. Janus always did enjoy making a grand entrance, but that didn't mean he had to pay attention to it. Let him grandstand all he wanted for an audience of one who simply didn't care.

Two, he corrected himself, but Veidar had as little inclination to indulge his brother's antics as he did.

"Fancy meeting you here, brother," Theros said once the clouds dissipated and the thunder stopped. "I didn't think there was much in the world that could drag you away from your palace in the clouds."

Janus planted his spear in the ground and approached him where he sat in the shade. "True. There isn't. Why do you insist on walking the earth as an ancient, grumpy turd with naught but a lowly donkey for companionship?"

"You mock the wisdom of an old ass," he muttered in response. "As if you didn't know the benefits of one's counsel.

You can stop pretending to be a tough god if you like. Only you and I are in this lonely part of the world—still alive, anyway."

"You must stop using the human dead as your followers, brother."

"Not all those who live are deserving of the gift. Not all who die are deserving of it either."

His brother waved his hand dismissively and with the gesture, his stature shrank to a much smaller state although still massive by human standards. Now, he was almost seven feet tall and still wore the powerful armor he was known for.

"Better, Janus, but still annoying," he said and motioned for the god to join him. He retrieved a heavy wineskin from his pack and offered it to his brother. "Have a drink. I know it's not quite the ambrosia you gorge on but it should still make your surly disposition a little more tolerable."

He could practically feel his brother's glare but he took the skin and tipped it back with a motion that spoke considerable practice.

"I doubt it," Janus admitted.

"Have something to eat as well." Theros waved to the small feast he had set out for himself. It was more than enough for two and he moved to a boulder about the right size and picked it up.

Only one hand was needed to lift it from the ground. He dragged it to the shade and groaned as he sat on it.

"Well?"

"Well, what?" Janus asked and took a bite from the dried meat.

"You didn't seek me out for my sharp wit and good looks." He took the skin for a sip of his own before he handed it back and helped himself to bread and cheese. "Out with it. What have you come to complain about?"

"We have a problem."

"We?" Theros chuckled and gestured to the bloodstains that faintly marked the sand behind him. "I would say I resolved my most recent and only problem rather well."

"Yes, we," Janus retorted. "I refer, of course, to myself and my ignorant brother who refuses to pay attention to the matters of the world around him."

"I assume you have a particular matter to discuss?"

"A dungeon has been recently possessed by an evil being near the Belvish Mountains."

"That is...south of Verenvan, yes?"

"Of course."

Theros raised his hand. "Pardon my ignorance. Not all of us have the Well of Vataan to see the world in the blink of an eye. I am a god but not omniscient by any means."

His brother sighed and shook his head. "This entity has killed more than two hundred of my followers in the last seven days and will likely kill another hundred over the next two if my visions are correct."

"Ah, that is heart-rending." Theros chewed thoughtfully on a handful of almonds. "Yet I fail to understand how this has anything to do with me."

"You have noticed that more than a few of your followers have defected to join the ranks of mine, yes? At this point, you must admit it is no small problem."

"Good riddance." He harrumphed loudly but his eyes narrowed. "And why did they change their allegiance?"

It was telling that his brother avoided his gaze and stared into the desert instead.

"I might have instructed my priests to offer a significant reward for the follower or group of followers who killed the evil in the dungeon."

"They were tempted by greed. How predictable."

"And glory besides. And a godly gift, a promise from my lips."

Theros paused and ran his fingers slowly through his beard as his bushy eyebrows drew together over his eyes. "That is...well, rare. Giving one of your gifts away as a reward, even for you, is unheard of. What prompted you to such an unusual measure? What is the evil in this dungeon?"

"A magus lich," Janus said softly. "I have no clue as to how it was created or who did it."

That was indeed worrying. Liches were dangerous to deal with in general and magus liches added a level of extreme difficulty to an already potentially lethal challenge.

"I see. Magus liches are…"

"Rare?"

"Godsbedammned near impossible. Aside from the one that almost killed you, the last one I heard of was destroyed not long ago."

"Yes, by one of your followers."

Theros tilted his hand from side to side. "I wouldn't necessarily say he is one of my followers. Barbarians rarely follow in the truest sense of the word."

"They are an unruly race but they have their uses."

"True. They have their moments," he admitted. "But they aren't exactly attuned to the letter of the law—or the spirit of the law for that matter."

"And not the world's finest listeners either," Janus added. "And sometimes, they are a little too smart for their tiny heads."

He tried not to let his amusement show as he saw the ire building in his brother's eyes.

"And the one who came out the victor of my yearly dungeon crawl is particularly annoying. I swear I heard him call me an ass. More than once."

That broke Theros' composure and he had to chuckle softly. "That cannot be the worst a human has ever called you, brother."

"It was the way he said it I found most annoying."

The amusement was good for another few seconds, but the old man brought his attention back to the claim his brother had made. It seemed almost impossible but while he was an ass, Janus was no liar, and he had never heard him exaggerate either.

"The creation of a magus lich without our knowledge concerns me," he stated finally. "Watch my donkey for a moment and do not antagonize him."

"Should I be afraid?"

"No, but I'll hear about it for the rest of the week."

Theros stood, put his hand forward, and a blueish crackle formed in the air and warped the light around it. He stepped through and felt a tingle that made every hair on his body stand on end for a moment before the desert around him was replaced by perfect blackness.

He truly didn't need to see much. His location had been carved with his hands and while it had fallen into those of others, he still knew every inch of it.

When he had adjusted to the spatial change, he placed his hand on the nearest wall, closed his eyes, and felt the energy seeping through. His pyramid was still in place, which was a good sign, but something was altered and warped about it.

No power remained in the place aside from what it created itself, but there were remnants and whispers. Something had happened and more recently than Skharr's cleansing.

He breathed deeply and finally discerned an energy that had no place there.

"Godsbedammed," he whispered, waved his hand again, and grimaced at the prickle of the portal across his body. A second later, his eyes were again assaulted by the blinding light of the sun.

"You were always better at those than I," Janus admitted, having brought a seat to the blanket for himself. "What did you find?"

"No demon and no lich, but I detected something that should not have been there," Theros whispered and tugged at his threadbare robes. "Someone from our family is causing problems."

His brother stood slowly. "Our family, you say?"

"Aye."

He looked at his body and allowed a gentle tug and prickle of energy to build powerfully within. Gone were the aching joints and sore limbs of a man determined to spend eternity in the twilight of his life. He could feel power coursing through him again. Shrunken arms gained muscle, the dreary gray beard and hair took on thick golden hues, and his eyes shed their previous weakness. He knew that small sparks of lightning could be seen in his brilliant blue eyes now.

"Someone took possession of the lich Skharr defeated and the demon he trapped and merged them into the magus lich your people have faced. I suspect it was created in the original dungeon where they were defeated and moved to another location. I could still feel the scar left there by the portal that was created."

"One of our own, then," Janus agreed and handed him the empty wineskin. "They will owe me when this is done."

"Truly."

"So, do I have your help?"

Theros flicked his fingers at Veidar, who brayed in protest and was instantly transformed into a small figurine about the size of his thumb.

He moved forward, picked him up, and slid him into his pocket. "You do, my brother. I will need to conduct research of my own, however. I must also insist that there be no harassment of each other's followers until this evil is destroyed, including Skharr."

Janus grinned, took his brother's outstretched hand, and grasped it firmly. "Agreed. Wait—isn't Skharr the name of the barbarian who defeated my dungeon?"

"Not now, brother mine." He raised his hand and another portal was carved from the air. Janus was right, of course. He was better at creating them but only because he didn't feel the need to provide pomp and circumstance for every occasion.

As his brother disappeared, Janus smirked and shook his head. "Theros, you are a bastard."

He'd expected that it would feel different.

Something would change and he would feel more ready to take on the role once his father was dead. So many were looking to him for answers, guidance, and leadership, and Tryam couldn't help but feel like a fraud.

And yet, no one had questioned him, narrowed their eyes at him, or thought he was unfit for the position of emperor. That might have had something to do with how he had come to power. Or perhaps the fact that he wasn't expected to do much in the way of actual ruling.

Or maybe, just maybe, he was making a decent job of it.

Being stuck behind a massive, ornate desk for most of the day didn't help matters. A considerable portion of his responsibilities could be delegated down the line to others, but a few matters stopped with him and he needed to deal with them.

When Elric entered the throne room, Tryam immediately felt as though the man brought yet another headache to be added to the pile.

His captain approached the desk, paused, and took a moment to bow dutifully.

"Come," he snapped and gestured for him to approach. "We need to find a way around all this ridiculous pomp and ceremony that surrounds the title of emperor."

"There is a reason for it," Elric explained and approached the desk. "It is to make sure that all who approach you do so with reverence. And it provides enough time to ensure that any who do approach you are studied by your guards to determine that they are not armed and ready to kill you."

"Like I said, we can find a way."

The man nodded, although Tryam had a feeling he wouldn't pay much attention to the suggestion. He didn't know how to order the man to do so without causing problems, and unnecessary issues with his Elites would not be taken well. They were already on the thinnest of ice as far as he was concerned after they attempted to have him killed before he was even crowned.

"What do you have for me?" He motioned again for the man to come closer.

"Rumors, for the most part, but not the kind that can be easily disregarded. The priests of Janus have been annoyingly silent on the matter, but I take that as only a sign that we are on the right track. They tend to be loud and vociferous otherwise."

"Godsbedammed assholes. "

"Indeed. Even so, they are a powerful group with connections outside the empire."

"I rather wish that they would use those connections to bother the Ishkalads. A good time could be had by both parties."

"I doubt there is enough liquor in the world to tempt the Ishkalads with a good time."

"True enough. What rumors have the priests been spreading?"

"There is trouble in the south. A dungeon close to the Belvish Mountains has given them more than the usual amount of difficulty."

"The…what?"

"The Belvish Mountains. South of Verenvan, where we have had the most trouble with the goblin tribes. We occasionally need to recruit armies to destroy them as they rut and spread like rabbits."

Tryam sighed and rubbed his temples. He didn't have the best memory for locations to begin with, and having to keep track of all the rulers of all the towns and all the cities in the empire was proving to be a little troublesome.

His empire, he reminded himself in a moment of self-realization.

"Verenvan?"

"Yes, Your Highness."

"I don't suppose we have enough men to deal with whatever is happening in the region?" he asked and checked a map on his desk to make sure that he had the right location.

"It is a dungeon crawl. We could throw ten thousand men at it and the result would still be the same. We will have to discover what is happening for ourselves and resolve it as ruthlessly as possible. My suggestion would be to send a few scouts to determine the nature of the problem."

"Or..." He held a finger up as an idea came to him. "We could learn what is happening from the mouth of a specialist."

"Skharr DeathEater?"

"The very same. Is he known to spend his time in Verenvan?"

"Yes. But I fear that he will not appreciate this. You know that, yes?"

"He wasn't appreciative of helping me either," the emperor recalled. "But I did tell him that I was paying him well, so he should at least hear what I have to say. Send messages to the barbarian and ask him to consider looking into it. Not as a demand, though. Skharr will like as not ram any demands I make up the ass of the messenger who delivers it and call it a teaching moment. He had many of those when we traveled together."

"You miss him, don't you?"

Tryam shrugged casually. "He had a way of making the world so wonderfully simple. I suppose I miss that more than I miss the man himself but yes, I do wish he were here in the capital instead of wandering the world."

"I understand." Elric nodded. "He certainly had a talent for cutting through bullshit better than most I've seen."

With a deep breath, the emperor pushed from his seat, stretched, and groaned. He'd been there for far too long. "See to it that the message is sent and that Skharr knows it's a request, not a demand. I, in the meantime, will retire to my quarters for food and rest."

"Of course, Your Highness." The captain bowed stiffly at the hips. "I am very glad you are making a request of it. I would not have been happy to deal with an angry DeathEater."

"And you can find the most convincing way to have him on our side once the time comes, yes?"

"Of course. Will you need someone to…tend to you while you rest?"

"I'm not my father. I won't put a bastard in the belly of half the women in the empire. Or at least I hope I won't."

The man smirked. "Very well, Your Highness. I will report to you once I learn something."

"Thank you, Elric."

CHAPTER ELEVEN

The Council was together again after such a short time. There had been no meetings in person for decades and yet there they were, gathered in the same room for the second time in less than a month.

If Micah made her mind up to kill them all, this would be a perfect time. Not many of them would be able to stop her and even the guards who were waiting outside would only come in when it was far too late for them to do anything.

It was an unsettling feeling, wanting to kill the folk she was in a room with, but they were unsettling folk. Perhaps killing them wasn't such a terrible idea after all.

"The gambling dens are doing quite well," Taurin told them. "Not many folk leave their seats with their wits about them. Free drinks and all kinds of games that lose them money more than make up for any losses that might be incurred. Otan is exceptionally good at making sure all debts incurred are paid, including mine. It's a fine little system we have here, yes?"

"A fine relationship forged, yes," Tera commented. "But my ladies of the night have concerns. Men leave your dens drunk and high on the opiates you peddle to them and angry over having lost the money. My ladies attract them and yet they pay the price for your victim's losses. A bruised woman will not be paid for, as you well know, Taurin."

The dwarf scowled but looked away. "If there is a problem, you could always engage the services Fakos provides in dealing with men who need lessons in how women should be treated."

Micah noted that they didn't make any mention of what lessons dwarves needed to be taught.

"My men won't bother to protect ladies of the night without serious incentive in the form of coin," Fakos answered quickly and shook her head. "They have far more lucrative work to tend to."

"And that might have something to do with how your men tend to be the guilty parties when Tera's ladies are assaulted," Micah commented. "Rats have ears in this city, and your men talk too much when they dive too deep into their cups."

The woman scowled and drew a deep breath. "I can speak to them, find the guilty parties, and make sure any protection provided will be paid for out of their pockets. The threat of that should make sure they keep their fists to themselves, should it not?"

The other council members nodded slowly in agreement.

This wasn't the reason why they had gathered, of course, but once they were all in one place, it was clear that some business would be discussed. This was mostly because the only relationship the members of the group had with each other involved the gathering of coin in massive amounts. They would find their way to the matter at hand eventually.

"And should there come a time when the threats no longer assure Tera's ladies of their due protection?" Taurin asked and folded his thick arms in front of his stout chest.

"I have some genuinely damaging information on several mercenary captains in the guilds of this city," Micah noted and tilted her head. "It would cost Tera, of course, but not nearly as much as it would to hire the mercenary groups outright. Once the fact is established that you have trained mercenaries from the guilds protecting your ladies, there should be little problem with drunkards with needs to abuse something after they gamble their lives away."

"That would be appreciated," Tera commented and pocketed some of the food on the table to consume later.

"But that is not why we have come together today," Otan muttered and slid his gaze over each member of the small gathering in the room.

"I've always considered that such meetings in person were a waste of time," Tera retorted and raised an eyebrow. "It is extremely dangerous. With one wrong payment in the wrong hands of the city guard, we'd all be dead in one fell swoop. We should never be in the same room as another member of this council, much less all of us in the same room at the same godsbedammed time."

"There are circumstances that call for dangerous meetings," Fakos snapped, her hand on the empty scabbard at her side. Not wearing her weapon was a requirement for her to enter the room. "The barbarian yet lives despite our finest efforts to change that."

"They weren't truly our finest efforts now, were they?" Otan asked and his tone sounded a little challenging. "The crossbowman with the poisoned arrow was certainly a fine attempt, but the one that preceded it and the one that followed were the kind that should be forgotten, wouldn't you say? A single man with a dagger in a brawl and five men with daggers on the street?"

Micah could agree that they had been miserable attempts. Assassinations were judged by their success and all three had been failures.

Which meant all three were miserable, although she doubted Fakos would want to hear it.

"Mine was the crossbow that should have killed him," the woman all but snarled to prove the point. "I haven't a clue who directed the other two."

All gazes moved to Taurin, who looked like he wanted to find the nearest, darkest corner to hide in.

"Throw enough knives at the man and eventually, one will find his throat," he whispered and shook his head. "They need not be held by skilled hands."

"That might be true for a lowly thief who needs to be silenced," Micah replied. "A DeathEater is another animal entirely, however. The kind of violence they face as youths would make any street rat in this city seem to be sleeping in the lap of luxury by comparison. Killers without equal need unique methods for their disposal. Otherwise, it will be like throwing naked soldiers at a walled fortress."

"Do you have any ideas then?" Otan asked and scowled at her.

"I already told you that I will not be involved in planning or accomplishing the man's murder. You should be able to do it without me."

"It would seem not," Fakos interjected. "And the fact that someone is out there helping him kill those assassins who survive his hands is even more worrying. Killing an assassin who has failed…well that is plain murder, is it not?"

"He has left the city walls," Tera whispered. "That should be the end of the problem, yes?"

"He will return, you moron," Taurin snapped. "He's with Sera Ferat and her company and provided that nothing happens to them on the road, they will both return."

"Unless, of course, something were to happen to them while they are on the road." Otan raised an eyebrow and looked around the room.

Micah stood quickly. "I will leave now. Discuss whatever plans you have for the man's death away from my ears."

They all nodded in agreement and waited for her to leave,

although she could feel their glares follow her out. They had hoped that she would join them in their attempts and her reluctance to do so would most certainly be the cause of some strife.

Not that she cared. The group as a whole could go and fuck themselves.

She circled before she reached the guards and pushed a few panels in the wall until she heard a soft, satisfying click that opened a secret door into the room that would not be noticed by the council members.

The fact that they continued to discount her ability to find information would be their downfall but for now, she only wanted to hear what they had to say about the assassination. While Skharr was in the city, she couldn't care what business or danger the man found himself in. But if he was traveling with her sister, she needed to know that Sera would be safe in any situation that put Skharr in danger.

There was no wall between her and the rest of the room, and the painting was created so she could see through it with only the slightest of distortions.

"The godsbedammed woman needs to question where her loyalties lie," Otan stated belligerently and shook his head. "I am beginning to worry that her mind might not be in the right place in this. She might care for the barbarian in some form or fashion. Perhaps she warns him of the attempts and makes sure he knows beforehand."

"Even we don't know beforehand." Taurin ran his fingers pensively through his beard. "What the other will attempt, I mean. The woman has ears in every corner of the city but she wouldn't know what we have planned if we do not even share it with one another."

"It doesn't matter," Fakos snapped. "We have been able to track the convoy the barbarian travels in and have discovered precisely where he will go next. A team already awaits him and his party in the next town they will visit—a small fishing town by the name of Creanda. Our assassins will be ready for him. Should they fail, a larger group of mercenaries has been assembled to meet them outside the town."

"What of Sera Ferat?" Tera asked and looked around. "Should she die as a result of the murders, I would not want to have Micah out for blood against any of us."

"Both women have cast their lots with the barbarian." Otan smoothed his greasy hair as he spoke. "Should they find themselves victims when he dies, that will be their doing."

"If she doesn't want to eat steel from her sister, I can't think they are overly close anyway," Fakos agreed. "I'm sure she will appreciate us getting rid of the bitch."

Micah narrowed her eyes, took a step back from her listening point, and moved through the walls toward a secondary exit to the building away from the guards who were at the front.

She might have murdered every one of them in that room if not for the kind of trouble that would inevitably come from it.

Not that she particularly cared about the trouble in and of itself but it would delay her immensely. She planned to leave the city immediately before any word of what they had planned reached the assassins they already had waiting for Skharr.

"The godsbedammed fucks declared war on the Ferat clan," she whispered grimly as she turned into the stables and mounted her horse quickly. "I'll be sure to bring that war directly to their doorstep."

It was an odd kind of irony, he supposed. Necromancy was banned from most practices for a variety of reasons, the chief of which was the fact that humans had a strange attachment to their dead. They intensely disliked seeing bodies used against them in the hands of a skilled necromancer.

Of course, such rules hadn't been truly implemented until

about seven hundred years before, after the last of the great wars where thousands of the dead on battlefields were raised to fight each other repeatedly and ravaged whole continents.

Memories of the war had faded but the rules remained fresh.

But the humans who invaded his domain continued to fight each other, even if they didn't know it.

"Now this is fun to watch. Humans fighting humans."

"Which are the dead humans?"

"Is there a difference?"

"Yes."

"Then…the ones fighting for us. Those are the dead ones."

"Ah."

The reanimated corpses were considerably less skilled than their living counterparts. Something about rotting muscles and torn ligaments made them less coordinated and more difficult to control, so the living humans carved into the undead who had been raised fairly easily. There was a limit to how many times a dead body could be brought up to fight, of course, and that was reached when certain bones were broken or certain muscles were missing entirely.

It all depended on the skill of the necromancer.

The lich was skilled but not enough to stop a paladin who sliced through the horde and raise a blessed sword to strike at the lich.

"That will hurt."

It did. He recoiled from the strike yet something was there. An anger drove it as the flames all around the fighters suddenly flared with rage and lashed out at the paladin for daring to strike at him.

"He does have spirit, does he not?"

"They. There are two of them in there, remember?"

"Who gives a shit?"

It was a fair point.

As battles went, it was fairly ugly. The lich couldn't so much as touch the blessed armor the paladin wore but he didn't have to. He swung his staff and shrieked at a pitch high enough to shatter glass as he tripped his adversary and proceeded to pound his staff into the man's helm.

It took almost a dozen strikes before he was sure that the head inside the helm had been crushed and the man was dead.

The battle continued all around. Tongues of flame reached out to catch those who were unaware and thus stood too close to them, and they engulfed them quickly in fire hot enough that their armor began to melt into their skin.

That would be useful later. Undead who had armor fused to them were a little more durable than the ordinary ones and far more stable.

A few of the maggots escaped the chamber, raced back the way that they had come, and left the lich alone with his dead.

"Not quite alone."

A slow clap echoed through the room, louder even than the flames that had begun to fill it.

The lich was already angry and irritable from the pain of a gaping wound in his shoulder, but as he raised his staff to strike at the newcomer, he paused. A familiar face was illuminated by the demon's flame.

"You return, Quazel?"

His visitor smiled and continued to clap as the undead began to collect those who would later be added to their ranks. "Yes. Yes, I do return. I trust you are enjoying yourself?"

"Fuck this! I have been trapped in this useless, putrid excuse for a body for far too long!"

The lich didn't sound like he was angry enough to sound off in such a manner. He was smart enough to know better than to speak to Quazel that way. No, that sounded like the demon, angry at still being locked inside the lich who had summoned it from its realm of preference. It was all the sweeter to watch them fighting.

Hating one's flesh was the ultimate incorporation of chaos and Quazel could only revel in what he felt radiating from the abomination before him.

"What exactly do you think you would have been able to accomplish without that body?" the deity asked and tilted his head. "Most demons summoned to this realm peter out and die in days. The lich would likely have done the same without you. I like to think of it as a symbiotic relationship between the two of you and I suggest you learn how to get along. Neither of you will survive without the other."

"But what next?"

That was the lich's voice. He was less angry and less aggressive and now attempted silly manipulation.

"Next?" he asked.

"This is not my dungeon. This was never my plan. You forced me into a situation in which I can do nothing but kill those sent to destroy me in self-defense without so much as being able to attack them in return. Even those who escape this chamber are allowed to live!"

Plan? Quazel had never been one for plans. Basic ideas and concepts were about the limit of what he was able to establish beforehand but anything else was left to chance. Chance created entropy, which was where his truest power lay. It wasn't the kind of thing that he liked folk to know about him, though.

Let them all think he had an endgame to all of this. It would keep them guessing.

"We were promised sacrifices," the demon reminded him. "Virgins for our sacrifices, yes!"

"Why...why virgins? Does it need to be virgins? Would any female do?"

The demon paused. "Virgins are preferred."

"Why?"

"They are pure in both mind and body."

"Not the virgins I've met."

"Their spirits are...never you mind why. I want to be the first to enter them and let us leave it at that."

Quazel sighed. "I have enjoyed you destroying my cousin's minions so handily, I must admit. It is driving Janus to drink. Well...more drink. Or to not enjoy the massive amount of drinking he indulges in most days."

"What about Theros?" the lich asked.

"That good-for-nothing cousin? He hasn't been seen yet. I doubt he even knows what's going on, to be honest. He is bound to find out and meddle at some point, but it won't do him much good. You'll need to make this dungeon larger and grander. Fill it with the kind of death and mayhem that will certainly catch the attention of those who look upon it and force them to despair. Break their spirits almost before they enter."

Neither demon nor lich had much to say to that.

"I would think you have a very specific vision for what you want this to be," the demon responded. "And I would suggest you carry this vision out yourself instead of calling on us to do the work for you."

"I like to be surprised and I cannot be surprised if I am the one who plans it." Quazel waved his fingers at the creatures inhabiting a single corpse. "Now, Janus does like involving spirits in his designs and used them as a way to kill those who are unwise enough to fall asleep inside the dungeon. I like the thinking behind it, but I wish to push it further. Spirits who are able to make those who enter think they are in the middle of a living nightmare."

"Have them kill each other, thinking they are killing the monsters that inhabit this place?"

"Yes, yes, yes, I like the way you think...which one was that?"

"The Mighty Wolfgod Togroz!"

"Of course. How silly of me. But yes, do as you will. Watch their spirits crumble even before they reach this chamber, knowing that theirs were the hands that felled their comrades. That's the kind of thinking we need."

The lich and the demon had considerable sadistic pleasure between them, although the lich had always lacked in creativity. Still, all Quazel needed to do was inspire them and point them to the right path and they would find new and fresh horrors to inflict on the creatures who entered their domain.

But they were looking at him and waiting for instruction. They were waiting for him to tell them what to do and that wouldn't do at all.

He took a few steps back, moved through the demon's flames, and slipped into the darkness that began to fill the room again. It pleased him to allow them to think they were alone with each other while he watched the turmoil that roiled through the creature he had created.

"Your attitude certainly does not help things," the lich muttered and moved them to the throne they used to gather and maintain power over the dungeon.

"My attitude? What exactly do you think would help things?"

"You are in the presence of a high god, imbecile. Act like it and show some deference."

The demon scoffed and pulled the body back a few steps. "Why the hell should I? I am at least as powerful as he is."

"Not in this realm you aren't. You'd have barely a puff of smoke in you if you didn't have a vessel to contain you."

"You wouldn't talk so mightily if you were in my home realm. The fires would consume you alive for eternity and I would enjoy every minute of watching your suffering."

"But we aren't in your realm," the lich answered and forced the body step by step to the throne. "So keep your mouth shut, your attitude one of servitude, and allow the adult to speak instead of screeching like an unhinged child."

It was all too interesting to watch the two engage in their struggle. They were evenly matched in that body, which had been by design. The lich had intended to summon the demon to be his servant, and the demon had been a mighty being in its realm.

Now, they were forced to work together. Quazel could watch the battle between the two for decades, and the fact that their strife would make the dungeon even more of a hellish landscape for any who entered made everything that much better.

It was truly a masterpiece of his own design. And lack of design, of course. Letting their creative minds combat one another was for the best.

"This has the makings of the most entertaining decade yet."

"It hasn't even been a week."

"Even so."

CHAPTER TWELVE

The caravan moved a little faster after their encounter with the local bandits. There was no way to tell who else might have had the idea to take advantage of the lack of patrols in the region, and none of them wanted to be mistaken for a group that couldn't defend themselves.

Skharr was well aware that the primary purpose of having a guard complement was to make any who might have foul intentions think twice before they attacked.

If too many chose to attack anyway, it would end in lives lost and not only those of the brigands. An errant arrow or a lucky thrust of the knife could kill almost anyone in the world, even him.

A collective sigh of relief heralded the moment when they saw walls rise in the distance. They were of simple construction, mostly palisades, but towers were visible along the length, both for defense and to keep watch on the surrounding landscape.

It wouldn't withstand a protracted and determined assault, of course—and there was no moat around the palisades—but it would do to keep the common bandits and goblin raiding parties away.

Once again, the threat of defense was far more effective than the defenses themselves. There were even a handful of armed guards waiting at the gates as they approached and they held their hands up to stop the group before they could enter.

"We've had trouble with the local criminal element these days," the captain told them. His armor was clearly not at the level of those used by the Verenvan city guard, but it was better than what most mercenaries were able to afford, at least. His thick gambeson and rough leather helm were both stamped with the sigil of the baron of the city. "Where do you hail from?"

"Verenvan," Sera said and retrieved the documentation issued for their caravan. "Supplies are required in the south and they need a larger cohort to defend against any possible goblin raiding parties."

"They would in these parts," the man mumbled and strained his eyes to read the papers. "The small fuckers steer clear of us but use the woods for cover from the sun. This enables them to travel much farther from the mountains than we'd like. Folk are saying we should clear the forest and sell the wood to the count for his ships."

"But then you'd have none for your use," Skharr pointed out.

The captain glanced at him and took a step back so he could look him in the eyes. A suspicious look slid onto his face as he tried to determine what he was talking about.

The barbarian suddenly had a feeling that he couldn't read the document in his hands and was only playing the part.

"Aye, well, I don't know much about that." The man grunted and handed the papers to Sera, who was still mounted. "I merely mind the gate and I leave the politicking to the politickers."

"Politicians."

"Whatever you say. Come on in. You don't want to be out there when night falls. Mind your manners within the walls and there won't be any trouble."

It wasn't the warmest invitation they'd ever received but far from the coldest, and they were all glad to be out of the wilderness for a while as they headed through the gates. A few in the caravan had business there and it was far from a small town.

While not comparable to Verenvan, Skharr estimated that at least a few thousand families lived inside the walls and a few hundred more made their living beyond. The port was a decent little inlet that provided a safe refuge from the more violent storms that swept the open water. He assumed the water was too shallow for the larger ships or there would be more movement in the port.

Despite this, a veritable fleet of fishing vessels and quick knarrs and longships could slip in and out without too much trouble. A few larger vessels had docked too—a handful of barges that traveled the river that flowed through the city and what looked like whaling vessels as well, all visible from the gate since the whole town sloped toward the port.

The barbarian wondered if any of the inhabitants were worried about large waves and floods given that they built their homes and livelihoods so close to the sea and on ground that was so low, but they knew the landscape better than he did. It reminded him of his time spent on the water but that was a little too long ago for him to think about with any real recollections.

He also hoped that no one recognized him from his time on the water. There were certain kinds of trouble that had a habit of following folk that he did not need to follow him into this little city.

Sera trotted her horse to where he was still leading Horse with the rest of the caravan and drew him out of his reverie.

"I need you," she snapped.

"I suppose it is about time you decided to have a taste of what others wanted, but you should know I do not mix business with pleasure. Often."

She scowled at him, shook her head, and decided immediately that she wouldn't engage in that type of banter with him.

"I need your help," she rephrased sharply. "Regor will escort the group to where they'll settle in. The town doesn't have a dedicated Guild Hall, but there is an area near the port where the caravan can rest and prepare for the rest of the journey."

"Do you need my help to organize that?"

"No, Regor has done so many times. He'll be able to manage that side of things. I will arrange for the resources we'll need for the longer push south."

"What do you need my help for with that?"

"Folk in these parts are traditional. They tend to not take a woman seriously, even when she carries a sword and could eviscerate them in fifteen different ways. I could deal with them and teach them the error of their ways, but I feel something might be gained if you went with me."

Skharr nodded and patted Horse on the neck. "Follow Regor and don't cause him too much trouble. If I hear from him that you were stealing apples, you and I will have words, do you understand?"

The horse nickered softly and moved away from where they stood to trot toward Regor, who was still mounted and directed the group with the easy confidence of long practice.

"I'll follow your lead," the barbarian said and gestured for her to walk in front. Even though she was mounted, there would be little chance that she would lose him in the small crowds in the town. Her horse seemed a little calmer than usual and didn't appear to avoid him like he was some kind of predator that would savage its hind flanks. He'd had to avoid a few kicks in the past but so far, on this trip, there had been no need.

Then again, she called the gelding Cody. How could a horse be a happy creature when it had a name like that?

Although he had noticed that she spoke to him a little more than she generally did and held conversations. That usually calmed horses.

Sera dismounted in front of one of the local merchants,

whose expression changed quickly from an odd smile to confusion when he saw Skharr standing a few feet behind her.

As she began to discuss the items they would need for the troop, the man continued to watch the barbarian like he expected there to be trouble from the huge warrior who stared daggers at him.

With a sigh, he ignored the merchant, folded his arms, and took a deep breath as they began to bargain over pricing. The man continued to slide wary glances at him and he could see that he was ready to settle as quickly as possible.

He had a feeling that he would have tried to haggle until the end of the day on the price of dried fish but his hulking presence had unnerved him. Skharr hoped it was only because his massive figure blocked his stall from other potential customers and not because he thought he would have trouble with him.

It wouldn't have been the first time folk called the guards simply because they felt threatened by his mere presence, but Sera already had what she needed and gestured for him to join her.

"What were you doing?" she asked in a whisper, laid the packs over Cody's back, and walked next to Skharr. "I thought you would say something or interject at some point, but you didn't say a word. The man was sweating like he was in a steam room."

"I did nothing more than watch him to make sure he knew that he wouldn't be able to cheat you even though you were new to the city."

She laughed and shook her head. "You never cease to surprise me."

"Not all barbarians are stupid. Some know when silence is more powerful than any words that could be used."

"How many are smart?"

"Fewer than you would like," he admitted. "More than you'd think but more than enough, I suppose. There are smart barbarians and smartass barbarians. Both can be equally cunning although not in the same ways."

"What is the difference?"

"Smartassed barbarians usually get a blade in their gut before they grow old enough to learn to keep their mouths shut and eyes open for a long enough time to become the smart barbarians."

"I see. And those who don't learn?"

"There are many ways for a young barbarian to die."

"None appear to have caught up with you."

Skharr smirked. "What about you?"

"My trainers beat me until I learned to keep my mouth shut."

"That seems to be the kind of thing a horrible father would do."

"My horrible father was the type to disown me, my sister, and my mother for politics."

He nodded slowly. "I wondered about that."

"It was rather obvious, yes."

Not all situations called for silence. The point of wisdom was, of course, knowing which situation called for which kind of action, and Skharr liked to think he had some knowledge in that particular area.

And not all the godsbedammed sellers in the city would be intimidated by his mere presence.

"I know this is not the price you asked of the folk who came through before," Sera stated and shook her head. "You're charging more for less of your supplies and I won't stand for it."

"Call it the tax we charge the folks who come from out of town," the man replied and grinned beneath his mustache. "These supplies are for those traveling out in the trawlers and if you want what they need, you'll have to pay a little more for it. Your purchase leaves less for the rest of us."

That made no sense, but the barbarian doubted that appealing to his better nature would work. Not for this one who seemed the type to simply dig his heels in.

"I'll need to talk to the guards about you charging taxes without the approval of the baron," Sera stated and folded her arms. "I am sure he will want to know what you charge the folk who visit so he can decide how much he will want to take from these taxes you levy."

That touched a sensitive nerve and the man's face turned bright pink. "You cannot come into my city and threaten me with such...such..."

"It's not a threat if you take a legal tax from the new arrivals to the city," she answered quickly when he paused, unsure of what he should call what she was doing. "It is only a threat if you are breaking the law—in which case, you are cheating my caravan."

The merchant laughed and shook his head. "If you think I'll be intimidated by you and your golem, you'll be surprised. They'll find your corpses in the river—if they find you at all."

He picked a small bell up from his counter and rang it once, and Skharr could feel as well as hear the footsteps in the room next to theirs.

"These situations, Skharr..." Sera began and shifted her focus to the opening door and the man who ducked to pass through it. "Would you say they are the kind that require you to be silent?"

He shook his head. "Occasionally, one needs to remind them why they need to be afraid."

She nodded and turned her attention to the giant who stepped out of the adjoining room.

With that said, the barbarian couldn't help but feel as though his words should have waited. The man who entered was taller than he was. It was an odd situation to find himself in, and he studied the newcomer cautiously. A thick black beard, dark hair that grew up instead of down, and hands that looked like blocks of granite painted an impressive picture that suggested brute strength.

"Big fella," Skharr muttered but stood his ground. There were signs that said his opponent wasn't pure human. His jaw was larger than usual, his fingers had no nails, and his eyes had a green tint instead of white. While he couldn't tell exactly what the giant's descent was, it didn't matter. He moved like most bipedal creatures, which said that almost everything vital or vulnerable had to be in the same location.

"Small fella," the large man rumbled. "Wants me to throw them out?"

"Crush them," the vendor ordered. "Leave their bodies in the river for the missies to devour."

The barbarian decided he would have to find out what these missies were, but not in the circumstances the vendor thought they would. The giant faced him and extended a beefy hand to grab him, having identified him as the larger threat.

He would have an interesting surprise if Sera removed both his arms, but Skharr doubted that help would be necessary in the circumstances.

After a moment of consideration, he took a step back, evaded the first clumsy punch, and stepped in closer. He drove his fist into the giant's stomach, high and a little to his left, held it like a spear, and dug in as hard as he could for a moment before he darted back to avoid another log-sized arm aimed at his head.

The giant didn't quite stop but he looked at his stomach and groaned. A moment later, he fell onto his knees and his noises of pain grew louder. The barbarian approached him again and this time, put all the power in his body behind his fist and hammered it into his jaw. His eyes glazed over immediately and he fell with a heavy thud.

After a nudge with his foot to the larger man's ribs to ensure that he was unconscious, he turned to look at the cheating merchant. The man gaped at his giant and tried to decide what he should do next.

"Perhaps...we started off on the wrong foot," he said and looked furtively around. "And...as you are aware of one of the ways in which I make money, perhaps—in exchange for your discretion—I could offer a special price for the items you require?"

Sera smiled. "I'm sure a reasonable exchange could be achieved."

She paid considerably less than what he'd originally asked and walked away with far more supplies than she'd first requested, although Skharr did most of the carrying.

"I am glad I did not need to intervene with the giant there," she whispered as he loaded the produce on Cody's back. "How did you bring him down so easily?"

The barbarian shrugged. "A man that large will have a larger liver. He had all the signs of one who liked to drink as well, so a quick blow to that region would bring him down if he didn't expect any resistance. He wasn't much of a fighter and relied on his size to intimidate people. I doubt he ever engaged in a fight with someone who wasn't already trying to run away."

That brought a small smile to her face. "Honestly, I would have simply kicked him in the balls and called an end to it then and there."

"It was the first thought to occur to me but in my experience, the bigger they are, the smaller that target becomes."

"Have you punched many giants in the cock, then?"

"Why else would I learn to hammer him in the liver?" he countered. "If kicking a man in the groin is your first attack and it fails, what do you have in its stead?"

"You make a good point."

"We're being followed."

Skharr looked up from tending to Cody's saddle straps when Sera spoke and he narrowed his eyes.

He hadn't expected his reputation to follow him to a fishing town almost fifty miles from Verenvan, but anything was possible. It seemed logical to assume that the numerous attempts on his life meant a contract was open on him and it wasn't a stretch of the imagination to realize that a would-be assassin might have followed him on the road.

After a moment, he nodded and turned his attention to the saddle straps again.

"Did you see them?" she asked.

"Aye—the tall, lean man at the apple cart. He's trying very hard to not look our way while mirroring our steps."

"Oh… I hadn't even seen him. I was talking about the woman on the far side. I can see the sword she's trying to hide and she's dogged our footsteps all afternoon."

After a quick pause, he tilted his head and tried to not look openly in the direction in which she pointed, her hand hidden by her body so no one else would see.

A woman carried a short sword and tried to cover it with a heavy coat. It was suspicious enough on its own, and if Sera had seen her following them before, that was the confirmation.

"Do you think there are any more in the crowd?" the guild captain asked, moved closer, and leaned on Cody as she patted the gelding's neck.

"Undoubtedly," Skharr replied, straightened slowly, and drew a deep breath. "They'll have a trap planned, somewhere they think they'll have some kind of advantage. My guess would be that they believe we don't know this city and if we wander into a blind alley or something similar, we'll make easy targets."

He scanned the crowd carefully, hoping to identify others that were following them, but he couldn't find any.

If there were others they would no doubt reveal themselves in short order.

"So...we find our nearest dead-end and trap those who hoped to trap us?" Sera nodded.

"Well...yes. How did you know?"

"I have been around you long enough, Skharr. I like to think I know how you think, more or less."

The barbarian nodded. He had sent Horse off with most of his weapons, but he still had his ax on him. It didn't appear as though any of the potential assassins wore any armor—unless it was the kind Cassandra was known to wear—and the ax would be able to cut into them easily provided they didn't have any ranged weapons.

Or poison, he reminded himself. He hated having to worry about that as well.

Sera gestured with her head to the side and guided Cody into a narrow street she had seen that ended in a wall at the back of a house of worship.

"This should be interesting," Skharr commented, unhooked the ax from his belt, and watched as the guild captain guided Cody to the back of the alley. He would be away from the fighting they still weren't sure would come to find them.

He hefted his weapon and grasped it a little tighter while he leaned against a nearby wall. From his position, it was easy to see the shadows approaching their location as well as hear the footsteps on the dirt streets.

They certainly hadn't wasted any time. Perhaps they couldn't believe the two of them had fallen into their trap and were a little too anxious to snap it shut. It would be their undoing, he decided as he attempted to count the number of footsteps.

At least four but perhaps more. He pushed off the wall and readied himself to meet the group he knew had targeted them. Whispering near the entrance suggested that they were trying to decide how they would approach the fight.

They numbered five in total, all accustomed to fighting if their bearing was any indication. All were better armed than those who had attacked Skharr in Verenvan. Two carried swords and bucklers, one grasped a small boar spear, and a fourth held a war hammer in hand.

The last one caught his attention, however, with a small recurve bow.

He didn't bother to wait for them to announce themselves or even for them to pretend they might have had better intentions. His gut instinct told him that if there was ever a time to act, it was then and there. Besides, the archer already had an arrow nocked and ready to loose.

Before he'd even considered a battle plan, he was in motion and had chosen his first target. He wouldn't be able to reach the archer with the crooked nose without engaging the rest of the group, which left him with only one available path.

The barbarian lifted the ax and leaned forward to launch it from his hands with as much power as he could muster. It spun once along its trajectory before it buried itself up to the haft in the archer.

The man hadn't even had time to draw his first arrow back and toppled slowly with a gaping hole in his chest.

He choked loudly as he fell, clutching his wound, and Skharr retreated and watched the assassins turn on him immediately, their weapons at the ready as they rushed forward.

The swordswoman fell back suddenly and a wound appeared in her neck as soon as Sera reached her. The guild captain slashed across her arm to make her release her weapon and turned her attention on the next assassin. He was no slouch, however, and rebuffed her assault with his buckler and retaliated with one of his own to force her back.

After a moment of indecision, the man bearing a war hammer rushed to the swordsman's aid, and a sixth assassin with an arming sword entered the alley to join the spearman to attack the barbarian.

"Come on then, you stinking globs of fucking maggot-brained, slimy troll snot," he yelled and made an obscene gesture with his free hand.

The spear moved quickly and sliced across his arm when he tried to reach out and grab it. The swordsman lunged and tried to avoid coming between the warrior and his comrade as he slashed high and followed with a low reverse to force Skharr to step away from them until he felt a hard wall against his back.

In that moment, both assassins decided they had the advantage and attacked at the same time. The warrior shifted to the right and growled when the spear cut into his shirt but missed the flesh to plant itself in the wall behind him. The swordsman rushed in and Skharr swayed, trapped the spear under his arm, and compelled his adversary to flip over the spear haft with a hearty shove.

Without thought or too much consideration, he lashed his fist forward and hammered it firmly into the spearman's jaw with enough power to catapult him back and make him release the weapon.

It was still trapped in the barbarian's shirt, and he twisted it and himself around as he drove the blade portion into the belly of the fallen swordsman.

He paused to draw breath but was alerted by a shuffling sound behind him. The former spearman held a dagger in his hand now, although he seemed a little sluggish. Before he could rush into the attack, the haft of the spear snapped to catch him unawares in the cheek. He fell, stunned for the moment.

Skharr managed to untangle the spear hastily from his shirt and drew it out to point the tip squarely at the assassin, who regained his feet although he looked a little unsteady on them.

Perhaps it was the two knocks on the head that had relieved

him of his senses. Either that or he truly believed he would be able to hit his target before the massive warrior hit him.

He was met by a spear to the chest before he had taken two steps. With a powerful roar, Skharr drove him into the ground again and the haft of the weapon broke on impact.

There was no time for him to celebrate his victory, however. He could see that the two who had engaged Sera were skilled enough to keep her impressive abilities with the sword contained and inched her slowly into a position where she wouldn't have the advantage of her blade to its fullest capacity.

"Not on my watch, you putrid fucking gutter-spawn."

Without a moment to spare, he took up the broken haft of the spear and sprinted toward them. He uttered a low roar as he hammered it across the back of the one who wielded the war hammer as he tried to flank Sera while his comrade attacked her from the front.

The barbarian heard the man's breath leave his lungs in a rush with the force of the blow. The assassin dropped his hammer and reached his hand to where he had been struck. Before he could recover, the barbarian grasped the back of his skull and with another roar, drove his head into the nearest wall. Bone crunched and his opponent dropped soundlessly. He assumed he was dead and turned his attention to the one who remained.

Sera was more than capable of dealing with him. The swordsman was distracted by his fallen comrade and she took advantage without hesitation. One stroke opened his throat from the right and it was followed by another nimble slash from the left that severed his head completely.

It had been difficult to even see that it had taken two strokes to kill him, not one.

"Well fought." Skharr nodded, drew a deep breath, and looked at the carnage around them.

"To you as well." She breathed heavily, took a rag from her belt, and used it to clean the blade of her sword. He wondered why she didn't simply flick it clean with the deft movement she usually used but decided that she was perhaps distracted. "We should search them to discover why folk are trying to kill us."

"So many have tried to kill me lately that I have stopped asking why," he admitted as she began to search the closest of the bodies. "And I assume they were trying to kill me. You might have simply been in the way."

She searched the headless body first and moved hurriedly to the others. When she stopped at the archer with the crooked nose, she slid her hand into his jacket and kept it clear of the blood that had already begun to congeal slightly.

"Skharr," she called and gestured for him to approach. "Have a look at this."

He stepped closer and narrowed his eyes at a coin she held up. "A guild coin."

Sera nodded. "It was a sanctioned assassination. Someone is determined to kill you, Skharr."

"Well, we knew that already," he muttered and yanked his ax out from the dead man's chest. "What do you think? Should we hide the bodies?"

"This isn't our business," she whispered. "Whoever sent them can deal with the bodies. For our part, I think we should simply move on with whatever we've collected from the bodies and say nothing."

"To where the rest of the caravan are camped?"

"No. They'll be waiting for us there. We need to find an inn that is reasonably safe and a random choice so there is no possibility that the food is poisoned."

He wanted to ask her how she knew this much about being targeted by assassins, but he followed her in silence, cleaned his ax, and hooked it onto his belt before he caught up with her.

Skharr trusted her to choose the right inn for them to spend the night in, although there were a few locations he would have selected closer to the port.

The Clucking Hennessy was an interesting establishment, but the rich scent of roasting boar was enough to drive all doubts from his mind.

"This isn't the first time you've had an attempt on your life, then?" he asked as a young woman brought two flagons to their table.

"In fairness, the attempt was on your life. But as my sword was already drawn and blood needed to be shed, I thought you could use a little help."

"And it is much appreciated." He tapped his flagon to hers and took a long draught of the thick, dark ale. "Why did you only ask for one room?"

"It would be better for us to stay together." She nodded and tugged her hair gently. "Should another attempt be made, we would be able to help each other in a fight. Don't you agree?"

While he could see how that was the wiser choice in the end, rooms in inns like this one tended to be small. And they usually only had one bed.

It came as no surprise to discover he was right about that. Once they had finished their meal and drinks, they retired to the room where he could see that the only bed was barely large enough for two with a thick straw mattress.

"Turn around," Sera said and began to undo her belt, "while I change into something to sleep in."

"You didn't do that when we were traveling."

"I have a real room now. I'll sleep in what I am the most comfortable in."

Skharr thought it wise to not argue and complied as she changed her clothes.

When he turned once she had finished, he realized that she was most comfortable sleeping naked.

"I guess...I'll sleep on the floor," he muttered and looked away quickly as she slipped under the bed linen.

"Are you sure?" she asked. "It looks hard and there's enough space on the bed for us both."

"The floor might be hard but it isn't the most...uh, problematic hard thing I need worry about."

"What?"

"Nothing. I can sleep here fine."

"Very well."

He nodded, pulled his shirt off, and unhooked the ax from his belt. He placed it carefully beside him and settled into an uncomfortable position using his shirt as a pillow of sorts.

"Sleep well," she whispered.

"Likewise."

It had been a headache to coordinate but she was finally seated for the evening, took a sip of the red wine that had been provided at the inn, and waited for her man to arrive.

Micah hated traveling. It was uncomfortable and she was left in a terrifyingly vulnerable position where all she could hope for was that no one knew where she was.

As if that wasn't bad enough, she was spreading the word to arrange for one of her spies to meet her.

After what seemed like an agonizing wait, the man slipped in. Nothing he did set him apart from the other patrons, of course, but she noted a distinct look about him. To her practiced eye, he seemed shifty and a little uneasy and his hand settled on a place in his cloak that showed no sign of needing it.

He caught sight of her almost immediately as well but gave no sign that he knew her before he sat across from her.

"What do you need?" he asked and lowered his head so his thin black hair covered his eyes as he studied the table intently.

"My sister. You'll find her traveling with a barbarian known as DeathEater."

"Skharr DeathEater? Do you want me to find him?"

"No, I want you to find my sister but they'll be traveling together so you'll be more likely to find her quickly if you search for him first. Do you understand?"

"You...want me to search for the giant barbarian but only because he'll likely be traveling with the person you want to find."

"Correct. I want you to learn what happened to them and where they are at this moment. Go."

He stood quickly, likely as uncomfortable with the meeting as she was. He had pigeons that would be able to deliver the message to his contacts in the fishing town and would have the information waiting for him once he arrived.

It would make everything a great deal faster but Micah feared it would all be a little too late.

CHAPTER THIRTEEN

Skharr shook his head. "I don't understand. How do they know there will be more movement now that the order has come from Janus?"

"They don't know, not really." Sera shook her head. "But the market is never a guaranteed system. Still, certain assumptions can be made. Creanda is the closest town to the dungeon they want attacked, so the assumption is that all those who travel from the north will want to come through the city. As such, there will be a boom in spending on everything from food to travel equipment and even magical trinkets that are taken in there. Based on that, they assume there will be a massive demand and they buy larger quantities in anticipation."

He nodded. While he wasn't sure he understood the concept, he had never been one to consider the intricacies of the trade that crisscrossed the empire.

The barbarian knew almost everything there was to know about war and the waging of it. The elements of trade, however—which he was willing to admit was a large part of how and why wars were waged—were far beyond him.

Creanda was a little larger than the fishing town they had left behind, and its defenses were built better. The walls were made of thick logs sharpened to a point with enough earth between to allow patrols to walk on top of the wall instead of restricting them to the towers.

It had a moat as well, filled with water and spanned only by a couple of bridges that led into the city. Unlike where they had come from, there appeared to be signs that fighting had taken place in front of the walls.

"And if all those folks don't come through the city?" Skharr asked from where he kept pace with Sera and Horse plodded behind him. "Or if they don't buy everything they expect them to?"

"At that point, there is a surplus," she explained. "Most of the supplies we are delivering to can last for months or even years. They'll have too much of them in their stores, which will drive the prices down."

"Could we buy everything back from them once they have the…surplus and sell it in Verenvan or another city where they need it?"

The guild captain nodded. "There might be a caravan for that. And we could escort that one as well."

"Where did you learn so much about trade and how it works?"

"It was expected of the daughter of the emperor," she explained and patted Cody gently on the neck as they approached one of the bridges leading into the city. "Even if we wouldn't be the next ruler, there was always the possibility that we would find ourselves in a position of some power and so it was expected that we be prepared. Or, at least, that was what our mother thought."

That made sense, he supposed. Even if she wasn't empress, perhaps her brother would want her to rule over some city or something of the like in his stead.

"The caravan will stay here for a while," she said. "And with that, our contract with them is up, which means we can speak to the local Guild Hall to find other work in the region. If there isn't, we might find another caravan returning to Verenvan and in need of our services. I can only imagine that what we offer will be more than welcome in the region."

"When the demand is high and the supply is low, we'll be able to raise the prices, yes?"

"Something of the kind, although we abide by the rules of the guild to not raise prices merely because folk need our services. But it seems as though we might remain in the area for another week at least."

"Will you need me with you when you do that?"

"As long as you don't find some work for yourself in the area. I'm sure there are many noblewomen interested in your abilities in these parts."

Sera grinned and he could only shake his head as they arrived at the end of their journey. Half of the prices charged for each of the merchants traveling with them was to be collected at the end, and she moved from one to the other as they set up their stalls and collected what was owed from each one.

Skharr wondered if there was perhaps a better way to perform the trade than to have her collect the coin herself. Perhaps the merchants could leave it on deposit with the guild to be held until the end of the journey.

A few of the merchants were from the region, he realized, and owned shops and buildings within the walls and had thus been traveling home.

None of them appeared to have any problems handing the coin over. All the haggling over price had already occurred at the beginning, and anyone who failed to pay what was owed would likely find it difficult to travel in any caravan again and certainly not under the protection of the guilds.

It was an interesting practice, a matter of give and take between them all that was based on mutual trust and the understanding that they relied on each other for their living.

The last of the merchants was one of those who had a home in the region. Skharr realized that the building the shop was in had two stories, and while he worked and plied his trade on the ground floor as well as the basement, he and his family lived on the top floor.

"Of course, of course," the man said and bustled around the shop despite his portly build. "My apologies. It has been a few months since I was home and there is something of a mess to tend to before I can open shop for the morrow. I have your coin in my bags upstairs."

The barbarian narrowed his eyes. The man was sweating but that could have been explained by his weighty body moving around much faster than he expected him to.

But that did not explain why his amulet vibrated gently against his chest to alert him to danger. His body stiffened and he inched his fingers toward the ax he still carried on his belt.

With so many trying to kill them, it was best to simply remain armed. He wondered if there was any way for him to armor himself like a certain paladin in his past, even if he had to wear what looked like chain mail undergarments. Walking around in full armor would prove to be tiring and hot, especially when they continued south.

Sera noted his sudden change in demeanor, narrowed her eyes, and looked around the room. She didn't appear any more tense or ready for battle as before. Her hand was nowhere near the sword at her hip, but the barbarian knew for a fact that she could draw it in the blink of an eye.

"Is something wrong?" she whispered.

"It's only a feeling."

She nodded. It was nice that she trusted him to the point

where she didn't need to hear more than that it was only a feeling before she readied herself to fight.

He tilted his head, took a deep breath, and heard heavy boot-steps moving on the top floor. More than one, he realized and frowned. Either the merchant's wife and children were as heavy as he was or they had company.

"Do you think you can reach the top floor using the windows?" Skharr asked.

After a moment's pause, Sera nodded. "You draw their attention from the stairs and I'll attack from behind?"

"Yes. Although I think they might have hostages so have a care."

"Of course."

He waited until she was out of the room before he approached the stairs. Before he could ascend, however, the merchant took a couple of steps down. The man looked more flustered than before and his eyes widened when he realized that Sera was gone and only Skharr remained.

"Captain Sera," he said loudly. "If you and your man could… accompany me upstairs? I might need some help to carry the coin down."

The warrior looked pointedly at the ceiling and then at the merchant, who nodded quickly and his jowls shook with the movement. Genuine fear lurked in his eyes—fear that the warrior wanted to put to rest once and for all.

"We'll come up," he answered and spoke perhaps a little louder than necessary. He gestured for the man to remain on the lower level while he climbed the steps.

The merchant looked confused. Perhaps he wasn't sure how both his visitors knew there were unwanted guests up there or he was merely flustered by the whole situation.

There was no way to tell what went through his mind, but Skharr could appreciate that the man had at least tried to warn him about the danger.

He unhooked the ax from his belt, climbed the steps slowly, and inched toward the doorway, hoping against hope that he wouldn't wander into a kill zone created by a group with crossbows. Unfortunately, asking the merchant to explain the situation for him would only have made things worse.

Sera would have to save his skin.

The barbarian continued upward and heard boots scuffling across the floor. He stepped into view, his right knee already loosening to lower him by the time he saw three men standing at the back of the hallway. A portly woman and a young boy were seated on wooden chairs, their hands tied behind their backs, and all three men carried smaller crossbows.

Before they even registered that he had stepped out in front of them, Skharr had dropped to roll over his shoulder. Crossbow strings twanged on the other side of the room, followed by the thuds of the bolts embedding themselves in the wood of the walls above him.

He already had his ax in hand as all three dropped their crossbows quickly, drew daggers, and moved out from behind their hostages to attack him.

Under the circumstances, the daggers were a better choice than his ax. The hallway was narrow and there would be little room to swing his weapon effectively.

Before he could even try, however, one of the men fell and clutched the back of his thigh, quickly followed by another, his throat opened and gushing blood. The third turned to see what was happening to his comrades but not in time. Sera sliced his arm with a deft swing that severed the tendons needed to hold the dagger.

She spun her sword to hammer the hilt between the man's eyes and thrust him back a step, which gave her the space to drive her blade into his chest between the ribs and directly into his heart. The fatal blow had been delivered too fast for him to realize the danger.

Skharr stepped in quickly to stop the man whose leg had been wounded from reaching for his fallen dagger. The assassin pulled back and showed surprising alacrity as he dove toward one of the windows, broke through the blinds, and fell hard on the ground below.

The barbarian rushed to the window and saw the man limping away as quickly as he could. He doubted that he would be able to make that leap without injuring himself and even then, his assailant would likely be able to disappear into the city, wounded though he was.

"You should have killed him," Sera commented and flicked her blade with the deft motion she usually used to clean it.

"I thought we could take one alive and question them to find out who was paying to have me killed, but that... Well, it went out the window."

She smirked. "So we survived again and saved the family in the process. I would call that a good job, no matter what the circumstances. Even so, we should consider nipping this in the bud. If it has reached this far, we can be sure the guilds are involved."

"Do they take on assassination contracts?" Skharr asked. "I thought they were illegal almost everywhere."

"They are, but there are...well, ways for the contracts to be offered. It's usually through those guildmasters who are less than scrupulous and take coin for themselves from those who want someone killed. Where there is coin, there is a way, as they say."

He nodded. "We should find out who the guildmaster is in this city. See if he is willing to talk."

"Agreed." She sighed and smiled. "Tefre, are you well?"

The merchant had climbed the steps, likely fearful of the result, and looked red in the face and not from the exertion. "I...I am so sorry. I never wished...but they..."

"They threatened your family, and you did as every father and husband would," she interrupted him smoothly. "And it all turned out well in the end so you have nothing to worry about, although I would suggest that you lock your doors and keep the windows locked as well over the next few days."

"Of course."

She motioned for Skharr to join her as she collected the coin that was owed to the caravan from the man's extended hand. The warrior fell into step beside her as she exited the building and they strode quickly through the city.

It was elevated and extended into the hills. The lower section continued to the river that transported most of the wood and other supplies the city produced to the larger cities.

Most of the lords and ladies lived in the higher areas of the city away from the river, and the Guild Hall was in the same section. It was easy to identify by the massive marble columns that made it stand out from the other buildings around it and gave it the look of a temple.

Sera appeared to know her way around the city as she approached it directly without any distraction by the folks who recognized her and called her name out as she strode up the steps.

Skharr couldn't recall a time when he'd seen her thoroughly angry like this. This was a chilling, icy fury that wasn't comfortable to watch. It seemed that the smallest thing would have her sword drawn and folk dying.

Of course, she wasn't the type to simply attack without thinking, which meant she had someone in mind as a focus for all the rage she had pent up inside her.

"Sera Ferat!" the guildmaster called as she approached his desk. "It has been a few moons since you graced us with your presence. I don't suppose you are in need of any work here? Or will you rush back to Verenvan?"

She placed her hands on the table and drew a deep breath. "I will ask you something, Salvin, and I'll only ask once. I trust that you respect me well enough to not lie to my face."

His dark brown eyes narrowed and he dragged his fingers through his thick red hair. "Of course. I have nothing but respect for you and your sword arm."

"And so, when I ask you who has an assassination contract out on Skharr DeathEater, will you tell me the truth?"

"Assassination contracts haven't been sanctioned by the guild for over two hundred years. You know this."

"That isn't an answer."

"If you're saying you think I had anything to do with it, I'll think you have no trust in me."

The guild captain smiled when he said that. It didn't even remotely suggest anything like happiness or joy but rather the look of a woman about to engage in imminent violence. Skharr already had his ax in hand when she jerked her hand out, grasped the guildmaster by the collar of his shirt, and slammed his head violently on the desk.

This drew an instant reaction from the mercenaries around. They all reached for their weapons but paused instantly when they saw the barbarian who stood guard. Either they knew him by reputation or they were not sure if they wanted to engage the giant who stood between them and their guildmaster.

It was a wise choice, especially as Sera drew her sword and pointed it at the group until she could see them inching away from her.

"I'll get a straight answer out of you if it kills you, bastard," she snapped and returned her attention to the official. "I know you've taken coin from the criminals in the city on the sly, which means that if there's any guildmaster on the continent who will have sanctioned an assassination, it would be you. Now answer the fucking question."

He gasped for breath as she pressed his head into the surface of his desk, looked around, and hoped desperately for some help.

It soon became clear that no one would come to his aid.

"Fine," he conceded in a rough tone. "I took a contract that was sent from Verenvan. I didn't open it and I didn't see who it was for and merely passed it along to those who manage such things in the city."

"What were you paid to pass the contract along?"

"Come on—"

"What were you paid?"

Sera had a way of raising her voice that made even Skharr's eyebrows raise.

"Shit...fifty gold coins."

She nodded and looked at the mercenaries who were watching. "Your life is worth fifty gold coins to this man. I would suggest that you elect a new guildmaster."

After a moment spent inspecting the group, she pushed the man to the side and moved away from the table as the mercenaries gathered around the guildmaster.

Skharr could hear the man trying to explain his position to them but he had a feeling he would have little luck with it.

"Guildmasters are elected in these parts?" he asked.

"Aye. It's not a terrible system. I would suggest we have it in Verenvan as well but the count wishes to have control over who the guildmaster is in his city."

That made sense, although so did the concept of allowing the mercenaries to choose who would manage and distribute their contracts. As much as he liked the one they had, if he was popular with the others, he would have little trouble being elected.

"I need food," Sera said and broke the silence that had hung over them since they left the hall. "Are you hungry?"

"I could eat."

"There is a nice little establishment nearabout that most of the mercenaries use when they aren't working. We should pay it a visit."

"Agreed."

Word of what had happened to the guildmaster spread quickly, as well as word of what he had done while in his position. Rumor stated that he was already removed from office and placed in a cell at the Guild Hall to make sure he didn't try to escape.

"I'll bet you he's dead before he ever leaves that cell," Skharr muttered from behind the chilled glass bottles their beers had been served in. It was a novelty the like of which he hadn't seen before and would likely fade before too long.

Still, the colder beer made it palatable, especially in the clammy heat of the region.

"What makes you think that?"

"A man like him doesn't stay in power that long without the help of more than a few of the mercenaries in his employ. Those would see him dead before they allowed the word to spread that they were involved as well. The chances are the next guildmaster will find himself in the same position."

Sera tilted her head and shook it despondently. "I wish I could say that I didn't believe what you were saying."

She paused in her sip at the sound of a scuffle entering the tavern they were in. It wasn't uncommon in an establishment where dozens of men and women who were used to fighting their way out of trouble had access to large amounts of spirits and liquor.

The group who entered the tavern looked like they were coming out of a tussle, although Skharr couldn't make out why they were fighting.

"Sera!" one of the men shouted and approached their table. "I thought we would never find you."

"Is that why you've been in a fight?" she asked and sipped her drink. The barbarian recognized two of them as part of the group she had recruited for their caravan, although he couldn't recall their names. He truly needed to get a magical amulet for that.

"What? No." The man shook his head and joined them at the

table. "Merely an honest tussle between fighting folk, is all. But we did discover what they were fighting in that fucking dungeon. The Janus bastards are keeping it close to the chest but we managed to get it out of them."

"You beat it out of them?" Skharr asked.

"Not...not quite. There was a bet. It wasn't started by us but we joined in."

"What are they fighting?" Sera asked.

"They...they said there is a lich inside the dungeon. Tessana... Well, she was knocked over in the fighting and...uh, she won't join us for the return trip to Verenvan."

Sera looked at her bottle and studied the contents through the thick brown glass.

The barbarian realized they were having a short moment of silence for one of their fighters who had fallen, although he now knew the name of this one, at least.

"A lich?" he asked when they stirred and the moment of respect seemed to have passed. "I've fought one of those before. It almost killed me when I stood against it."

He stopped talking the moment he realized they were all looking at him.

"What?" he asked.

"I guess we all expect you to volunteer your ax and bow for the occasion," Sera said softly.

"I've never volunteered to head into a dungeon," he protested. "I've been volunteered many a time but never took the task upon myself."

Before he could say any more, another cacophony came from the entrance to the tavern. It wasn't the sound of fighting this time but yelling in sharp voices with odd accents in the tavern's courtyard. These were accompanied by the sound of at least five or six horses that stamped nervously and whinnied.

"More assassins?" Sera murmured and she inched her hand toward the sword at her side.

"I doubt it," the barbarian whispered. "If I know those accents at all, they sound like they come from the Imperial City. I doubt assassins would travel that far to kill me."

After almost a minute of the same noise beyond the doors of the tavern, those who were responsible stepped inside to reveal imperial uniforms with a sigil of a hawk carrying an arrow in its talons.

"Although I have been wrong before," Skharr whispered.

"What would my brother's Swift Hawks be doing here, I wonder?" she asked in a matching tone.

"Why are you asking me?"

"Well, you were the one who put him in power. I assume they are here for you."

She wasn't wrong, and the captain of the group immediately located Skharr and strode to the table.

"Skharr DeathEater?" he asked and removed his helm.

"Who is asking?" he countered. It was a stupid question. How they could mistake him for anyone else was almost insulting.

"I am Captain Evon Paris of the Emperor's Swift Hawks and I come bearing a message from the emperor himself."

"Tell the boy the right boot goes on the right foot and everything else should work itself out from there."

A small ripple of laughter rose from the rest of the room, although it quieted quickly. Speaking ill of the emperor, it seemed, was not taken lightly in these parts.

And Parish did not look amused, although he pretended to ignore it while he offered Sera a polite bow at the waist. The gesture suggested that her identity was no secret to the man.

"A message," Parish repeated, pulled it clear of a pouch tied to his belt, and handed it to Skharr directly. "From the emperor himself."

The barbarian took the message and read the contents.

"Quick and concise," he muttered. "The emperor wants me to inspect a great evil that appears to have made itself known in the same dungeon to which the rest of the Janus fuckers are headed. His court would be deeply grateful if I were to find the time to inspect the dungeon."

"Deeply grateful?" Sera asked with a snort. "I would say my brother has no intention to order you to do this. He thought if he asked you nicely, you would be more amenable to doing his bidding."

"You said we have a week in this city, yes?" Skharr asked. "That might give me the time to travel to the dungeon and back without delaying you overmuch."

"Give you?" she asked. "Do you honestly think you'll do this on your own?"

"I didn't think it was my place to ask—or assume."

"You're right. It isn't. But I'll go with you, of course. What about you, Norik? Vita? Do you feel like clearing a lich from a dungeon?"

The two exchanged a look and shrugged.

"I need the coin," Norik mumbled.

"I'll likely as not find myself in fights here in the town anyway," Vita agreed and pushed a few stands of her short blonde hair behind her ear.

"There you go." The guild captain smirked. "The last time, you killed a lich on your own. You'll have our help this time to make it a little easier."

Skharr chuckled. "We'll need to buy supplies before we leave."

The Hawks captain raised a hand, untied the pouch from his belt, and handed it to him. "From the emperor for your supplies."

He took the pouch and weighed it in his hand. It was not a small amount. "I suppose this will help."

"We received word upon entering the city that there is an open contract on the barbarian's life," Parish noted. "They have been instructed to cease any and all attacks until your duty to the emperor is fulfilled."

"You couldn't have asked them to cease any and all attacks permanently?" he asked and raised an eyebrow.

"That would not be enforceable."

"You won't be able to enforce these instructions anyway," Sera muttered. "Come on, Skharr. We have a trip to the market to get out of the way."

CHAPTER FOURTEEN

News traveled quickly in the city of Canan.

It was almost impossible to determine how so many had heard that the emperor had called on him to attack the dungeon. Nevertheless, by the time they finished their search through the town's market for potions, amulets, and the other supplies they needed, those who were selling the items already knew what they were for and had pushed their prices up.

"The emperor can pay for it." The last of them stated that unless Skharr was willing to meet the prices demanded, his items were no longer for sale.

Even finding a room for the night was well nigh impossible. The possibility that assassins had targeted the barbarian resulted in innkeepers rebuffing them at almost every turn, which left only a few who were willing. Predictably, these were the establishments that were more expensive than usual.

A suite with two rooms and two beds was the best they could afford, only to discover that Norik and Vita both took it upon themselves to keep watch over their rooms for the night.

"I suppose this is better than you sleeping on the floor," Sera admitted as she unbuckled her sword from her belt. "It made me feel as though I was inconveniencing you."

Skharr shook his head. "You wanted the bed," he muttered. "And I had no intention to join you in it, not while you were naked."

"Did you think you wouldn't be able to control yourself around me, DeathEater?"

"I feared that if you felt something poking at you, you'd feel the need to poke me with your sword."

She laughed. "The worst I would do is tell you that I was tired and you should turn over. Not that it will be a problem now that we have two beds. I have a feeling we should have an early morning tomorrow and so I will bid you good night, Skharr."

He nodded and wandered to the room that had been designated as his. An early morning would probably be best, of course. The chances were that the whole city knew they were acting on the emperor's orders. The Swift Hawks had made no attempt to mask their presence or to ensure any privacy for the announcement.

The barbarian grimaced and realized he should have known. He pulled his shirt off, placed his ax next to the bed where he would be able to reach it smoothly and quickly, and settled into the soft bed. The comfortable give of the down mattress brought a sigh, although not of satisfaction. He should have pushed the emissaries into privacy, met with them in secret, and only then discussed what they had planned.

Not only had they effectively declared the emperor's request to anyone willing to listen, but they had all but announced that there was a price on his head. Only the desperate would ever try to take advantage against the emperor's orders, of course, but there were many desperate folk in the empire.

A deep sigh escaped him as he settled into the bed and tried to make himself comfortable.

"It's the heat, isn't it?"

The voice in the room made Skharr reach for his weapon but before he could take hold of it, he looked into eyes that were awfully familiar.

And at the same time, he thought bemusedly, quite foreign. The man who stood before him was almost as tall as he was, with long, golden locks and beard, a powerful frame, and eyes that glowed like they were possessed by lightning.

His robes were long and white instead of the tattered rags he usually wore, but there was no mistaking who had joined him in his room.

"Theros," the barbarian muttered and settled back in his bed. "You look...different. I guess not all those potions sold to make a man appear younger and more virile are shit after all."

"Your lack of deference is still amusing, Skharr," the god replied and folded his arms. "I am curious to see what will happen should you encounter one who is not so easily amused."

"That will be an interesting day. Is there anything I can do for you or are you also interested in finding out what is in that fucking dungeon?"

"I am not curious. I already know what you'll find in that fucking dungeon. I only fear that you have entered this situation a little too...dismissive of the dangers you will encounter."

"It would be unfortunate, then, if I were to find myself heading into the situation without any proper sleep."

"Fear not, barbarian. You are, in fact, sleeping and will awake feeling more refreshed than you have in years. I am visiting you in your dreams as I often have."

"Bothering me in my dreams, I would say."

"I have come to warn you of what you will face in that dungeon."

"If you tell me, what makes you think that I won't simply hand the information over to captain...whatever his name is and consider that particular problem of mine solved? I could simply return to Verenvan to discover who is trying to kill me and kill them instead?"

"Do you honestly think an envoy from the emperor will believe that you were visited in your dreams by a god who told you what is in that dungeon? What is the world coming to where an emperor believes that a barbarian is a sage who speaks to the gods in his dreams?"

"I give no shits whether he believes me or not. And not gods. Only the one god. You."

Theros raised an eyebrow. "Are you serious? You truly have no plans to enter the dungeon?"

"I didn't say that, but I've faced a lich before. Even if there is someone to help me, I doubt I would survive another one. I am capable but not insane. Magic is beyond my realm of understanding. That kind of magic is—"

"You're afraid."

Skharr nodded. "Aye. Had I known what you were sending me after, I would never have left my farm. And I so appreciate you leaving that part out of your tale."

"As you say, if you had known, you would not have left and in the end, we would have had a lich bound to a demon. Which…as it turns out, is exactly what we have now. Have you ever heard of a magus lich?"

The barbarian's eyes narrowed as he straightened in his bed. "Legends from the war. Liches summoned demons to infuse them with their power. They slaughtered entire battlefields and feasted on the dead when they were drunk with power. It is a cautionary tale against the use of magic in my homeland."

"The stories were only slightly exaggerated. I fought in those battlefields, and…well, they slaughtered almost everything on the field. Then they brought them back as undead armies to fight for them."

"Are you saying there is a magus lich in that dungeon?"

"A unique form of the same. The lich you destroyed was

infused with the demon you trapped. Not only with the power of it, but the actual demon. I…well, I wasn't sure that such a thing was possible. I would imagine both entities are fighting for control, but once the fight is settled, it has the potential to be one of the most powerful creatures to ever exist."

"I know there isn't much in this world that could bring a lich back when its phylactery is destroyed. Who did it? Janus?"

"No. As much as my brother is a troublemaker, he is deathly afraid of magus liches and what they are capable of. He is trying to rid himself of the creature and has already lost hundreds of his followers in the attempt. In this effort, his followers and mine are to support each other."

"If they don't piss me off, I'll not crush their skulls," Skharr offered.

"I would suggest that if they do not attack you. Your patience is legendary."

"I don't have much of it so it must be the stuff of legends."

"That was my point, Skharr." The god sighed and shook his head. "Unfortunately, if you go as you are now, the creature will kill you, even in its comparatively vulnerable state."

"So why don't you go?"

"There are rules. As a deity with followers, I am not allowed to involve myself to that extent."

"I would say that if a god created this, you are allowed to involve yourself." Skharr stood from his bed and scowled deeply. "It was a god who did this, correct? From what you tell me."

"Yes."

"And?"

"A god with no followers has…more options for involvement." Theros looked like he tried to explain the situation in a way that he would understand and it had begun to frustrate him. "Suffice it to say that the consequences of my involvement in the matter would only be permissible should the fabric of reality already be endangered to the point where my direct action would prove a minor fluctuation."

The barbarian nodded, his expression grim. "I...suppose that would be bad? Imagine that I don't speak the language of the gods."

"If only." Theros sighed. "A hundred magus liches would be better than altering the fabric of reality. You...you are our finest hope, but not as you are. I could only help you to the extent that you need if you were a paladin."

"A paladin?" Skharr ran his fingers through his beard and paced in agitation. "Perhaps it is my time to die then because I cannot be a paladin. Rules, remember?"

Theros sat in one of the chairs in his room. "I suppose... Perhaps there can be a special type of paladin."

"What type?"

"Would you agree that you are a barbarian?"

"A DeathEater."

"You chose to follow me."

"Aye," he agreed. "I had to follow someone for the guild and the Lord High God Janus—"

"Is an ass." Theros chuckled. "He's heard."

"Oh?"

"That's not important at the moment." The god waved his hand dismissively. "It isn't the most ringing endorsement, it should be said."

"As you said, I am a barbarian. I could not give a shit about the divine niceties if I squatted for over a week."

"Which is why certain rules could be bent," Theros continued. "As you pointed out the last time we spoke, if I wanted a different response, I should not have chosen a barbarian for the task."

Skharr held his tongue for the moment. Despite his lack of deference, he did know what the god was capable of and had no intention of bringing Cassandra's name up if he did not have to.

"Skharr DeathEater, the Barbarian for Theros, will you follow my rules, my precepts, and bring honor to my name in exchange for my support as you follow your heart and engage the strength of your body to deliver justice to those who would harm the people of this land?"

That sounded a little too formal for his liking, and the fact that Theros was standing as he said it only made it worse.

He sighed deeply. "Theros, you have never done me wrong and have pointed me to evils which have needed to be destroyed. As a DeathEater...I will follow those rules I know, being true to the barbarian as I was when you found me, and...I will not purposefully bring dishonor to your name."

The god narrowed his eyes. "Is that the best you can do?"

"I think I might have pulled a muscle saying it, but yes."

Theros laughed, grasped Skharr's outstretched hand, and shook it firmly. "Then I'll take it."

"You know I won't break that promise, at least."

"Now that I am willing to place coin on. Rise, Skharr DeathEater, the first Barbarian of Theros. When times are beyond your abilities, call on me and I will answer."

"I wasn't kneeling."

"Yes, well, certain things must be spoken. Now, arise!"

"I wasn't—"

His voice cut off as he jerked from his bed. The candles in his room had already gone out, which meant it had been hours—too many hours. Perhaps talking to a god who visited him in his dreams made time pass a little quicker than he realized.

He shook his head slowly, lay down again, and rolled over. "At least he didn't bitch about me being a mostly naked paladin."

She should have seen that coming. Again and again, folk underestimated Skharr. They thought he was merely another stupid barbarian and expected him to be an easy target in any plan that showed even a modicum of brains.

And each time, they were taught their lesson.

"Eventually, someone will grow wise to what you are," Micah whispered.

"Ma'am?"

She narrowed her eyes and looked at the spy master like she was surprised that he had spoken.

"Why are you still here? You've delivered your message and you have your coin. Get the fuck out."

"You haven't— What are our next orders?"

"There are no orders. Merely the usual and keep your ears open for anything else. This is beyond your abilities to help me with. I'll need to do this myself."

"Of course."

CHAPTER FIFTEEN

She could practically hear their eyes rolling.

"Hold for a moment," Sera interjected, closed her eyes, and shook her head like she had difficulty believing it as well. "Theros visited us? While I was sleeping? And you didn't even bother to wake me to meet him?"

"That is what you have trouble believing?" Skharr asked and narrowed his eyes.

"Well, yes. You should have called me. I have a couple of questions for the bastard, if you don't mind."

"We are working under the assumption that this barbarian is telling the truth, then?" one of the Swift Hawks asked and looked around in bemusement. "He could be lying simply to find himself more of the coin the emperor sent for him."

"I am still going to the dungeon, am I not?" the barbarian asked.

"So you say."

"Enough!" Captain Parish stepped in, took his man by the shoulder, and dragged him back a step. "If the Barbarian of Theros says he spoke to the god, you will believe it as long as you wear the emperor's sigil. He believed the barbarian. Are you questioning the emperor's judgment?"

"No, but this is beyond madness."

"Madness or no, you will stand under the emperor's will or fight under a different banner." Parish turned his attention to Skharr and straightened. "What message shall I convey to the emperor?"

Sera smiled at the man's almost instant about-face, but when she saw the serious expression the warrior wore, her eyes narrowed.

"You believe me, then?" he asked.

"The emperor trusts you. As such, I do as well. If you say Theros came to you in a dream with a message... Well, I will relay the message to the emperor and he will decide whether to believe you or not."

"That is fair enough." He nodded and appeared to steel himself. "Well, Lord High God Theros told me in dream that what we will face in that dungeon is a magus lich—a lich and demon merged through the power of another deity."

Even as he said it, Sera knew he realized how utterly insane he sounded.

The captain showed no sign of doubt but shook his head and chuckled. "What a godsbedammed asshole."

"It wasn't Janus," Skharr corrected him quickly. "Theros Well, he confirmed to me that Janus is working to correct the abomination as well."

Sera tilted her head and her brow furrowed as she studied the barbarian in front of her. Something was off about the man if he defended Janus.

"Another deity then?" Parish asked. "Did the lord high god happen to mention who that might have been?"

"He told me he was not strictly sure himself."

The captain sighed and tapped his leather breastplate idly. "The emperor must learn of this at once. If there is this much power involved, he must be warned. Do you know if the mages at the guild hall have speaking stones?"

"I…yes," Sera replied before Skharr could tell them he didn't know.

"We shall send the message that way then. Will there be anything else, DeathEater?"

"You can tell the emperor that I will attack the dungeon."

"But the emperor merely wished to know what was inside. Now that we know, a proper response can be assembled."

"Yes, but Theros wants me in there. This evil cannot be allowed to fester while Emperor Tryam gathers his forces. He can do so anyway in case I am unable to contain the power within. Should it break out, I would advise that he marshal the full might of his empire to stop it."

"We," Sera interjected.

"What?" Skharr asked.

"On the chance that we are unable to contain the power within," she corrected. "You can tell my brother that I'll not let the Barbarian of Theros attack the dungeon on his own."

"You know that we'll probably die, yes?" he inquired.

"Probably," she admitted. "But if we don't, what will we be afraid of then?"

The warrior studied her for a moment. She knew he was considering saying it was too dangerous and that he needed to fight it on his own or some such nonsense. It was the kind of bravado that struck a man when his ego grew too large.

She prepared to cut that ego down to size when he nodded, drew a deep breath, and turned his attention to the Swift Hawks.

"Inform the emperor that the Barbarian of Theros and his sister send our regards."

Parish beat his right hand on his chest. "Of course. Move out!"

Sera grinned as the group mounted their horses, kicked them into a gallop, and turned them toward the Guild Hall.

"You don't have to look so pleased about it," Skharr muttered and patted Horse's neck. "We are likely riding to our death, after all."

"I thought I would have to teach you that you have no authority to tell me where I can and cannot go."

"I've watched you fight, Sera. I know what you're capable of. The chances of survival are dim but slightly brighter if you are with me."

He'd traveled with her for some unaccountable reason. Micah had no idea what she'd done to inspire so much loyalty in the man, but he was there with her at every turn—ready to help, either in drawing a bath, cooking a meal, giving advice, or listening to her when she needed someone to talk to.

The fact that he had practically the same name as her half-brother was not lost on her, although she wondered if that had been a cruel joke on her mother's part or a simple coincidence.

It didn't matter, though, not when there was so much else to occupy her thoughts.

"Triam?"

"Yes, ma'am?"

"I hoped I could talk to you for a moment."

He nodded and placed the tray of dirty dishes on a nearby table. "I am always willing to assist wherever I can, ma'am."

"Why didn't my mother leave Sera with a guardian like you?"

"As I recall, she did, although the poor sap died on the road she took to where she was trained to be a blademaster."

"Oh. Right. Do you remember his name?"

Triam sat across from her and shook his head. "I'm afraid I do not. Is it important? I could probably peruse the old files your mother left when she died."

Micah shook her head. "No, it's not important. I'm merely considering the fact that I'll likely go head to head with the

Verenvan Council before this is done. They won't stop their attempts to kill Skharr and whoever he might be traveling with simply because the emperor ordered it so. It's an atrocity that I have to deal with them at all, of course. I am royalty dealing with pigs. They should listen to me as a superior, not an equal."

"Of course. However, you must take into account that you have only shown yourself willing to engage on their level. They fail to see you as anything but their equal because you have failed to act as anything else."

"It's how I make a living. Would you have me traveling the world, keeping musty caravans safe and coming home to a piddling farm?"

"That is not royal either, which is likely why they have no compunction about killing Sera to get the barbarian."

She sighed deeply, sipped her watered wine, and shook her head. "Those were simpler times when it was only Sera and I against the world. And you, of course. I would have killed anyone who so much as looked at her the wrong way, and now I'm considering the consequences of doing that instead of charging into the fray without a second thought."

"Now that sounds like royalty."

"It's not like they'll respect me if I stand against them. If anything, they'll decide I'm not worth their time and try to kill me as well."

"Royalty does not care what her inferiors think of her actions. She does as she sees fit and kills those who stand in her way."

Micah looked at him and narrowed her eyes. "Saving my family is what I should do, regardless of what they might think. I'm not the one standing in their way, but they are standing in mine."

Triam smiled and stood slowly. "That does seem like a royal attitude to have. Should I see to it that your horse is ready for departure?"

"Yes, thank you."

"Of course, ma'am."

The man was right in his roundabout way. She needed to stop pretending that she was there to pander to their needs as an equal. The simple truth was that she couldn't be half-swine and half-royalty at the same time. They would learn to fear her or they would die.

Now that seemed like the attitude of an empress. Perhaps she was more suited for the role than her bastard brother.

CHAPTER SIXTEEN

The early departure had been an inspired idea. Not only were the streets empty of the throngs that usually filled them, but it appeared as though they were leaving before any of those who had death on their minds could act.

Or perhaps folk had listened to the warnings from the Swift Hawks to leave them alone, at least until the dungeon had been cleared.

Either way, they reached the gates in good time. The guards glared at them through bleary eyes and it appeared they were only now getting ready to open them for the day.

"We'll get to it when we get to it!" the lead guard snapped and gestured for his men to get back to work instead of ogling the four who waited impatiently for the gates to open.

Skharr sighed and tensed a little at the clatter of about a dozen horses approaching from behind them. Most folk had the good sense to avoid galloping through the city, which meant there was only one group of self-entitled asses who would ride in this manner.

It seemed they had sent their message and were already anxious to leave the city.

"Open the gate!" Captain Parish snapped and reigned his horse in savagely. "Open the gate in the name of the emperor!"

That put a little spirit into the steps of the guards, who hastened to lift the bar that kept the gate closed and pushed it back.

Skharr scowled at the way the men treated their horses. Folk who spent so much time on their mounts should have learned to treat them better.

But instead of rushing through, Parish turned to face Skharr, who was feeding Horse a few of the apples the stallion could already smell in their saddlebags.

"The emperor has commanded that we escort you and your group to the dungeon, DeathEater," the captain said as the gates were dragged slowly open.

"What?" he asked. "And…why?"

"We have been commanded to ensure your safe arrival and that none harass you on the road. It will be a perilous journey, and the emperor wants you to be well-rested and in good health and spirits before you embark on the most dangerous part of it."

"So you won't enter the dungeon with us?" Sera asked and raised an eyebrow.

"No. Our services are needed elsewhere. Besides, we are told that large numbers are not required to clear the dungeons."

"Not very many are needed to get there either," Skharr muttered and gestured for Horse to follow him through the gate.

The Swift Hawks fell into formation behind him instead of ahead of their group as he'd expected. It was a nuisance because if they were following him, he would have to decide where exactly they were headed for their next stop.

That meant reading maps and the like. It wasn't that he didn't know how to do it, but Sera had managed the logistics thus far. Folk expected him to take the role of leader, it seemed, and he needed to play the part however reluctantly.

"There's no time to dally about," Skharr stated and retrieved another apple for Horse to munch on as they moved onto the road that led farther south. "We have a dungeon to clear."

"Of course." Parish motioned to his men, who quickly took positions around the troop and acted like an escort even though the roads were still abandoned.

A few wagons came in from the farms in the outskirts, as well as three that were led by teams of massive draft horses dragging tree trunks out of the forest, likely to be split and sent to Verenvan.

The barbarian assumed that the larger logging yards were able to use the river to transport their goods. Working in the woods was not a terrible way to live. It wasn't something he had ever done himself, but he thought he would do it well. There would be no time for him to deal with godsbedammed fucking dungeons and emperors if he was too busy cutting trees, removing the branches, and sending them to be used elsewhere in the world.

How hard could it be?

"I hope you don't mind if I ask you a question?" Parish asked once they were well on their way and the sun began to beat down on them as it climbed in the sky.

"Me?" Skharr asked.

"Well, either one of you," the man said and leaned forward to pat his horse's neck and stop it from moving too close to Horse. Both were stallions, and while Skharr knew his beast was mellow enough that he didn't bother to pick fights with younger horses, those younger horses would be a little friskier. "I was curious as to how a barbarian and the former emperor's daughter came to travel together. The very same barbarian, of course, who assisted the current emperor to claim his throne."

"We met before he helped my half-brother," Sera explained. "He needed a caravan that would travel close to a dungeon he planned to visit, and we needed real fighters among the group. It was...an eventful journey."

"Oh?" Parish asked. The barbarian assumed that the man didn't have much opportunity to listen to these kinds of stories from first-hand witnesses.

"Aye. At one point, he decided he would scout ahead and find out if brigands were waiting for us farther down the road. He said he would report back if he found any and we would attack them together. But instead, he decided to attack their camp while they were waiting for us, killed them all, and wounded himself in the process."

"I didn't wound myself," Skharr protested.

"You know what I mean. Anyway, he returned and we determined that there were likely traitors in our camp. We found them and dealt with them together. I think you left our caravan the next day to find yourself a nice little dungeon to attack, and then we met up again once you were finished."

"You attacked a dungeon on your own?" Parish's voice mirrored the disbelief on his face.

"In fairness, the dungeon had already been cleared and had only recently been inhabited by a new evil that needed to be destroyed," the barbarian explained.

Sera nodded. "What of you, then? I've always assumed that there is some kind of process involved in the selection of the Emperor's Swift Hawks, but I never discovered what that consisted of."

"Ah. Well, there is an interesting history to that. In the early stages of the empire, there was a small tribe of horse nomads who were incorporated early and named the Swift Hawks. They were skilled horsefolk to a man and woman with a few ceremonies that bring a youth into adulthood, mostly consisting of testing their riding skills. The tribe has since melted into the empire, as it were, but their tribe name is honored among the Swift Hawks now. Those chosen must pass the same ceremonies that the tribe children needed to."

"And how is it that you were selected?" she asked. "I assume a leaning toward riding skills was part of the process?"

"Yes. I was part of the scouting troop in the Wesforn campaign. There, I earned three medals for bravery in battle but was also a part of the communication group that General Yosun organized in the largest battles of the war. At one point, I spent seven straight days and nights traveling between the platoons, helping to coordinate the attacks."

"And so, for all that effort, you became the messenger for a decaying old man?" Sera asked.

"There… Well, yes. But there is great hope among the ranks that your brother will prove to be a finer example of how an emperor should act."

"He might be for the first few years," she said a little acerbically. "But you'll remember that my father was a mighty warrior in his youth and once he had taken all he wanted, he discovered that dallying with women a quarter of his age was as amusing as engaging in war."

"We shall see."

That was the trouble with succession the way it was decided in the empire, Skharr decided. All the tests in the world would not prepare any man or woman for the position and the corruption that came with it. Even the kindest, purest heart would be heavily laden by the power of the office.

"Do you think it was worth it?" Skharr asked and patted Horse on the neck. "Leaving the front lines to join the Swift Hawks?"

"It has been so far," Parish replied. "Should we not be mounted by now? Or do you choose to walk instead of ride everywhere you go?"

"Oh, gods, not this again," Sera whispered.

"Horse is my brother," Skharr explained. "I don't ride my brother."

"Your…brother?"

"Aye."

"Is he under some kind of enchantment?"

The barbarian turned to look at the beast. "Not as far as I know. Have you been put under an enchantment, brother?"

Horse nickered softly.

"I think he's asking if Horse was a man turned into a horse using magic," Sera explained.

"Not to my knowledge."

"And yet…he is your brother?"

"It is a barbarian concept," she interjected before there was any more misunderstanding. "Horses are considered brothers among the DeathEaters and usually carry heavy loads but not the barbarians themselves."

"Ah." Parish looked pensively at his horse. "What about in matters of emergency? Should you be rendered unable to walk, for instance."

"Horse will decide if he wants to carry me to safety," Skharr replied. "It has not been an issue to this point."

"I see."

When they drew closer to the dungeon, Sera could see that more than a few parties were already in the region. A veritable army had been summoned and all were anxious to find themselves in the good graces of one of the lord high gods.

Not much could be done about that, although she did note a few foul glances at them as they approached the larger encampment where most of the mercenaries had settled to wait their turn. Skharr muttered something about the logistics of the group, but the fact that he didn't say it as loudly as he could to anger those who listened was something new.

He was different. There was no disputing that, and Sera had a feeling that the visit from Theros the night before had something to do with it.

"These are all the Janus' followers then?" she asked and narrowed her eyes. They had organized in the camp like they were in the military, which begged the question of why they weren't all attacking the dungeon at once. A few hundred had assembled already, and there wasn't a force in the world that could stand against that many fighters if they assaulted them at the same time.

"Those who were interested in the coin that Janus could pay them, yes," Skharr said and shook his head. "We should make camp here for the night. There is time enough to find out why they are waiting and attack the dungeon come the morning, I think."

Sera nodded and it appeared that the rest of her little troop agreed. Despite an uneventful day on the road, the heat had begun to tell on them. A little rest felt like it would be beneficial to prepare them for the attack.

"I thought the dungeon was restricted to the followers of Janus, yet I see the man known as the Barbarian of Theros has come to take the honor that belongs to us."

She pulled her horse to a halt as a small group approached them.

They were all well-armed and armored but despite this, they showed no indication that they were looking for a fight with the newcomers. Instead, they seemed curious about their arrival.

All of them looked like real mercenaries, the kind who would generally be paid well to fight in one war or another.

But no lord was willing to pay the amount of coin a god could. Sera was surprised that there hadn't been mass desertions from the local armies to engage in the dungeon quest.

Or perhaps their greed was not enough to overcome the fear of what would likely be waiting for them inside. No matter what riches might be found in the dungeons that still existed in the world, the dangers inside were enough to dissuade all but the bravest or the most skilled.

Occasionally both, but not always. She knew that thousands of corpses of men and women lay in the dungeons scattered across the continent. They had all thought they were the mightiest warriors on the planet until the moment when they found themselves pinned to the wall by a troll's spear.

The Tower still had folk flocking to the invisible gates every year, even though it was extremely rare that a survivor emerged at the end of it.

"The problems to be found in this dungeon are enough of a threat to call on the followers of Theros," Skharr said and took a step forward. "Even though we were not promised the same glory and riches that the followers of Janus were."

"I suppose that would be because your god wanders the earth as a penniless old man who can't afford to pay his followers for acts of greatness."

The barbarian smiled and nodded. "That is very possible, yes."

Sera tilted her head. That did not sound like the man she knew. At any other time, he would have spewed the kind of vitriol that would bestir all the followers of Janus into a fight and then show them why it was such a terrible idea to engage him in battle.

"You wouldn't be stealing our glory anyway," the Janus follower said and calmed himself in the face of the giant's non-confrontational attitude. "But we certainly do appreciate the support. I've heard that you have been in more dungeons than any other man alive. Do you have any suggestions for when I and my group of merry adventurers enter in the morning?"

"What is your name?"

"Savas," the man replied, took a step forward, and shook Skharr's extended hand. "And you are the Barbarian of Theros, Skharr DeathEater."

"Yes. Well, this barbarian would suggest that you not enter the death trap at all, but if you are intent on doing so, I would suggest that you avoid sleeping while inside. Dungeons tend to punish those who do by venturing into their dreams."

The mercenary took a deep breath and nodded. "Your advice is welcome indeed. Will you camp here for the night?"

"Aye."

"There is a place next to our camp that is close to the river. It's a little cooler and far from the latrines that have been dug on the east side."

Perhaps there was something to the warrior's use of comradery instead of hostility. It would prove profitable for their group but even so, it was uncharacteristic of him. Sera decided she would ask him about it but at another time when they weren't in a position where division would prove costly for them.

Surprisingly, as they settled into their campsite, she noticed the Swift Hawks quickly started work to set their tents up and build a fire. A couple of them began to put food out for the group, which didn't leave much for her or Skharr to do.

Most in the camp chose to turn in early for the night so they had no opportunity to find out what kind of organization had been put into place. She still wondered why all those present hadn't entered the dungeon immediately and instead, camped out as if waiting their turn.

But there would be time for that later. For now, rest certainly seemed like something she could enjoy.

A tent had been set up for her, a small structure that still allowed her to stand at her full height. Skharr had one as well, although she doubted that he could stand in it without having to stoop considerably.

Any thoughts of asking him questions disappeared when he retreated quickly into his shelter as the sun slipped out of sight. She could follow him into the tent but decided against it. They would find more than enough time later for that kind of thing, and she didn't need any of the others to talk about her joining him in his tent for the evening.

CHAPTER SEVENTEEN

When they broke camp the next morning, it appeared that the group they had camped beside had already headed out earlier. Skharr had heard the bustle of them leaving and he could see where their camp had been, but they were long gone.

Sera emerged from her tent a moment later. She looked like she hadn't slept much and wasn't in the finest of moods as a result as she approached where the Swift Hawks had already begun to make breakfast.

"I could get used to this business of not having to cook for myself," he muttered as she approached.

"I thought you lived in an inn where you bought all your food from those who cooked for you."

"True. But I could still get used to it."

She shook her head. "Do you think we should speak to someone about what happens next or should we simply... approach the dungeon and see what happens?"

He frowned as he looked at her. "What do you mean?"

"I assumed there was some kind of order these groups were placed in. Each team waits to head into the dungeon and so avoids fights over who gains all the glory and whatnot."

"That is sadly not unlikely," Skharr admitted. "But there does not appear to be any kind of order. The groups simply head off on their own and don't come back."

She raised her eyebrows like the thought hadn't even occurred to her. "I suppose they might be waiting for someone else to do the job while they gather the courage to do it themselves."

He nodded slowly and rolled his shoulders. "In which case, we should probably not delay. It will keep the others from dying pointlessly in there."

"Are we moving out then?" Parish asked and walked toward them holding two steaming bowls of stew and a slice of dark bread for each of them.

"I thought you would be ready to return," the barbarian admitted. "You've escorted us this far but we will make the last push toward the dungeon from here."

"I had a word with the men last night," the captain said as they took the food he offered. "And if you don't mind, we thought we would continue with you. There is always the possibility that someone among the mercenaries in this camp might know there is a price on your heads or perhaps individuals who would kill you to avoid splitting whatever reward there is with another group."

Skharr took a mouthful of the stew and nodded in appreciation. It could use a little more spice but it was not necessarily bland. It was warm and filling, which was oddly comforting despite how warm it was in the morning in the region.

"How far do you plan to travel with us?" he asked. "Because turning back halfway through the dungeon might mean you've already gone too far."

The man chuckled and shook his head. "I think we'll see this through to the end if you don't mind. Too many would choose to stand aside and let whatever evil a magus lich can create rip through that dungeon and kill hundreds. The emperor told us to see that you had the time and means to complete your task, and we will see it through to the end."

He nodded and patted the man on the shoulder. "I can honestly say that is probably the dumbest thing you have ever said in your life, but I do appreciate the support."

"It's not quite as stupid as heading into multiple dungeons, however," Parish retorted.

"True. True."

No one appeared to stop them as they packed their camp and immediately started their journey. A few watched them but aside from the same dour gazes that had followed them in, there was little change.

"I guess I was right," Sera whispered. "They are all waiting to die here."

"The idea of glory is far more appealing than having to earn it," Skharr agreed. "All the bards in the world somehow forget that for every hero in their ballads, there were about fifteen others who died in the attempt."

It wasn't quite the note he wanted to start their quest on, but there was no point in trying to encourage them with a rose-tinted view of what they were facing.

As he followed the map that directed them to the dungeon, he could see the changes that had begun to come over the region. He had never seen it quite this early before, but there was a price to be paid for the kind of magic that kept a lich alive—or whatever the term was for the undeath it experienced—and that took a toll on the plants and the animals for miles around.

Never quite to this extent, however, he realized. The trees had begun to shrivel and the ponds and rivers stank from the animals that lay dead in them. The grass and moss that covered the ground where the trees didn't was dry and dying, all thanks to the creature inside the godsbedammed dungeon.

"Hold for a moment," Sera called and held her hand up.

"What?" Skharr asked as he approached her. He hadn't felt any tremor in his amulet, which meant they were probably not in any immediate danger. Still, he would always trust her instincts over whatever magic his trinket contained.

"It's merely...odd. The troop that came through here before us should have left tracks, yes? There were a good twenty of them and all on horseback, but I see no sign that the landscape was disturbed by so much as a bird's landing."

He looked around. She was right, of course. The dead and dried landscape should have shown some sign of the group but from all appearances, it seemed as though they were the first ones to come through.

"Maybe they took another route to it," Parish suggested as he eased his horse closer to them. "The map shows at least three different approaches that would allow them to reach the dungeon. This is the shortest one, but they might have used another for some reason."

Skharr nodded. That was the most likely scenario and he didn't want to say there was something wrong immediately, but now that Sera had pointed it out, he wouldn't be able to shake it from his mind.

The hills that surrounded the dungeon grew even worse. There were no trees now, only pockmarks of burnt stumps, and the farther they went, the harder it became to ignore the fact that they still saw no sign of any of the other companies that were supposed to attack the dungeon.

"This place is cursed," one of the riders muttered and Skharr could see the same hesitation in Vita and Norik, the two mercenaries they had brought with them from Sera's original group.

All of them looked like they suddenly wished they had not come along for the journey. He had begun to feel the same sense of impending dread himself, although he couldn't determine why. Perhaps that had persuaded all the other parties to hesitate before they attacked.

But, unlike the dungeon with the lich he had faced before, it didn't feel like there was an invisible force actively trying to prevent them from approaching what he could see looming, built into a narrow ravine that delved deeper into the ground.

A path led down into it and they traveled less than a mile until they reached what appeared to be a small city built directly into the walls of the ravine they were traversing. All signs of life were gone from the area, however. If it had ever been inhabited, it certainly hadn't been for the past few hundred years.

Even longer than that, probably. The stones the buildings were made from had been gradually eroded for centuries until they were crumbling to pieces before their eyes.

Skharr took his bow from Horse's saddle, somewhat tempted to tell the stallion to remain where he was for the moment. He strung it quickly and deftly, immediately selected five arrows from the quiver, and kept four in his hands and one on the bowstring, ready to fire at a moment's notice.

"Is something about?" Sera asked and moved her hand to her sword. The way her voice echoed through the ravine walls made him wince visibly as he tested the pull on the weapon.

"It's only a feeling," he whispered. He didn't want to say that he was getting ready for a fight on the basis that the amulet around his neck had begun to vibrate gently.

When the shaking grew in intensity, he looked around as they began to approach the areas that led directly into the ground.

"Weapons ready," Skharr shouted and scanned their surroundings. He'd heard something. He knew he had, although there was a niggling doubt in the back of his mind that perhaps it was merely his nerves or his mind playing tricks on him.

Sera didn't have any doubts, however. She immediately drew her sword and the others did as well. All the Swift Hawks had small bows on their saddles and while a few chose those and made them ready to loose, the others drew their sabers and hefted their shields.

Something moved in the abandoned town around them, and

Skharr could hear it coming closer, even though it hid in the buildings.

Suddenly, one of the archers on horseback loosed an arrow. All eyes turned to see the projectile bounce off of one of the nearby building walls.

"There was something there!" he shouted and took another arrow from his quiver. "I swear it."

There was doubt in his voice too, but the fact that the horses had grown increasingly nervous was the clearest indication that they would be in danger very soon.

Something shook the ground as it advanced and almost out of pure instinct, he was already turning when he felt the steps approach them from behind.

"Look out!"

He didn't know who had called the warning and he didn't care much. The beast that stepped into view was already in his sights as he drew back on the powerful bow and launched his arrow a moment later. He doubted that he would have been able to hold the bow back for very long even if he'd needed to.

The arrow whistled toward its target and punched hard into the beast's shoulder, but he suddenly doubted that it had done much damage. It was the size of a massive bear and stamped on the hardened earth on what looked like fists, parted its jaws, and uttered a thunderous roar. It looked at where Skharr had shot it, ripped the projectile clear of the wound, and tossed it aside.

"By Janus' hairy fucking ballsack, what is that?"

While it was difficult to explain, something about the beast made it difficult to look at. It was like chunks of it didn't quite fit. Heavy arms emerged from its back, smaller than those that secured it on all fours. It roared again and he already had another arrow nocked and ready to fire as it began to rush toward them.

Sera was quick to react, turned Cody, and spurred the gelding into a charge at the monster, possibly to run it down. It was clear that attacking the beast on foot was not a good idea.

"There's another!"

The cry came from Parish, who was already firing his arrows at the second of the creatures that appeared. It also had four legs and two arms jutting from its back. All the limbs had a red sheen and reflected the sunlight in a sickly gloss that made Skharr uneasy simply by looking at them. He loosed another arrow and this one caught the monster low on its forelimb and continued through.

It stumbled, and chunks of the creature were left behind as it continued its attempt to attack Sera.

She shouted and swung her horse around to charge directly into the creature. The horse was slightly larger and forced it back, but the arms from the monster's back immediately reached for her and tried to drag her off her mount.

Another scream turned Skharr's attention to a third creature, which had used the distraction of the other two beasts to climb one of the nearby buildings and pounced from the higher vantage point. Two of the SwiftHawks were crushed and mauled almost immediately, along with their horses.

"Bastards!" Vita shouted, her sword drawn as she rushed at the creature, but it thrust her back with an almost dismissive strike from one of its forelimbs before it turned its attention to the men who now launched arrows at it.

Skharr released another arrow, which cut deep into its hindquarters and dragged a cry of pain from it before he turned his attention to where Sera was still beating the first of the creatures back.

She had lopped one of the arms off but the other swept out, dragged her from her saddle, and hurled her down. The creature tried to attack her, but Cody was there to stop it. He rose on his hind legs and proceeded to beat the beast back with his front hooves, neighing furiously while his rider regained her feet. The beast's claws sliced into him but the gelding held his ground and snapped and bit at the creature as Sera surged

"Are these..."

"The mercenaries who attacked the dungeon?" Sera shrugged. "It's hard to say, but yes. This odd substance all around them and mixed with the blood infuses them with a will and a means to kill."

The barbarian dropped to his knees and grimaced when his fingers dipped into the filth and pulled one of the claws clear of the monster's arm.

It didn't surprise him that it was a spearhead. From the shapes of the others, there appeared to be swords and even a few clubs mixed in to make the beast even deadlier.

"What the godsbedammed fucking asshole kind of craziness is this? Janus may be a fucking ass, but even he wouldn't stoop so low," he whispered and inched away from the dead. "I've never heard of magic like this. What kind of magic would be capable of doing this?"

Sera shook her head. "You said the lich is possessed with a demon's powers beyond anything we've ever encountered and beyond what we know to be possible."

The shaken Swift Hawks had come to the same realization and backed hurriedly away from the monster they had killed. A few of them staggered a few paces, fell to their knees, and threw up.

He couldn't blame them. His stomach was a thing of steel, or so he'd thought until he tried to wipe the red goo from his fingers.

It left a hint of a tingle that faded quickly once he'd cleaned it off.

"I wonder if anyone knew," Sera whispered. "If they fought these monsters, realized they were the fallen, retreated, and never bothered to warn any of the others."

"It would be difficult to prove that," Skharr responded and tried to shake the unnerving reality of their situation from his mind. "And it doesn't matter. We know now what happened to the party that went out before us and there is little more to discuss on the topic."

"What do you want to do?"

"What we came here to do. The creatures are venturing out of the dungeon and attacking folk in the open, which means the lich's power is growing. If we allow it to continue, it will gather the dead to power its army. We need to stop it now before anything else happens."

Parish approached them, his face green and his balance unsteady.

"You know, then?" he asked and looked at the bodies. "How... What on earth can do that?"

"A magus lich," Skharr stated as though he had only now realized what that meant. "Are you certain that you wish to continue down this path with us?"

There was a clear shadow of doubt in the man's eyes, but he nodded firmly. "If that...entity is able to continue to spread its influence through power over the corpses like that, I would not have it anywhere in the empire. The fact that it was allowed to fester this long is an abomination."

He placed a hand on the man's shoulder. "You are a brave man, Parish, but I would not think less of you or your men if any decide not to head into the dungeon with me."

It didn't look like any would remain behind, though, even those who'd thrown up. If anything, seeing the true nature of the monsters steeled their resolve further.

"What are our casualties?" the barbarian asked.

"Three dead," Parish replied. "A handful are wounded and already being treated."

"Those who aren't wounded or treating those injured must burn the bodies," Skharr instructed.

"Burn them?"

"We don't know if whatever magic brought them to life will be capable of doing so again. I happen to know that ash is more difficult to raise from the dead than corpses. Use what pitch you brought with you and see to it that nothing but ash remains."

The captain nodded and jogged to his men, who jumped into action at the thought that the monsters might come back to life if they weren't careful.

"What do you think we'll find in there if this is what was waiting for us here?" Sera asked and shook her head.

"Something considerably worse," the barbarian muttered. "It's not too late to turn back, you know. I wouldn't hold it against you if you wished to stay and watch the horses."

She scowled and punched him hard on the shoulder.

"That's my answer, then?" he asked and rubbed the injured spot.

"Aye. And don't you think of asking me that ridiculous question again, DeathEater."

CHAPTER EIGHTEEN

No one in the group wanted to talk about what they had killed at the entrance of the dungeon. They would probably prefer to not even think of it if that were possible. Skharr doubted that he would have been able to think about it and retain the contents of his stomach.

Once they had donned their armor and taken what they needed from the horses, the barbarian assured them that the beasts would be safe with Horse who would lead them a short distance away to await their return. The absence of any other horses, attended or otherwise, was cause for concern. Either they had been killed by the same monsters the group had encountered, or they had fled from the location.

The Swift Hawks were a little dubious but when they saw their horses follow the stallion without too much anxiety, they were a little reassured. Still, they found it hard to believe that Horse would know when they had emerged and return to the entrance.

All those who had survived had chosen to continue inside. It was good that they were alerted to the stakes they would be facing early on before they started the actual attack, but there was nothing to fully prepare them for what they would face.

The barbarian wasn't sure what a magus lich was capable of, and it felt like they would find out far too soon without any knowledge of how to defeat it.

The sound of fighting could be heard deeper inside the tunnels, and his eyes narrowed as he took the lead and strode ahead of the group as they began to move through the abandoned, dark hallways.

"Do you hear that?" he asked and turned to look at Sera, who was right behind him.

"There's fighting down there," she agreed. She was skilled in wielding her long sword in close quarters and wore a glove to grasp the blade and use it almost like a spear. "Do you think the Janus followers survived the creatures?"

It seemed like the only reasonable explanation unless the monsters were fighting amongst themselves.

The tight confines were not suitable for his bow so he held his ax in one hand and a dagger in the other, as ready as he could be for anything that might attack them at close range. Already, a few smaller, unarmored creatures had rushed them in the darkness, but aside from the surprise, they were easy to deal with.

"Pick up the pace!" he snapped. If there were any survivors from the group that had left earlier, he wanted to be there to assist them.

The more who could be added to their group, the better.

They walked through a chamber that opened into a longer hallway. This seemed like it was cut directly out of a stone castle in the north except for the lack of windows, and torchlight flickered ahead of them. The sounds grew louder and told them a fight was ongoing that they likely could help with.

A few of the Hawks settled in with their smaller bows and felled their targets from a distance while two of the others remained behind to defend them. It was fairly impressive how they were able to act tactically without the need for orders from their superior. Perhaps that was what came from fighting for the emperor.

Skharr raced forward, grasped his weapons a little tighter, and hoped he could trust in the armor provided to him by the dwarves in Verenvan. A roar began to build within him as he charged at the undead that were attacking the group.

Some of the mercenaries turned, their weapons raised to defend themselves against him as if they expected him to attack them instead, but he barreled past them into the group of undead that had gathered to assail them. He resisted the urge to snap at them and tell them where their minds needed to be—which was not on him—and soon, the first team and his group flung themselves into the fray as well.

The creatures were a far cry from those they had faced outside. There was very little meat left on their bones, which made them shuffle about and swing their weapons wildly and without much coordination. It didn't matter. Skharr already knew that much. What made the creatures the most effective was their lack of fear. They were already dead and controlled by a creature that wouldn't feel their pain.

The second biggest danger was their numbers. They surged forward in swarms, climbed over one another, and tried to attack at the same time. While they lacked any coordination, they were powered forward by the sheer will of another creature. They felt no pain and nothing other than an unabated hatred for anything living that crossed their paths.

"Brainless fucking hell-spawned bone sacks," he muttered. He roared defiance at them and swung his ax hard into the skull of the closest one. The force of the blow catapulted it into the group that came in behind it.

"Kill the godsbedammed brainless fucking soul-suckers!" he shouted and a handful of arrows thunked into the skulls of the beasts that surged forward while the rest of his team shored up the battered and beaten group they were trying to help. He adjusted his grasp on his weapon and thrust the dagger out to catch and deflect a heavy club that was swung toward his head. In a smooth motion, he buried the ax in the undead's neck, severed its head, and grinned when the rest of the body froze for a tiny moment before it fell.

The Janus followers felt a surge of encouragement from those who came to their aid. They were an enthusiastic group and needed only a little push to drive forward as a line as they shouted out a chorus of battle cries. Most revolved around their adoration of the ass, but Skharr chose not to point that out. Let them have whatever upheld them in battle for the moment. He was more than capable of keeping his trap shut for the betterment of the group as a whole.

The skeletons were driven back, crushed to a man, and no new ones approached to supplement those that had been destroyed. He knew for a fact that most mages put the enchantment of the skeletons in the skulls of the fallen. It seemed an odd thing to do but he'd heard dozens of different explanations from it allowing them better control over the creatures to making it safer for the enchantment.

None of the tales were definitive of course, since all studies into necromancy were theoretical by necessity. This meant that anything learned would always be questioned.

With the fighting abated for the moment, the Janus followers turned to make sure that the folk who had come to help them were not some kind of cruel trick played on them by the dungeon.

"Thanks be to Janus that you came to our aid, barbarian," one of them shouted. He was a powerful-looking man yet wore the robes of a cleric. Skharr assumed this was one of the battle clerics Janus liked to field.

"Thank Janus or Theros, but I have a feeling the danger has not passed," he replied and noticed Sera watching him curiously.

His gaze settled on the group in front of him, now with considerably smaller numbers than they had started with. "Were so many lost here in the tunnels?"

"Most were lost before we even came in," Savas, the captain of the group, stated as he approached him and the Swift Hawks. "Monsters waited for us outside. We managed to kill one but it cost us ten of our number. When two more appeared from the buildings, we were forced to either enter or risk losing more. How did you get through them?"

The barbarian didn't want to tell them what they learned about the beasts. Knowing their own dead were likely part of the perverted creatures he and his team had killed and burned would be a blow to their morale that he doubted they would recover from.

"We powered through the beasts," he told them. "I don't think the one you killed was fully dead, however. We took the time to burn the bodies and make sure they wouldn't be waiting for us when we come out again."

He chose his words very carefully. Seeing the low spirits of the group, he had a feeling they could use a boost of confidence. A few reminders that they would leave the dungeon alive would tell them there was hope in the world.

New determination infused the group and their captain wanted to make use of it immediately.

"We'll keep moving then," Savas said loudly. "Check your weapons and collect yourselves. We move in a few minutes."

The group responded with alacrity and a little more enthusiasm in their movements than there had been previously. Skharr retrieved a small vial of potion meant for healing and handed it to the mercenary leader.

"I'm fine," the man said and shook his head.

"Your right leg limping says otherwise," he insisted.

"They...one of the creatures bit me. I'm dead already."

The barbarian narrowed his eyes. "What? No, zombies are

another form of undead. These were simple dead humans that were raised from the dead. There is a whole other process to it. Keep yourself healthy."

Savas sighed, took the potion, and dabbed a few drops of it on his wound before he drank the rest and tossed the clay vial aside. "It is appreciated, barbarian. I would have expected less from a Theros follower."

"In these parts, there is no division between the followers of one god or another. There are those who live and those who die. I am determined to keep as many as possible among the former."

"That is appreciated," the man whispered and patted him on the shoulder. "For what little it might mean to you, I feel the same way."

"I can fight alongside any who feel the same way, no matter who the asshole is they worship."

That drew a laugh from Savas, who shook his head and collected his weapons again as his group assembled and readied themselves for the fight to come.

"Something's happened to you," Sera grumbled half under her breath as they continued down the hallway.

"What do you mean?" Skharr asked.

"You're…not shouting at folk to keep them in line. It's odd to watch."

He smirked. "We are all survivors here. There is no need to berate folk who had no idea what they were wandering into."

That didn't prevent the sideways glances darted continually at him, but for the moment, they needed to keep moving. They were approaching a larger hall that opened out like it was a throne room ahead of them.

"This…isn't right," Skharr whispered and tightened his grasp on his weapon. The amulet on his chest seemed close to shaking itself free of the chain that held it around his neck, but he couldn't see any sign of danger inside the chamber. Still, he was learning to trust it more with each time it warned him.

Sera looked like she was similarly worried, her sword already in her hand. The barbarian caught a flicker of light from the corner of his eyes. He turned and realized immediately that it was not from any of their torches. Instead, a flame flared from the back of the room and grew quickly until it followed the walls as the teams pushed forward. It illuminated the statues lined up along the length of the room and drew their attention slowly to the opposite side of the large space.

He knew what he was looking at almost immediately. The throne brought his mind back to the creature he'd fought before so it came as no surprise to see something seated there with his staff pointed directly at him where he stood at the front of the group.

"You!"

The sickening voice echoed through the chamber, unnaturally amplified as the figure pushed slowly to his feet.

He was larger than before but the armor was oddly the same as when they had faced each other last. The staff was not the same, but there was certainly something familiar about the creature and he seemed to feel the same about him.

"That decides that," Skharr stated grimly. "Without a doubt, he's the same lich I fought before."

"How is that possible?" Sera asked. "I didn't think liches could be brought back from the dead. Second...death? Is that the term?"

"Fucked if I know. It's something gods can do, I suppose. But he's the same creature."

Savas either didn't hear them or chose to ignore them and motioned for his team to take their positions and prepare for an attack.

"Kill them all!" the lich roared and swung his staff around the room. "But I want the barbarian to suffer."

"You and I have to talk about how you've managed to anger a lich and a demon this much," Sera commented.

Skharr didn't understand why defeating the lich had caused

such a grudge to form. The creature had been the one to draw him in, hoping to possess him with a demon. The only thing that had stopped him from succeeding was the fact that he had under-estimated the barbarian.

Then again, liches didn't seem like the type to acknowledge their mistakes. He shook his head but put these ramblings aside when he realized that the statues had begun to come to life. That was a weapon he hadn't expected when they'd entered. In truth, he hadn't expected to reach the magus lich so soon in the dungeon. He had hoped to have more time to prepare.

The statues were fully animated now, and more skeletons rose from beyond the flames and marched through them quickly. A few were still on fire as they drew inexorably closer to the group.

"Skeletons." Sera shook her head in disgust. "Why does it always have to be fucking skeletons?"

The combined teams looked ready to initiate the attack, but Skharr couldn't help the feeling that they needed to find another way. They were not yet ready for this kind of fight.

"Pull back!" he shouted, but none of those present heard him or if they did, they didn't care. The cleric called on a bolt of light-ning that left the barbarian's ears ringing and his eyes watering. One of the statues was reduced to a pile of dust and small rocks as Skharr took a step forward, still shouting, but he could no longer hear himself.

That likely meant the others couldn't hear him either.

"Sons of Janus' poxy whores, the lot of you!" he snarled and pushed to the front of the line as the first of the statues reached them.

It was a little smaller than he was, although he knew that wouldn't be the telling factor. He flipped the ax in his hand to use the spike on the opposite side of the blade, swung it as hard as he could, and hammered it into the statue.

The blow left an odd ache beneath his numbed arm and he

drove his foot into the creature and forced it back to shatter under his next blow.

"Pull back!" he shouted and gestured to reinforce the command as more of the undead surged toward them.

A few of their men fell under the assault, but as Skharr attacked the monsters and thrust them back with repeated blows with his ax, he cleared enough space that they finally realized they were not in a position to fight in this situation.

It wasn't the most comfortable thing to do, of course, but a little injured pride was better than death, he decided, and they needed to clear the room while they were still able to do so. Hopefully, they could regroup and find a way to kill the magus lich.

"Go now!" he roared when even the cleric fell back as well. The man continued to launch a couple of bolts of lightning in slow succession that almost blinded and deafened the warrior each time.

Skharr decided to have a word with the man about that. He adjusted his hold on his weapon but he'd cleared a path for them to use to escape the room.

Finally, they took it. Each and every fighter there realized what they now faced and all agreed when he said they needed to withdraw and regroup.

They managed to retreat in an orderly fashion, at least. His arm still felt like it had been stung and ached all the way up to his shoulder. They rounded a corner away from the chamber and he looked back, expecting the monsters to follow them.

Thankfully, none of them did. He almost didn't believe it but reminded himself that something was odd about this dungeon. The sense that something didn't feel quite right persisted and he looked around before he settled onto his haunches.

Fear coursed through his veins, fueled by the knowledge that the entity within the throne room was powerful beyond imagining. Despite the almost crippling terror, he knew he had to attack it again.

The barbarian rubbed his fingers in an attempt to restore some feeling to them as the group assembled to decide what they would do next.

"Parish," he said sharply before anyone else could speak. "You saw what we faced in there, yes?"

The captain nodded.

"You must leave here," Skharr instructed firmly. "You and your Swift Hawks, and if we don't join you out there in two days, you must send word to organize a force unlike anything that's been seen before to defeat what awaits anyone who ventures into this dungeon, do you understand?"

"What?" Sera asked and seemed ready to argue.

"Numbers will not win us this battle," he responded. "And we need to prepare for the eventuality that we might fail."

Parish clearly did not like the idea of leaving either. He was a warrior above all and running from a fight went against every instinct in his body. Still, he knew the importance of relaying intelligence to win battles.

He nodded grimly. "We'll take the wounded to the surface and hold our position there for the next two days."

Skharr grasped the man's shoulder in what he hoped was an encouraging gesture. "We'll join you as soon as we can."

Sera looked around and gestured to Vita and Norik. "You'll join them on the surface."

"What?" the woman snapped.

"Go. And if the two days pass and we do not join you, send word to the rest of the caravan."

None of those commanded to leave liked the idea, but Skharr had a feeling that they were more than willing to admit to themselves that they were a little relieved. If so, he could not blame them for it.

CHAPTER NINETEEN

Those who remained shared a somber disposition. Skharr had seen the kind of morale that now surrounded him in a handful of the armies he'd been a part of.

Thankfully, his experience told him that their attitude didn't mean their spirits were low or even that they were falling into despair. Instead, they shared a grim resolution to do what they had to do to finish the contract, even if it claimed their lives.

He doubted that fear wasn't chewing at their insides, but he knew that Janus' followers were not cowards, no matter how awful they were or how well they represented their ass of a god.

Courage alone wouldn't win the battle for them, however. He looked at each one, grateful for the good fortune that none of them seemed to realize how perilous their situation was.

The statues and the skeletons were merely the first wave, the kind of thing the magus lich used to amuse himself and eliminate the lesser threats. A creature like that reveled in the violence he caused, even if he wasn't directly involved. But once the entity joined the battle, he had a feeling they would face something that even he had no idea how to defeat. He didn't even know if their adversary had a phylactery like the other lich had. What if it was sustained purely by the will of whatever god had raised it?

Skharr took a deep breath and lowered his head. They needed a god's help to stop a god, and he doubted that Janus would listen to him, even though he was trying to save the lives of the asshole's followers. Perhaps they were all doomed, but he knew it was foolish not to use every weapon that he had available.

"Theros," he whispered under his breath, "this time, it is too much. A DeathEater is not enough to defeat a magus lich. What you can give, Skharr will gladly accept."

He hadn't prayed in his life before, but he assumed it was the spirit that counted, not the actual words. Then again, gods were mealy-mouthed characters who got their undergarments in a twist over the smallest things.

Still, he hoped Theros wasn't a stickler for decorum when it came to his barbarians praying to him.

His eyes opened and he realized that Sera was studying him closely.

"What?"

"Are you going to explain your praying?" she asked and raised an eyebrow. "Or will we simply pretend that I didn't see you doing so? I am not usually this nosy, but you did call for us to retreat rather quickly in there and I would assume this has something to do with it."

Skharr shrugged and pulled his helm on. "Yes. When Theros gave me the knowledge of what I would face here, he asked me to help. But he told me I would likely die if I tried to gain the victory under my own power."

"And?"

"And it turns out that he was right." He chuckled. "I did have to make an attempt, though. I have a hard head that way."

"I could have told you that."

"I am unsure if that would have been any help." He tapped the side of his helm. "A hard head, remember?"

"True," she admitted.

"And so, with that in mind, Theros…offered me a position as a paladin."

Sera took a step back and narrowed her eyes. "You…didn't take it?"

"There are too many rules I would not be able to follow. I don't know if I've told you, but I recently traveled with a paladin, and with that knowledge in mind, I knew the position would not have suited me well. At the same time, he knew he would not have been happy if I carried his name like that. Instead, we came to a…mutual agreement that I would be the best Barbarian of Theros I could be."

"So that is why you provided no argument when Savas called you the Barbarian of Theros."

"Yes."

"So…what did you get?"

"From?"

"Theros. Usually, when they extend you that kind of consideration, you receive something from it, yes?"

"Oh, right." Skharr nodded. "Aye, he did mention something along the lines that he would be aware of my need should I happen to pray."

"It seems nebulous," Sera pointed out.

"I cannot say that my vow exactly promised clarification of what I would do for him."

She laughed. "Well, I suppose that bit you in the ass."

"Not yet," he muttered and noticed that the group was once again ready to start their assault on the chamber. "But I might find out that I bargained poorly soon enough."

"I cannot say I'm happy about that," she answered and followed him as he moved to join the others. "I only hope Theros thinks you are worth more to him than you seem to think you are."

"So, you do not have anything to say before we go in there?"

"No," she answered. "Nothing comes to mind."

"Fair enough." The barbarian hooked his ax into his belt and drew his sword instead.

"I thought you were more comfortable with the ax," Sera commented as he inspected the edge of the blade. "If I'd known you planned to use it, I would have told you that you need more practice with your sword."

"I am and I do, but this blade is…powered, somehow. The ax is simply another weapon and I don't like ignoring any possible advantages we might be able to bring to the field."

She nodded. "You do need more practice with the blade. We could have done a little training while we were on the road."

"I needed that time to condition myself with the new bow," he replied as Savas approached.

"Have we a plan, then?" he asked.

"Aye. You hang back and wait to support us. Sera and I will advance to determine what we'll face. I very much doubt that it will be anything like the undead in our first encounter."

The man nodded and brandished his weapon. "We will be ready to support you."

"Are we truly going ahead?" Sera asked.

"Aye. Is that a problem?"

"Not really. I had a feeling the Janus followers would get in our way so being the vanguard is probably a good thing."

The chamber looked different when it was dark—almost peaceful like a tomb, with the statues barely visible in the faint light from the embers that had been left burning where the fires had been. They would go out eventually but still left a warm, red glow in the room that would otherwise have been completely dark.

It was good they had at least some light. Skharr imagined the lich had better vision in the dark than they did, so if they wanted to sneak in, being able to see where they were going was important.

"And you simply let him go!"

The sickening voice echoed through the chamber and made both of them freeze their slow and cautious approach.

He tightened his hand on his sword instinctively, but the amulet wasn't vibrating on his chest yet, which likely meant that they weren't in any danger for the moment.

"How many barbarians run away from a fight like that?" a second voice asked, although it sounded hauntingly similar to the first. "I think he's grown smarter since we last faced each other."

"Didn't you say he knew more about you than most? That he knew to look for your phylactery when he killed you?"

"Semantics. I meant that he might be growing more intelligent. I had hoped to catch him before the others and make him watch while we killed all his friends."

"And I tried to close the doors to prevent their escape."

"We didn't need to do both."

"We could have shut the doors, then done whatever you wanted to do with him later."

"All right. I'll admit that does sound like the better plan, but you should have told me. We are still growing in power and we can't control all our creatures, hold the flames, and coordinate the rooms in the dungeon at the same time."

That was interesting to know. Skharr had a feeling that he heard a discussion between the lich and the demon who both possessed the same body, although he hadn't expected them to be at odds.

Perhaps the demon didn't like being summoned by the lich.

"We should find a way to continue growing our power," the voice he assumed was the demon's grumbled. "Waiting to kill the bastards who wander in here so we have the power to grow takes too long."

"We have ventured out to gather more but it is slow work," the lich replied. "We'll grow slowly at first but as time progresses, our power will increase faster."

"I suppose, but—wait."

"What?"

"Shut your mouth."

"Our mouth."

"Shut it! I smell something. Virgin blood."

Skharr paused with a small frown and glanced at Sera, who looked anywhere but at him.

"You?" he asked in a breathy whisper.

"What?"

"Are you?"

She didn't answer the question but she didn't deny it either. Even in the semi-darkness, he thought he could see a flush touch her cheeks.

"And you didn't think that was important to mention?" he whispered.

"How the hell was I supposed to know that my inability to find a man or woman I was willing to fuck would be a problem?"

"When I told you there was a demon involved you should have mentioned it." He shook his head. "They always think with their cocks."

"You just described half of all males, human or otherwise!" she retorted.

The barbarian opened his mouth to disagree but stopped. She wasn't necessarily wrong, after all.

"All right, you make a good point," he admitted but before he could continue, his amulet vibrated to warn them of danger. "I believe they know we're here."

"They?"

"The lich and the demon," Skharr snapped and pushed up from where he had been hiding. The heat of the flames around them grew stronger as he advanced on the creature with his sword in hand.

The heat wasn't only from the flames, he realized. The magic dampening amulet he wore as well had begun to grow hotter and he could practically feel the gaze of the lich on him.

"Yes, we can see you there," the entity said coldly, stood from the throne, and descended the steps slowly. "You can sneak all you like, but this dungeon is my home now and I know it better than the back of my own hand."

"I'll admit that I don't know the back of our hand," the demon interjected. "Which means I know the dungeon better than that."

It was odd to watch the same mouth producing two distinct voices. They sounded the same but were also undeniably different.

"We did manage to sneak a little," Skharr answered and stood his ground. "You'll need to get to know the dungeon a little better."

The magus lich laughed. "You came this far because I wanted to kill you myself. I was disappointed when you ran but I knew you would return and walk within my grasp again."

"Is that why you haven't summoned your monsters to fight us?" the barbarian asked.

"I want to squeeze the life from your body with my own hands."

"Our hands."

"Godsbedammed, that is what I meant. Would you please...shut up!"

He wasn't sure which voice belonged to which entity, but he could see the power gathering in the aberration's staff in preparation for an attack and tried to ready himself as best he could.

"If there ever was a time," he whispered, "it is now, Theros."

Sera doubted that she could stand against the creature alone. She could practically feel the power radiating from him and her damper amulets began to heat to the point where they felt painful on her skin. Their magic was probably the only reason why she managed to stand her ground against the evil emanating from the creature instead of bolting from the chamber.

But Skharr was there. She knew he felt the same fear she did and he was out there in front and refused to back down.

That was the kind of thing that couldn't be taught. It was either in him or it wasn't and in this case, it was most certainly in him.

"Come on, then, you godsbedammed soul-sucking self-fuckers!" Skharr roared in response. "Is it good to pleasure one another while you fucking connive and plot and feast on others to grow your power?" He swung his sword to loosen his wrist before he lunged at the creature.

The lich's laugh was more of a cackle, a loud, deep, shrill, and unpleasant sound that triggered a painful spark from the amulets on her chest. One of them cracked and fell from the chain she'd used to keep it in place.

That didn't stop the barbarian, however, and she thrust her terror aside to join his attack. The power growing around the lich's staff transformed into a ball of fire that he launched quickly across the room at his large adversary.

The entity didn't seem to realize that she was there, but when she took another step forward, the second amulet shattered and something stopped her physically. It wrapped her in a tight hold, froze her in place, and forced the blade to fall from her numb fingers.

Something was horrifyingly wrong. Sera tried to push against it, but all her effort achieved was a blinding pain that seared across her whole body and dragged a scream of agony from her.

Skharr glanced over his shoulder at her. If she could, she would have told him to continue the fight. She was in no real and immediate danger. Whatever held her wanted her alive and likely far away from the destruction the battle would cause.

Perhaps he understood as he turned away from her and resumed his attack on the lich. The fire that issued from the being's staff suddenly launched forward to fill the whole room with a bright yellow light.

He dove to the right, rolled over his shoulder, and regained his feet to push into a sprint toward the entity.

He might not have seen the second fireball launched at him but even if he had, there was no way to avoid it.

Sera tried to look away and close her eyes, but she couldn't stop herself from watching the flames strike Skharr in a blast that washed her face with heat.

"That was a little too quick," the lich complained.

"It's for the best. Now we have a virgin to toy with. Keeping her separate from the destruction certainly will pay off for us, I think."

"I'll never understand your fascination with untouched women."

She couldn't make anything out in the flames for a moment, but as they began to fade, relief washed over her, even if she couldn't act on it. Her entire focus was on the figure of the massive barbarian in the flames, untouched by them and still standing.

Skharr looked as surprised as Sera felt. It seemed like the lich was similarly shocked as he glowered at his staff as if to determine what was wrong.

"This is impossible!" he roared.

A second voice echoed the same word loudly enough to make the floor shake in the chamber. Her bones ached even from the sound of it.

Something in Skharr's eyes drew her attention. She had seen it before—a gleam in a man with violence on his mind. He moved forward again with his sword ready and lunged toward the throne.

Another blast of fire missed and the lich raised his staff to deflect his adversary's blow.

His form was still a little stiff around the hips, but Sera felt a flush of pride as she watched the barbarian flow around the lich's attempt at a counterattack, circle the being, and slash his blade across his back.

A painful screech echoed through the room as the creature stumbled forward and tried to look at the wound Skharr had carved into him.

"A sanctified blade?" he demanded indignantly. "Where does a dimwit barbarian get his hands on a sanctified blade?"

"Dimwit barbarians have friends," he said in reply and darted deftly to the side when the staff was swung to catch him in the chest.

It missed and he sliced the lich again with a smooth swing of his blade. A glow emanated from where the blade cut deeply.

"A house divided," the lich whispered and scowled at its wounds when Skharr took a step back and readied himself for another attack.

The warrior drove forward, brought his blade up over his shoulder, and arced it down with as much power as he could muster. His adversary raised his staff to block the blow.

The sword cut through the staff and continued its swing to cut into the lich's neck.

As the blade sliced through, a blast of white light flickered through the room and shook it to the point where chips of stone fell from the ceiling.

Suddenly, the power that had constrained her was gone and Sera dropped to her knees and sucked in a deep breath as if she had held it from the moment when the invisible force had taken hold of her.

The blast upended Skharr and as they both scrambled to their feet, she realized that the lich was still standing.

No, that wasn't right. The armor he wore crumbled and transformed into piles of dust around it. In its place, standing where it had been, was something else.

A creature wreathed in flame and darkness looked at its hands and around the room.

"Now...that is better," the demon said gleefully.

It must be one of the other gods interfering. No human, no matter how large or powerful, would withstand a blast of that power.

Theros...or Janus. Perhaps Sarea or even Illia or one of the other gods and goddesses. It was possibly one of the lesser deities, but Quazel doubted it. He would have been able to sense their presence.

"Hello again, cousin."

He whirled and swung the dagger in his hand at the neck of whoever stood behind him.

"You—no." He shook his head. "What are you doing here?"

Theros' usual pitiful appearance of a decrepit man who could barely stand without the help of his staff was gone. He looked like the warrior he had been in times of old, standing tall and powerful and ready to fight.

"I have a message for you," he said calmly and placed a hand on Quazel's shoulder. Flickers of lightning and smoke appeared behind the huge deity. "My brother would like a moment of your time."

In a moment, the dungeon vanished around him.

Skharr hadn't even seen what he now assumed to be another god until Theros appeared. He had no idea where the high god had come from, but he took the stranger with him without so much as looking back until the other god disappeared.

"Good luck with this one!" he shouted to them, drew a dagger from his belt, and flicked it through the air.

The barbarian lunged forward to snatch it mid-flight, but Theros was already gone and the dagger was in his hand.

He looked at it but could see nothing that made it exceptional or remotely special. It was merely a dagger with a leaf-shaped blade and a leather grip.

Still, the god wouldn't have given it to him if he didn't think it would help.

Sera seemed to have recovered from whatever had overcome her. She moved to his side and looked a little winded, but she held her sword firmly and stood squarely and surely.

"What was that?" she asked.

"I don't know." He turned his attention to the demon, who was still distracted by self-examination. The creature seemed to enjoy the freedom from the lich he had possessed. "Here, take this."

"A dagger?" she asked as she took the weapon from his hand. "That was Theros, wasn't it? He gave you this?"

"Yes, and I have a feeling the demon will be focused on me for the moment. Look for an opening and we will trust that it works."

She nodded and inched away from him as the demon finally seemed to return to a consciousness of their presence.

"Do you feel more yourself?" Skharr asked.

"Youzzzzz have no ideazzzzzz," the demon hissed through the flames. "Trapped....insidezzzz a bodyzzzzz not my own. Horrifying."

"So you'll thank me for releasing you, then?"

"I will spare your life if you give me your virgin companion."

"Ah. Well, I cannot do that."

A hideous smile appeared with long, dagger-like fangs shaped from flames visible. "I thoughtzzzzz...not. It's best to jusszzzzt kill you anyway."

Skharr nodded and lifted his weapon as the creature of fire and smoke began to expand. He grew taller than he was and only stopped when he was twice his size. What had once been fingers were now tongues of flame that flared out to catch him around the neck.

He cut through two of them but they continued to writhe and wind themselves around him like snakes until the aberration dragged him off his feet and lifted him high to stare into the lidless eyes. There was nothing inside them, only a black void that brought visceral discomfort to settle in the pit of his stomach.

The fire didn't burn his skin, oddly enough, but the barbarian groaned as the tongues of flame tightened around him and twisted his body beyond its limits. Something cracked in his right shoulder and pain seared through his whole body.

"Whatever protected you from my blast of fire before appears to still be in place," the demon whispered in a voice that physically pained him to hear. "No matter. I'll tear you limb from limb! That'll be more fun anyway!"

Skharr screamed when the flaming tentacles wound around his arms and began to pull.

"Oy!"

The demon stopped and Sera surged forward to vault onto the creature's back.

"That barbarian is my friend, you piece of hell-spawned shit!" she bellowed and drove the dagger deep into the demon's back and used it as leverage to climb higher. It shrieked in pain, dropped the warrior, and flailed to reach her.

She moved too quickly and yanked the dagger free before the clawed flames could take hold. With a yell of defiance, she plunged the blade into the demon's temple.

"Next time you go hunting for virgins, I suggest you look for those who can't defend themselves," she snapped, dropped off the monster, and rolled away. The flames flared and burned brighter as he tried to yank the dagger out.

His tentacles pulled away from the handle like they had been stung and he began to shrivel slowly and lose his vast size.

Skharr laughed, although he wasn't entirely sure why. A few bones had been displaced in the fall, which hampered his efforts to struggle to his feet. The demon was gradually sucked into the dagger in its skull, which glowed like it was in a forge.

Finally, the being wisped into the blade, which fell and spattered on the floor, so hot that it had been turned to liquid.

He continued to laugh as he rolled onto his back and reached over to his side, grasped the arm that had been pulled from his shoulder socket, and with a grunt, pulled it into place.

"Hurts…" he groaned and the laughter stopped abruptly. The ache traveled up his arm and told him that even with the healing amulet, he would need a few days before he was in any condition to travel.

Sera dragged herself closer to him and the barbarian realized that while he had been immune to the demon's flames, she was not. Her hands and knees looked badly burned yet she was still moving.

"Do you…have any health potions with you?" she asked, her voice rough and raspy.

Skharr groaned, pushed to a seated position, and searched through his pouches.

They were wet inside, which was already not a good sign, and he peered into one. The flames had crushed all the potions and left him with pouches that would be in perfect health for years to come.

"One," he whispered and withdrew the small vial that had survived, placed it on the floor, and pushed it gently to her.

"No," she whispered and winced with a groan of pain as she forced herself to sit. "You look like you need it more than I do."

"You are joking, yes? You look worse than a pig that's been roasting on a spit for three hours."

"I'll be fine. I had worse injuries than these when I was training."

"I suppose they allowed you to rest after taking those injuries?"

She sighed and nodded.

"We do not have that luxury here." He nudged the vial closer to her. "Besides, Theros would not approve of my making use of a healing vial when others are in need."

"Shit to that," she retorted but took it gingerly. She had to work at the cork with her injured fingers but eventually pulled it out and sipped the contents to empty it only halfway.

She gritted her teeth immediately as the potion began to take effect. The burns scabbed over and gradually transformed into soft pink skin instead.

After a few seconds, she pushed the vial to him.

"I can make it," Skharr insisted.

"I give this to you freely, so there is no need to worry about dishonoring your god, Paladin. Besides, I won't carry your barbarian ass if you are lying, so drink it and we can drag each other from this place."

"Fine." He took it and tilted the contents into his mouth.

The effects were almost immediate and he growled as his ribs snapped into place and the other bruised and battered bones began to mend. It didn't complete the healing but it would make walking a little easier.

"Better?" Sera asked and grunted as she stood cautiously. She collected and sheathed her sword before she offered him a hand to help him up.

He took it gratefully. "Much. But next time…"

She narrowed her eyes and helped him to retrieve his weapons. "Yes?"

"The next time we fight a demon and I ask you if you have

anything important to share, please let me know if you are still a virgin."

"Should we fight another demon," she stated and made sure he was able to stand without assistance before they started walking to the doors. "And should I still be a virgin, I'll ask the Barbarian of Theros to help me rid myself of that problem."

"As the Barbarian of Theros."

"And as my friend," she added.

Skharr nodded. "Of course."

"But until then, you won't speak a word about my choice."

"As the Barbarian of Theros and a DeathEater, you have my word, Sera Ferat."

"Good," she snapped. "I'd hate to have to explain to Theros the reason why I stabbed his pet barbarian."

"Trust me." He chuckled. "I'd rather have to explain to Theros why I stabbed you."

"Ha...oh, fuck." She winced and shook her head. "It still hurts to laugh. As for that virgin shit, I still don't understand how it knew. Anatomically speaking, I lost my virginity while riding a horse."

"That is a complicated way to do it," Skharr muttered. "But I have a feeling...yes."

"And if I happened to fuck another woman, there would be none of the usual physical signs I don't think. Do you have any idea why the demon was obsessed with that?"

"They are perverts," he answered simply.

"Ah. I see. Wouldn't they prefer someone with more experience if that is the case?"

"I would. But then, I'm no demon."

CHAPTER TWENTY

There were problems that Skharr hadn't accounted for. The magus lich had been in control of the troglodyte tribes and now that his control was gone, the creatures rampaged through the tunnels accompanied by shrieks and screams.

"This isn't fucking fair!" Sera shouted and swung her sword to cut through two of the marauders that broke away from the rest. "We killed the godsbedammed lich. They should be throwing us a fucking parade."

The beasts didn't focus only on the adventurers and seemed as determined to kill one another as they were to attack the teams. The barbarian realized that they were likely a few dozen different tribes that had worked together under the control of the lich. Once they were released, it was clear why they were separate tribes.

He arced his weapon as a small group rushed into an attack and he killed one of them before he wounded two others. His whole body still ached but this new enemy, thankfully, didn't provide much of a fight.

There were merely so many of them.

It was a relief to rejoin the Janus followers as it gave them greater safety in numbers.

"Did you kill it?" Savas asked. "What happened in there? And why are all these fucking brainless shits attacking us?"

"The lich is dead," Sera snapped. "And...well, I can't explain the monsters but we need to leave this place. Now!"

No one voiced any argument.

Finally, they reached the entrance of the dungeon. It felt impossible, but there was even more pandemonium outside than there had been inside.

The horses neighed loudly and tried to drive the monsters away. Those who had gathered outside were fighting the troglodytes. There were far more of these creatures out in the open than there had been in the tunnels, and they appeared to be gathering with the intention to attack the humans as invaders. It seemed that even these primitive beasts knew the concept of uniting against a common foe on the odd occasion.

The cleric blasted a hole through the creatures that allowed them to pass, but it spooked the horses even more than all the previous mayhem.

"We need to go!" Parish shouted. "Is the work done?"

"Yes!" Skharr roared as most of them mounted up. The Janus followers had lost their horses already and he wasn't about to let any of them ride Horse. That would be even worse than if he rode the stallion himself.

"Then we ride!" Parish shouted and cut one of the troglodytes down with his saber as the other mercenaries hastened to leave the wretched place.

It would not be a gentle ride, but the foul creatures appeared to have a sense of where their territory ended.

"I suppose this is what amounts to a coup among these hell-spawned brainless fuckers!" Skharr declared and tried to keep pace with the rest of the troop. He did better than most of the others who had to walk but he felt as though every bone in his body begged for release. He desperately needed relief and perhaps a little more healing.

Parish finally brought the group to a halt and before the barbarian realized it, he was on his knees. He gasped for breath and held his sides like the old geezer Theros pretended to be.

"Are you all right?"

He wasn't sure who had asked the question as he was focused on trying to push through the difficulty he experienced in breathing. Finally, he managed to look up. Sera and Parish stood over him.

"Do I...fucking look all right?" he gasped belligerently. "It feels...like a rib's...poking into...my lungs. I can't breathe."

"I told you he'd be fucking ungrateful," she muttered.

"Why don't you take a healing potion?" Parish asked.

"Yes, Skharr, why don't you take a healing potion?" Sera echoed.

"I...fucking hate...both of you."

The Swift Hawks' captain grinned. "Are you all out then? I think I have a few to spare."

He took a vial from his belt and proffered it with a neutral expression. The barbarian wasn't the type to drink simply anything that was handed to him and paused to inspect it before he swallowed all of it in a single gulp.

In moments, his ribs felt better, although they were still a little sore, but he felt spent. The potions were magical but took most of their power from the body's ability to heal to accomplish what would normally take him weeks or months. This was bound to take a toll.

"I need an ale," he muttered as he pushed slowly to his feet. "The cold kind. This godsbedammed fucking heat will kill me as sure as a lich will."

"You're being dramatic," Sera replied. "We need to keep moving. Parish thinks we can reach the camp before dark."

"I don't want to meet whatever else might turn rampant thanks to the death of that lich," the captain agreed.

"All right then. It means I'll die on my feet at least."

———

Micah scowled at the woman who served tea from an ancient clay pot.

"I told you I am in a hurry, yes?" she asked and raised an eyebrow.

"You cannot rush the tea," the older woman muttered and tucked a few errant gray hairs behind her ear. "Too hot and it can crack the pot. Too cold and all you have is warm water with a few leaves in it."

All tea was warm water with a few leaves in it, but she was too wise to make that observation. The woman was clearly devoted to the craft of making tea and it was delicious enough to make it easier to endure the wait.

"We could have done this without the tea, Margo," she pointed out.

"I don't do business without making tea," Margo answered, sat with a soft groan, and sipped her tea. "Now, how can I help you, child?"

"You oneiromancers are a dying breed these days and hard to find."

"They stopped teaching it in the universities. Something about there being no scientific accuracy to the practices. Of course, they also considered the magic they practice to be unscientific back in the day until they discovered the truth of it. If you stop studying something, you cannot establish its validity."

Micah had a feeling the woman had practiced that speech for a while.

"I need a message sent," she said, withdrew a small purse of coin from her sleeve, and placed it on the table.

"A message is complicated. I need an item that belonged to the person you wish to contact."

She nodded, took a small dagger from the same sleeve, and placed it on the table. "Do you need anything else?"

"No." Margo hefted the bag of coins before she picked the dagger up. "What is the message you wish me to send?"

"Tell Sera that there are certain projects that need her attention before her return."

The woman raised an eyebrow. "Is that all? Will she know what it means?"

"She will." Micah stood and brushed the flecks of dust off that had collected on her travel clothes. The room irked her, which of course led her to understand why oneiromancers were generally avoided unless their services were needed. Every square inch was littered with amulets and books "Do you need me to remain?"

"No. I cannot sleep when there is someone else in the house, which means that no message can be sent."

"If I have to return here because you took my coin and did not do what I paid for, you will regret it."

"Of course, of course." The woman already looked sleepy as she pushed her portly body out of her seat. "Go on now. The message will be sent and your sister will hear of it when she wakes."

Micah paused on her way to the door. "I never said she was my sister."

"You didn't have to. The dagger did. Now go on, Micah. Know that your coin is well-spent."

"We'll see about that," she whispered and advanced toward the door of the house. Hopefully, she could put it behind her forever.

CHAPTER TWENTY-ONE

Another caravan and another trip to Verenvan were not what he would have chosen at this point in his life.

Skharr's body still ached from his encounter with the magus lich. It was painful to even think about, but he chose to not complain too much. He assumed Sera and the others were already a little weary of hearing his complaints. Even Horse was less conversational than usual, likely so he wouldn't think he was interested in hearing how fucking old he was.

The total anticlimax after they escaped the dungeon and the troglodytes was disconcerting—it felt almost like nothing had happened. He wasn't sure what he had expected after the battle. Some kind of remuneration, certainly. He didn't work for free, after all, even as a barbarian. But there was no word from Theros and it hadn't been a proper contract either so he couldn't expect compensation from the guild for his intervention.

He also doubted that the Janus followers would spread word that he and Sera had done most of the killing. They would all live in luxury for the rest of their lives thanks to their ass of a high god while he trudged his painful ass to Verenvan.

The journey wasn't for free, of course. The merchants paid

good coin to be escorted although it wasn't what he usually earned from dungeons.

"Gods like it when we work for free, don't they?" Skharr muttered and gave Horse an extra apple to compensate for any frustration the beast might endure. He had complained far more than usual, and it had been all about him. The stallion could only take so much before he reminded him that their relationship was a give and take.

Horse made no reply but took the apple from his hand.

"I am sorry I've been difficult to deal with lately," he whispered and patted him on the neck. In fairness, he had healed considerably faster than any human had a right to without the help of magic—mainly because he had a little magic to help him. It certainly had its uses.

When there was still no response from the stallion, he turned to leave but felt a nip on his shoulder.

"Ow!" he snapped and glared at the beast, who now chewed his apple like he hadn't tried to take a bite of the barbarian's shoulder. "Fucking donkey."

At least it meant the beast was talking to him again. The barbarian was happy enough about that and more than willing to offer his shoulder if it meant he could speak to his friend again. He could always take a potion for the nips.

"You look to be in a good mood," Sera muttered where she was seated outside her tent and stared into the fire while breakfast was being prepared.

"And you don't," he answered and moved away from the stallion to sit beside her. "What's the matter? You look like someone stuffed your bed with hornets."

"They might as well have. I had the oddest dream last night and I can't shake it from my head."

"Dreams can be portents of things to come."

"Well, my dreams generally involve a well-endowed merman who turns into a centaur halfway through our coupling. I don't know what to make of that."

"Centaur cocks are too large for a human woman your size to accommodate. Orcs, on the other hand, consider it something of a feat of strength to mate with a centaur, although most don't survive the encounter."

"Are centaurs—"

"I take it you've seen a draft horse's cock?"

"Ah. Never mind then."

"Hmm. What about this dream?"

"It was odd. Micah looked like she was seated across from me, drinking tea in an old house full of dust, books, and amulets hanging from the rafters. She told me there are certain projects I need to attend to before my return. It's an odd turn of phrase and she only ever used it when she tried to warn me of dangers— which hasn't been very often lately."

Skharr narrowed his eyes. "The amulets hanging from the rafters. What did they look like?"

"Like…little nets that were stretched across wooden circles. Or maybe spider webs. I'm not sure."

"They are called dream catchers, the kind oneiromancers use to protect themselves against others invading their thoughts and dreams."

"On… Onei…what?"

"Oneiromancers. Mages who use dreams either to divine the future or to reach out into the world and pass messages on as required. I think Micah tried to send you a message."

"That I'm in some kind of danger? I thought I had left the most dangerous part of this trip behind me in that fucking dungeon."

"There are still assassins who seek to kill me. They might know that you and I are together, which would put you in a great deal of danger."

"Oh. Right. I'd almost forgotten about that."

The barbarian nodded. "I might need help when we get back

to Verenvan. The chances are that they will scale their efforts up once they know I've returned."

"True." She sighed. "We could always speak to Svana. She still owes you for giving her everything she has by killing that poisoning bastard Tulius."

"True. But she won't do anything I need for free. She will want something in return."

"If it is more than you can pay, I can probably help you cover the costs."

Skharr looked at her. "You are not their target and need not involve yourself any more than you have already. In fact, the only reason assassins might try to kill you is because of me."

"I would kindly remind the Barbarian of Theros to get over himself." Sera smirked and popped a prune into her mouth. "I think we are past thinking that we aren't in a mess of things together."

"Are you—"

"Yes, I'm fucking sure. Now get along. We need to start moving or the merchants will get pissy about delays and the like."

Sera whistled loudly to catch the attention of her troop and Skharr wandered to where Horse was still waiting for him and looked around for another apple.

He sighed, took one from the saddlebags, and let the stallion munch on it happily. "I don't think I'll ever understand that woman."

Horse snorted.

"I know, but she's…different. We help each other, yes, but I was always paid for my efforts and frankly, so was she. Besides, she is royalty, whether she likes it or not. I've dealt with royalty in my past, of course. Before all this Theros business. I'd like to stay away from such entanglements in the future and avoid having my balls strung up by some zealot or another."

The stallion had little to say, which wasn't surprising with his mouth full of apple.

"She confuses me, is all," the barbarian admitted and shook his head. "And she would confuse you too if you cared to think about it too much."

That drew a whinny from Horse and he smiled as he began to put the saddlebags in place for the day's journey.

"Skharr! Get the fuck up, you big bastard!"

He hadn't heard anyone approaching and the fact that Horse hadn't made a loud noise to wake him told him that the voice was a friendly one.

It didn't seem like it, however. He mumbled and turned over, hoping the person would go away.

"I will drag you up by your red hair if I have to."

Skharr opened one eye and vaguely discerned Sera in the dim firelight.

"Not tonight," he muttered. "Have someone else help you."

"What?"

"What do you want?"

"I had another dream," she snapped. "We'll meet Micah a little way from the camp. Come on."

Perhaps he was too tired but her having a dream did not connect with him heading out with her to have a word with her sister.

It seemed, however, that she had no desire to wait. She was already standing and he had a feeling she would start to kick him if he didn't scramble to his feet. His ribs had barely healed and were still a little sore so it was best to avoid that.

After a few moments during which he muttered about his rotten luck, the barbarian finally dragged himself to his feet and followed her out of the camp, his eyes still bleary from sleep.

At least they were still far enough south that the night wasn't quite as cold as he thought it might be.

Sera appeared to already know where she was going and he simply followed at a discreet distance. If she didn't want him involved in the conversation and only needed him to watch her back, he wouldn't ask any questions. He'd simply get the job done.

Finally, she paused in front of a small pond and crouched to dip her hands in the water and splash some of it on her face after she'd made sure it was clean.

Skharr grasped his ax, ready to attack when he saw movement in the clearing. She saw it as well, however, and smiled broadly in the light of the full moon.

"Micah," she whispered, stood hastily, and wrapped the other woman in a warm embrace. "You don't have to jump through all these hoops to see me. What is wrong with a normal message?"

"A normal message can be intercepted by those looking to kill you," Micah replied and kissed her sister's cheek. "And on that topic, tell your barbarian he need not lurk in the shadows for this conversation. It would be best if he were part of it, I think."

Skharr had thought he had been quiet enough to avoid detection but he shrugged and slipped out from the small thicket he'd hidden in.

"Skharr, what the hell are you doing?" Sera asked. "I didn't ask you to watch the conversation."

"I am still fairly certain this is a dream of some kind," he muttered. "What other man can have two princesses wake him to talk?"

Micah looked oddly at him and tilted her head as if she wasn't sure what she had heard. He realized what she'd most likely heard of him—that he had difficulties speaking the common tongue.

Rather than comment, she shook her head and moved quickly past it.

"Those whose lives are in danger," she said before he could

explain more about what the dream might entail. "I assume both of you know there is someone out to kill you by now?"

Sera regarded her sister with a frown. "Well…yes. They have hunted us since we started on this journey."

"They hunted me far longer than that," Skharr muttered.

"Yes, but they only tried to kill both of us once we left the city."

"Right."

"Do you know who is trying to kill us?" Sera asked her sister.

The barbarian didn't know much about the woman, even if she was the spitting image of Sera, but there was a clear indicator of shame or at least some guilt. She didn't look to be the type who was ashamed often.

"I do," Micah answered. "The criminal underworld of Verenvan was not pleased with Skharr's return and decided that everyone would be better off if he were no longer among us. I didn't mind much since he had interfered with my business ventures in the past as well."

He narrowed his eyes. "What made you change your mind?"

"When they were informed that you would be traveling with my sister and decided that sacrificing her life to take yours was an acceptable risk. No offense, barbarian."

"None taken," he replied. "We don't know each other but a bond between siblings should be enough to spur anyone into action."

"So, what can we do next?" Sera asked and changed the subject quickly. "If they continue to attack me as well, that should give us a few more options, yes? They will need to be a little more creative."

"I'm afraid they have taken the route of throwing any who will take the coin at the problem until it is solved. This will continue until the end of time, unfortunately, so the only real way to stop them from trying would be to kill those who want to see the barbarian dead."

"If they run the underworld of the entire city, I assume that finding them will be the greater challenge," Skharr commented wryly and folded his arms in front of his chest.

"You would be right. They have grown a little paranoid since all this started and assume—correctly—that you will attempt to kill them when you have the chance."

"So they aren't the dumbest of folks," he noted. "I hate it when they aren't stupid. It makes things so much more difficult."

Micah looked at him like she was trying to decide if he was making a joke or not but shook her head and moved the conversation forward quickly. "We won't be able to do this alone. It will be difficult and we'll need warriors on our side."

"I was already talking to Skharr about that," Sera agreed before they could get into an argument. "We might find success if we send him to have a word with Svana."

"The noblewoman?"

"The very same. Having some noble support on our side would make things easier and could open avenues of investigation that would have been closed to us otherwise."

"If I know the woman, she won't do anything for free," the other woman noted and the expression on her face looked like she had accidentally bitten into a lemon. "Very well, but there are other matters that need attention. The Council will be watching the Mermaid and Sera's homes in and out of the city."

"I might be able to sneak into the city," Skharr suggested and rubbed his chin idly in thought. "I could go ahead of the caravan and find a way in to speak to Svana."

"You?" Micah raised an eyebrow. "As happy as I am to allow you to stroll into the den of vipers, you have to know you are far from the least conspicuous man to wander Verenvan's streets."

"I'll find a way," he insisted. "And should it go wrong, I will be dead anyway and the threat to your family will be at an end."

"At a pause, at least," she muttered.

"How soon can you leave, Skharr?" Sera asked.

"Immediately."

"Do that. I need to have a word with my sister before we continue."

The barbarian nodded and withdrew but remained in earshot. As much as he believed that Micah had no intention to harm her sister, he wouldn't leave Sera alone with her.

Although the blademaster probably wouldn't need his help.

And, as it turned out, he had been worried about the wrong sister turning violent. As soon as he stepped out of sight, Sera caught hold of her sister and thrust her back until she was pinned to a nearby tree.

"What?" Micah protested through clenched teeth and tried to dislodge her vice-like grip.

"I saw that look when I mentioned Svana. The same godsbe-dammed look you had on your face when you stole pastries from the kitchen and blamed me when mother found the crumbs."

There was no accounting for what two sisters would know about each other. Skharr assumed Micah knew of Svana and didn't like her.

"What do you want to share with me?" Sera insisted.

"I…fine. But let me go."

The guild captain complied and her companion took a moment to suck in a deep breath. She rubbed her neck where her sister's hands had tightened around it.

"You were involved in the whole process of getting that noble-woman married, yes?" Micah asked and Sera nodded. "As it turned out, I was on the other side of that dispute. Tulius paid me a great deal of coin to see to it that Skharr was dead before his wedding day. He didn't care much how it happened as long as the barbarian died."

"You were the one who tried to poison him, then?"

The woman nodded slowly. "It was before I knew you had any connection to the man."

"Do you think that is an excuse for what you've done?"

"I don't need to make excuses for what I've done," Micah snapped suddenly. "We are daughters of the emperor, forced to scrounge for scraps in the dregs of the city we should be ruling over. We should be princesses in the Imperial City but instead, we're one of a thousand bastards spread across the fucking continent."

"What would you have changed?" Sera asked and put her hand on her sister's shoulder. "To have some measure of royalty in our blood or perhaps a father who left in the night like a thief like so many other children?"

"We never saw the man in our lives. At least I cannot remember it."

"But we are still connected to the emperor who is on the throne at the moment."

"Us and a thousand other sycophantic shits? I'll pass on that, thank you."

"You do realize that the emperor who currently reigns sent his royal messengers to find the barbarian you tried to kill to ask him—not demand, ask—a favor?"

"Skharr?" Micah looked into the darkness he had disappeared into.

"Yes."

"Who is he? What did he do?"

"I am not sure who he is, at least not completely, but he has a good heart."

"That is not the only good thing about him." Micah smirked. "I hope he is enthusiastic between the sheets as well as energetic. You know men can be the type who simply…attack with a great deal of vigor for a few minutes and consider their job done."

"What?"

"Oh, please. Are you telling me you have not created the proverbial beast of two backs with the man?"

"Micah, for a woman with aspirations as high as an empress' throne, your mouth is at home in the gutter."

"So is most royalty when they think no one is listening. Trust me, I've heard worse from them. The men are terrible and the women are sluts dressed in precious silks. Or do you still wear that chastity belt of yours?"

"That is none of your business," Sera replied firmly.

"Well…" Micah looked in the direction in which Skharr had gone again.

"And you had better keep your…kitty empty of the barbarian's milk," her sister told her sharply

She raised her hands. "I see. I did not realize he wore a ring. I generally notice such things."

"He does not. But if I happen to change my mind, I'd rather be with a man who hasn't been with my sister."

"You know the man is far from celibate, yes?"

"That isn't the same and you know it. There are thousands of men you can choose from. Leave it alone."

"It or him?"Sera laughed, shook her head, and embraced her sister again.

CHAPTER TWENTY-TWO

It was not the first time Skharr had needed to sneak into a town and would likely not be the last either. Still, he needed to grow increasingly creative to gain entry without being noticed.

He recalled the last time it had been necessary. That was nigh on five years earlier when he was told to infiltrate a city so he could help with the assault that would come from the outside. One of the downsides of being a mercenary in an established army was that most generals considered mercenaries expendable.

Those officers who did certainly weren't the best. The most effective knew to use their finest and most experienced warriors as shock troops, but not all commanders knew how to handle the power of commanding an army.

This time, there was no order from a superior officer. It had been his idea. He had spent too much time in the city and much of that time was passed studying the defenses. This was mostly because it was how his mind worked without any real intention to do so.

The walls were impregnable and even if there was a way to

scale them and climb down again without being seen, Horse would not be able to join him.

Of course, the city's weakness was the most obvious solution. That particular vulnerability was known to many but had never been shored up by the local nobility as Verenvan had not been attacked for a long time. Time had made them complacent and they believed it never would be.

As a result, they left the slums in the swamps to grow unabated which provided Skharr with a clear route into the city.

There was a downside, of course. Most of those who looked to collect coin on his death made their living in the swamps that were fed by a river that ran north and was shored up by the walls and forced into stagnation before it finally crawled to the sea.

Still, it was better than going through a group of guards who would say his name loudly and clearly, then likely warn those who paid them coin that he had returned.

Horse followed him as he pulled a massive cloak over his shoulders. He forced his shoulders to slump and his knees to bend like he was older and had trouble walking. A staff helped him to maintain the facade and to remain in that somewhat awkward position for hours on end as he wandered the maze of flooded streets and stilted sections that comprised the slums.

He was merely another stranger who came to Verenvan hoping for refuge from the wars that ravaged the continent. It was better to be miserable without a war than with one. Even he could understand that.

Despite his efforts, he was a larger man than most and while those who saw him barely noticed him, Skharr knew that only one keen mind was needed to identify him, put it all together, and decide there was something odd about the old man who hobbled through the streets.

Most would search for the famous Barbarian of Theros in the regular part of the city. The more cunning, however, would simply look for all those who were a little larger than usual, no matter how disguised they were or which part of town they were in.

The barbarian knew he'd attracted two of those. They trailed him slowly with curious, greed-filled looks on their faces as they tried to catch a better glimpse of him from a distance.

His slow plodding would not work for him. He knew how to stay ahead and look away without seeming too suspicious but that wouldn't redirect the curiosity of the two men following him. They were no doubt willing to potentially waste a day trailing a fat old man or lady when the possible upside was that they could kill a man with a price on his head if their suspicions proved correct.

Skharr knew he had to deal with them quickly and quietly. It was a good thing he was in the swamps. Folk often died without explanation in the area. He slipped into a small inlet that brought him to a section of the road that was supported by stilts and looked into murky, foul-smelling pools.

"Stay," he muttered and Horse moved to the far side of the alley, likely offended by the smell that emanated from the water. He leaned against one of the walls, pulled his trousers down, and relieved himself into one of the larger holes into the swamp.

He could hear the voices and footsteps of the two men who approached him from the rear.

"Turn around, big-un," one of the would-be assassins said roughly. "Let's have a look at your face."

"You'll see more than my face if I turn," the barbarian answered and tried to disguise his voice.

The effort probably wasn't necessary. Not many in the city beyond those at the Guild Hall or the Mermaid had heard his voice or would recognize it.

"I said turn around!"

A hand grasped his shoulder and he whirled without warning and caught the man across the jaw with his elbow. The blow was powerful enough to spin the assassin off his feet and Skharr advanced quickly on the second man, who fumbled desperately for his dagger.

He didn't reach it in time. The warrior held him by the back of the head and pushed his lower jaw with his other hand to snap his neck in a single, smooth motion.

It would be a good time to make sure the first man was dead, he supposed, but he took a moment to cover himself first.

That done, he stabbed the first assassin's dagger into his chest to make sure and after a moment of thought, pushed him through the hole into the swamps.

"It's not the finest of resting places, floating around in my piss," Skharr muttered. "But maggot-brained fucking bottom-feeders like you don't deserve the best, do you?"

The oddest part, he realized, was that his amulet hadn't vibrated even once while he had engaged them. It likely knew he faced no threat to his life.

They wouldn't answer him and he wouldn't have listened to them anyway. The fools had wandered into the situation on their own and he wouldn't act like a parent who was there to teach them to be better.

He had more important things to worry about.

Once he confirmed that the bodies were sinking in the mire, the barbarian adjusted his cloak and his body to look like an old man again, whistled for Horse to join him, and continued along the road.

Thankfully, no others appeared to want a piece of him and he felt a little more comfortable once he reached the better areas of the city. Not that he thought the guards wouldn't try to kill him, of course, but among the higher-class citizens who were on the streets, they would at least be discreet about it.

He could deal with discreet.

Night had begun to fall over the city when he approached the Palatine and followed the steeper roads toward the more beautiful villas that were enclosed by the city walls. Skharr grimaced and realized that he needed to move faster as the guards were ushering folk from the streets and telling them to move along. He quickened his pace as much as he could without compromising his disguise.

It wasn't long before he found a small alley created by a handful of businesses that were closed for the evening. These gave him enough cover as he inched toward the walls that surrounded Svana's estate.

"Hold here for me." The barbarian motioned for Horse to wait for him as he pulled his cloak off. The wall was not as high as the one that protected the city but it required a fair amount of effort on his part to scale it.

The nearby buildings were close enough to the wall to provide useful handholds and traction and he finally grunted as he dragged himself over the top and dropped smoothly into a soft flowerbed waiting for him on the other side.

"Sorry," he whispered to the plants that had died to cushion his landing. Thankfully, most of the injuries sustained at the hands and flame tentacles of the demon were healed and allowed him to move comfortably and easily through the estate. He paused now and then to wait for guard patrols to pass and kept to the shadows to avoid notice by a handful of servants still working as he approached the main building.

One room in particular had his attention. The serving staff who hovered seemed to avoid it, which told him it was where the lady of the house was sleeping. It was something of a challenge to steer clear of the staff and rather than risk discovery, Skharr crept through the gardens again. This time, he scaled the side of the building to reach the low-hanging balcony outside the room.

It took considerable effort but he finally slid over the ledge and moved to the room, creeping on the tips of his toes.

Unfortunately, he wasn't quiet enough. A small gasp from inside gave him pause before a woman's voice stopped him.

"You should hope to Theros that I know who you are,"

Svana said curtly. "Because if I don't, I'll scream and my guards will be here in moments to cut your balls off and feed them to you."

"I would have knocked," Skharr replied in a hushed voice, "but there are too many who want me dead. I do hope in Theros' name that you know me, however."

"Skharr? Tell me that is you!"

He could see her slender frame clamber out of the massive bed and move to pull the sheer drapes aside for him to enter. She wore a thin, almost translucent silk nightgown with her golden hair contained in a thick braid.

"I will tell the guards to leave your balls intact," she said and grinned as he stepped inside. "I was told you wouldn't be in the city for a few more days."

He raised an eyebrow, which prompted a laugh from her.

"Are you surprised that I've tracked your movements?"

"A little."

She poured watered wine from a carafe into two goblets and handed him one. "Now, I know you didn't come all this way to provide me with the wedding night you robbed me of. How can I help you, my friend?"

"I need to speak to you. And ask for a favor, if you have one to grant me."

"You know I am the head of my house now, Skharr." She took another shallow sip. "What do you wish to speak to me about?"

"If you have tracked my movements as you say, I assume you know there is a price on my head that makes my life a little more…dangerous than I would like."

"I thought you enjoyed living a life of danger."

"Outside these walls and on my terms, where I can look my enemies in the eyes as I kill them. That is not possible inside the walls of the city. At least not as directly as I would hope. And I think the city guard will not be happy if they find me surrounded by a pile of bodies for the third time."

She nodded. "I knew there was coin offered for your death. Do you know who is trying to kill you?"

"According to certain sources, those in charge of the city's underworld dealings dislike my interference in their business in these parts. I suppose their continued failures only led them to put more effort into it. Perhaps having someone escape their grasp as I have so far would reflect poorly on their reputations."

"I see. I suppose you already have allies."

"Of course. You remember Sera Ferat?"

"The emperor's daughter. Yes. Well, I suppose she would be the emperor's sister now, wouldn't she?"

"Indeed. And her sister will join her efforts. It seems neither is happy that these underlords of the city were more than willing to kill Sera while I traveled with her. But they said more help was likely needed. These…cretins have a certain amount of power in the city and have lurked under it long enough to know how to avoid detection."

"If you need warriors, I am afraid I wouldn't be able to help you with many," Svana admitted. "But those I can spare are yours. I've had issues with some of the bastards myself since the death of my erstwhile husband, and I know there are others among the gentry who have suffered at the hands of the underworld and would be willing to help. I am sure they would be more than happy to improve their credibility with the sisters of the emperor."

Skharr noted that there was no commentary on how he was tied to the boy's legacy as well. Perhaps word hadn't reached Verenvan yet or the gentry simply refused to believe that kind of thing was possible.

It was a curiosity but of little importance and he focused on Svana as she continued.

"I'll see to it that they hear your proposal, at the least. And that they don't do something so stupid as try to turn you in themselves."

He nodded and ran his fingers through his beard. "That would be appreciated. I honestly didn't think there would be this level of cooperation."

"You could always pay me a gold coin for my efforts." She winked and refilled her goblet. "Where will you remain for the moment while there are still daggerhands waiting for you?"

"Honestly, I had hoped that I could find a quiet place on your land to remain while I dealt with the bastards. And a place for Horse as well. I doubt the assassins will think of him as a weakness in my defenses, but one of them might decide to use him to their advantage."

"I could always give your...Horse a place in my stables for the duration." Svana sat on her bed, pulled her sheets back with one hand, and casually removed the right strap of her nightgown with the other. "As for you, I suppose you wouldn't mind having a bed for the night? The charge is only a little physical effort. As you find yourself at the tail end of the journey, I'll be gentle."

"Not too gentle, I hope," he responded and smiled at her suggestion.

"Perhaps not, but I want to make sure you are too. I've heard tales that you can make it difficult for a woman to walk, although such tales are rife with inaccuracies that need correcting."

His gaze traced the gentle curves of her body as she undressed, illuminated only by the moonlight.

He pulled his shirt off, tossed it to the side, and caught her legs to drag her into a prone position on the bed. Her thighs parted around his hips, which elicited a pleased squeal from her.

"Allow me to prove their veracity," he murmured as she reached eagerly to undo his trousers.

Skharr had just finished a long journey, half of which he had undertaken on his own. His body was still recovering from a sound beating as well, even if he was mostly healed. Perhaps he should have taken his time and been gentler, but that wasn't who he was and he knew it.

Thankfully, he had managed to outlast her and had left Svana sleeping contentedly on the bed while he found a bath to cleanse himself and then joined her. She had, after their first frenetic coupling, allowed him to accompany her men and retrieve Horse, who happily clopped to the stable when he was told he would receive a good supply of apples for his patience. Thereafter, he had returned to her bed.

Having her sleeping soundly in the crook of his arm was the kind of thing a man could get used to, although he doubted he would be given the opportunity. Posh ladies of Verenvan's gentry could not be seen to openly cavort with barbarians, no matter what their affiliation.

When he noticed an old man in the corner of the room, he reached reflexively for the dagger he usually carried on his belt—when he wore one, of course—almost before he realized what he was doing.

"Another dream?" he asked and lay back on the bed.

"I thought that would be wise, yes." Theros smirked as he tilted his head and studied the woman in bed with him. "Do you have a woman in every city? And I suppose she asked you for this treatment?"

He shrugged. "She offered me her bed for the night in exchange for the kind of fucking that only a barbarian can provide."

"I see. And barbarian fucking is what the women want, it seems."

"She failed to offer any complaints after the third—no, fourth —time she tried to muffle her screams with the pillows."

"Four?"

"Aye," he answered and narrowed his eyes.

Theros raised his hands in a placating gesture. "I do not doubt you, Skharr. I'm merely impressed. But now to business. Your effort alongside Sera Ferat has been noted by myself and my brother. Of course, the fact that you follow me has left Janus a little bitter as his followers waited for you in the tunnels outside. Which does make it sweeter, I'll admit. You do fine work, Skharr."

"Thank you." The barbarian studied his visitor, who swept his gaze around the room again. "I don't suppose I could claim payment for my work in the form of a favor from you?"

"Which is?" The god raised an eyebrow. "Bringing yourself to full mast again?"

He chuckled. "Hardly. I'm a DeathEater, not dead. I'll die still able to salute womenfolk."

Theros waved him off. "If you say so. What is your request? Listening to it is the very least I can do, but depending on what you need, it might be the most as well."

"I assume a god of your talents was able to determine that I have a problem of a price on my head in this city that follows me wherever I go."

"Aye, a price put up by the local slumlords with more than enough rats hoping to collect."

"Any help offered in dealing with that problem would be appreciated," he stated and stroked Svana's hair idly as he spoke.

"So, you need warriors to dispose of those criminals who prey on the weak and helpless of the city?" Theros asked and folded his arms. "And to stop those very same bastards from killing you as well?"

"I could probably keep my head above the water, but there are others who could be caught by their poisoned arrows. Sera among them, of course. I wouldn't have that go unanswered."

"Of course not." The old man smirked. "You wouldn't be the Barbarian of Theros if you did."

"Can you help, then?"

"I can advise. That is mostly what us gods do, after all. As long as you are not fussy about where the help comes from, I know where to find what you need." Theros nodded. "I'll be off and you should get some rest. It is obvious that even a barbarian such as yourself is capable of running himself ragged."

"She proved a worthy challenge," he admitted. "But I am a DeathEater and rose to it."

By the time the last word slipped through his lips, he was talking to himself in a room empty except for himself and Svana.

Skharr leaned against the pillows, but it felt like he had barely touched them when he noticed two men in the room with him.

"Four times, you say?" an unfamiliar voice asked.

"So he says."

He narrowed his eyes and focused on the tall, powerful-looking man with flowing, jet-black hair who had joined Theros in the corner of the room. He looked every inch the warrior, and the barbarian recognized him immediately from the hundreds of statues and busts erected around the world by his followers.

"Janus, I take it?" he asked and continued to toy with Svana's hair.

It was one thing to call the god an ass generally but saying so to his face suddenly lost its appeal. He even considered showing a little deference, although he knew he would eventually regret it.

Still, he decided it was best to keep his insults to himself. Only a stupid and eventually dead DeathEater called Janus an ass to his face.

"I was telling him about your current situation," Theros explained. "And reminding him that he owes you a boon for the work you did for him."

"That was meant for my people," Janus protested and shook his head.

"And yet he killed the monster you needed dead," his brother reminded him. "Oh...did your folk not tell the truth? How unlike them!"

"Shut up, brother," the god snapped.

"He hasn't said a word to anyone as to who killed your magus lich," Theros continued. "And if your people will keep their word to you that they won't say anything about helping Skharr and Sera Ferat—the woman who helped to kill the monster—the assumption will be that your folk will be able to claim credit for its death."

Janus studied the barbarian carefully. "Do you swear it, barbarian?"

"All godsbedammed day," Skharr admitted. "And night too, if necessary."

"Droll. Very droll. Do you swear that you will not tell others what happened in that dungeon?"

"In exchange for your help to destroy the underlords of this city, I will," he agreed.

The god took a talisman from his belt and tossed it onto the bed. "Crush this when you have need of my support. You will have five hours before they leave."

Skharr picked the item up. A small clay coin with Janus' visage imprinted on it seemed appropriate for the situation.

"See to it that you don't crush it accidentally while fucking this one too hard. I doubt she would appreciate the audience." The god paused and tilted his head. "Then again, I would find it hilarious."

With that last word, he disappeared from the room.

"Asshole," the warrior muttered and placed the talisman with his clothes.

"I would wait a while longer before you air your feelings about him, DeathEater," Theros admonished him. "Watch out for him. He will do as he promised, as his honor is on the line. But should you crush it at the wrong time, he would only laugh at your misfortune."

He shook his head when the god disappeared from view like his brother had. The woman beside him moved against his arm.

"Skharr?" Svana whispered, looked around, and pressed her cheek against his bare chest. "Are you awake?"

"After a fashion," he admitted.

She smiled, ran her fingers across his chest, and moved them over his stomach and lower still. "Can you go again?"

The warrior leaned down to press a tender kiss to her forehead. "I am a DeathEater. I could go into the morning until you beg for a respite."

"I see." She grinned, placed a light kiss on his stomach, and shifted lazily down his body. "Prove it."

CHAPTER TWENTY-THREE

Despite the lack of sleep, Skharr enjoyed the time he had to wait until Sera's merchant caravan returned to Verenvan. It was surprisingly rather restful.

Word came to Svana the moment they arrived and she sent for both the Ferat sisters to join her for an afternoon meal. She made no mention that Skharr would attend as well.

They would discover this once they arrived.

Both women knew how to be proper ladies. They arrived with a retinue and sent word in advance of their arrival. This allowed the serving staff to be ready to greet them with refreshing drinks.

When they arrived, he noticed Micah nudge her sister in the ribs with her elbow as Svana walked forward to greet them.

"Barbarian legs," Micah said with a firm nod. "I would say someone has been milking the barbarian as much as she could."

"She isn't you," Sera retorted sharply.

Skharr tilted his head when he noticed that the woman was indeed moving a little gingerly. Perhaps he had gone a little harder than he needed to but she had asked for it—and almost begged, he reminded himself.

Once the traditional greetings were over—with Skharr left in the corner without so much as a look cast at him—their hostess motioned for the staff to move away and give them privacy before she motioned for the barbarian to join them.

"Tongues have wagged," Micah said as she sipped a drink cold enough that beads of water shimmered on her crystal glass. "They say you were bedding a barbarian and even housing him in your quarters, no less. I'm glad to see that they are true."

Svana smirked and showed no sign of shame. "I made the mistake of challenging a DeathEater, but it was the most delicious loss. And it will no doubt intimidate the suitors who have pestered me of late."

Skharr realized that he should have known there were other political motives behind what she did. Then again, he wouldn't complain about it either way.

"I've spoken to a handful of the other lords and ladies, including a few who have dealt with Skharr before," the noblewoman told them. "Many are willing to help in this endeavor but no one wants a protracted war on the streets of Verenvan. We would need to rid ourselves of all the godsbedammed bastards in a single fell swoop."

"The only chance of that would be to organize a meeting," Micah stated. "I would be able to arrange that but there would have to be something to draw them there—something that would bring all of them together."

"You can tell them that I seek some kind of reconciliation," Skharr suggested and leaned forward. "That I feel this has gone on long enough and we need to discuss our differences."

"You—that is mad." Sera shook her head. "They'll arrive with a small army and try to kill you."

"Aye, and we can have a small army waiting for them," Micah countered.

"Both are true," Skharr interjected. "But this will be tantalizing enough to draw them in."

"They cannot be outside the building," Micah continued. "Corralling them and attacking when they are inside will be for the best, but you'll need to be there. That means you will be comparatively alone until help arrives."

"I know. I'll be able to keep myself alive."

Sera shook her head. "I don't like it. They'll swarm you and kill you instantly."

"I can live with that," Micah responded.

"I can't!" her sister snapped.

"I agree with Sera." Svana shook her head. "There must be a better way."

"There isn't and you know it," Skharr insisted. "I'll be able to survive. I've dealt with worse before."

"I like it." Micah nodded and looked at the others. "And he is right. If we want this finished quickly, they'll need something significant to draw them in. Skharr offering himself like this would be precisely that."

"So, we are agreed," Skharr said.

"No, we're not!" Sera retorted.

"All right. Should we discuss this at great length and then decide that this is our finest option?" he asked. "I'm perfectly content to continue with this discussion."

He looked at the three women, waiting and hoping that they would be able to come up with a better option.

Not that he expected it. Ever since his meeting with Janus and Theros, he had considered what they could do to finish it. Killing them one at a time was an option, but the moment one died, all the others would go to ground.

It was best to get them all together, and it could be guaranteed if he offered himself as bait. Let them believe he was a dumb barbarian who thought they wouldn't fuck him over.

And he had a secret weapon besides, one he doubted any of them would anticipate.

"Fine," Sera whispered. "As long as Micah and I can be waiting to help him. We can find a way to avoid being noticed until the right moment."

"I can agree with that," Skharr replied and glanced at the other two, who nodded. "Excellent."

"I'll make it known that you are looking to negotiate," Micah said and pushed from her seat.

CHAPTER TWENTY-FOUR

Sera was still glaring at him when they settled in to wait for the Council to arrive. The die had been cast and they now had to deal with the consequences of their choice.

"Say what you have on your mind," Skharr said and inspected his sword carefully. "You look like you're about to explode."

"I still think this is a terrible idea," she said in a low tone. "One that will get both of us killed."

"You did volunteer to be in the thick of it with me," he countered and sheathed his weapon again.

"Yes, and I was stupid to do so. I have no idea why I continue to make idiotic decisions to get you out of trouble."

"Perhaps it's something in the water."

"How are you so calm?" she asked. "If I were the bait in a trap or the worm on a fisherman's hook, I would lose my mind... unless I had a plan of some kind. You have a plan."

The barbarian smirked. "It took you long enough."

"Why did you not share it before?"

"I am not entirely sure I can trust your sister with the information." He took the clay talisman from his pocket. "Janus gave me this and promised that when I needed his aid, I should crush it and the aid would come."

Sera inspected it closely. "That ass?"

"Aye. But I am assured that his honor depends on helping me when I need it."

"And you trust in the honor of that ass?"

He shrugged. "Yes, oddly enough."

She laughed and shook her head but before she could say anything, Micah entered the room dressed in dark brown and black clothes that helped her almost fade into the background when she was in the shadows.

"They are on the way," she stated and checked the dagger that she carried on her belt. "All five of them are coming but they are escorted by a small army and they are insistent that Skharr turn over any and all weapons he carries on his person. I assume they think that as long as he is armed, he has a chance to kill the four or five dozen fighters they are bringing with them."

"Shit." Sera hissed a sharp breath and shook her head.

"It will work out," Skharr insisted and stood. "You'll arrive as one of them, yes?"

Micah nodded. "How did you know?"

"It wasn't difficult to deduce. You are a member of this Council."

She smirked. "You're not quite the idiot you appear, DeathEater. Now, Sera, hide yourself. They should arrive at any minute."

Sera paused and patted Skharr on the shoulder. "Good luck."

"I don't need luck. I have my sword."

"You won't when they relieve you of it."

"Then I'll have my fists."

She rolled her eyes. Skharr could hear the sound of hooves clattering outside the building and when he looked back to where she had stood, she was gone. She'd disappeared into whatever cubby she'd found to hide herself in until the time was right.

He drew a deep breath to calm the hammering in his chest as the sound of dozens of feet approached the courtyard he'd positioned himself in.

The truth was, he had his doubts about whether Janus would do as he'd said he would. Killing Skharr and silencing him forever would be as effective as an oath of silence.

Micah had not lied, however, and the courtyard began to fill with dozens of fighters, all armed and lightly armored with their weapons at the ready and pointed at him.

One approached him quickly, and the barbarian raised his arms to allow the man to draw the sword, dagger, and ax he carried on his belt.

It was clear that none of them were comfortable, even with him completely unarmed.

A few moments later, the group entered through the same doors. A tall man with a large belly was first and acted as though he was the leader of the group. He was followed quickly by a smaller, leaner character with thinning hair and a crooked nose that made him look like a mouse.

Micah arrived after that and her eyes betrayed no sign that she and Skharr had shared a meal before.

Another woman followed shortly after and looked like she could have been Micah's sister. She was a little shorter, though, and her face had a few scars and a little more muscle was visible in her arms and shoulders. Without a doubt, she was a fighter.

A dwarf brought up the rear, his thick brown beard crisscrossed with streaks of gray.

They all stood in front of Skharr as the man who had disarmed him presented the weapons he'd taken from the barbarian.

The heavyset one was more interested in the sword. He picked it up and hefted it carefully before he handed it back to his man.

"You are a man of honor then, barbarian," the stout one said loudly enough to fill the whole courtyard. "You arrived alone and allowed yourself to be disarmed."

"Yes," he responded softly. His amulet practically vibrated off of his chest.

"Unfortunately, we are not similarly honor...ful? Honorous?"

The warrior drew a deep breath. He had seen such displays before and this was not even a particularly good one.

"The point is that we could do what we spoke of and find a way to strike a deal. But that would make us appear weak and we cannot allow that."

Skharr tried to pretend shock when the men in the courtyard drew their weapons. He squeezed the talisman in his hand until it shattered and one of the sharp edges nicked his hand to draw blood.

"Instead, we will do what we planned to do all along and kill you," the man continued and gestured for the men to attack. "You were even honorable enough to surrender your weapons. They would have enabled you to kill a few of our men before they killed you. Go on, then." He gestured to the guards.

"My men," the woman who stood to his left corrected and shook her head. That established her as the muscle provider of the group.

For a moment, Skharr felt nothing. Nothing had changed. The talisman was broken without any result. Janus had made it sufficiently vague that if he didn't think he could help, he would simply weasel out of it. What exactly would the help be?

Suddenly, war horns blared around them and a smile settled on the barbarian's face as he advanced on the men closest to him. The noise made most of the guards cover their ears and look around to discover where it was coming from. He disarmed the first of them when he yanked his sword away and thrust it hard into the fighter's chest.

Sera barreled out of where she had been hiding, rolled over her shoulder, and deftly beheaded one of the men before she slashed the throat of another in two clean swings. From all sides, new forces began to arrive.

These weren't those sent by the nobles or assembled by Micah and Sera but men in full plate who bore the weapons of knights and men at arms and were ready to attack.

Skharr could have sworn they weren't there a moment before but they now stood near the Council fighters.

This was the kind of help that Janus had provided, then. The barbarian nodded and shifted his gaze to the group they were there to kill.

The fat one looked as if he might snatch the sword but thought better of it, turned, and motioned for the rest to join him.

With quick, smooth steps, Skharr swept his blade out of the other man's hand. Sera carved into a handful of the fighters who stood nearby. Her attack was eclipsed by the new arrivals who cleaved a hole through the group that suddenly had more on their minds than killing a barbarian.

Micah was nowhere to be seen, but the two members of the council who hadn't managed to escape yet were the focus of his attention.

"I will enjoy this, you slime-sucking fucking gutter-spawn. It's time that hard cock you get when you think of your godsbedammed stolen power fucks you in the ass."

He rushed closer, swung his sword over his head, and arced it in the way Sera had taught him. The blow severed one man's head and the blade caught on his spine, which slowed the stroke slightly.

The mousy councilman was dead, which left only the dwarf, who decided not to run. He yanked a short sword from his waist, shouted a battle-cry that wasn't audible over the combat all around him, and rushed forward.

The council member was clearly not a fighter, at least not regularly, and Skharr sidestepped the charge easily, parried the sword with his blade, and quickly reversed the strike to cut through the dwarf's thin clothes and slice his belly. The council member fell to his knees.

He came in behind the wounded dwarf and stabbed his sword smoothly through his back and drew it out quickly.

The other two were gone.

"Where is Micah?" Skharr shouted at Sera as she used the butt of her sword to crush the skull of an attacker before she stabbed him in the chest.

"I didn't see her go!" she called and swung her weapon into a ready position.

There wasn't very much left for them to do. The newcomers outnumbered the enemy and were far the superior fighters as well.

But none of it mattered if they didn't kill all four members of the Council.

Otan looked over his shoulder, a dagger still in his hand.

If the truth be told, he doubted he would have been able to do much with it. He was not a violent man—not if it meant he would be involved in it himself.

But he still felt more comfortable if he had a weapon.

"How did so many arrive so quickly?" Fakos asked and looked around the room they had sealed themselves in.

"Your men were supposed to have swept the building before-hand," he snapped and shook his dagger at her. "They didn't do their job."

"They did it perfectly," she retorted, flicked her saber, and easily knocked Skharr's dagger from the fat man's hand. "You were supposed to make sure he arrived without any help. They simply…appeared out of thin air."

"That's impossible," Otan muttered and shook his head. "No magic can mask that many men. No, you must have fucked up and now, everything is lost."

Not everything, of course. He had come back from disasters before. Never quite this disastrous, of course, but they would have to address that later.

"Fakos?"

He turned and expected the woman to at least continue to insist that her men had done their work when they had not.

Fakos clutched her throat and blood seeped between her fingers as she sagged onto her knees and revealed a figure clad in black who stood behind her.

"Who…who are you?"

He gaped when the figure drew her mask up and he recognized a very familiar face even in the darkness of the room.

"Micah?" he whispered. "You…you betrayed us?"

"This coming from the man who turned down an offer from the barbarian and decided to betray him instead?" She cleaned her dagger and picked up the one Fakos had knocked to the floor.

"We can find a way out of this," Otan whispered as she advanced on him. "You— They are all dead, and…you can take over all of their branches of the council but you will need help to administer it all. I can help you!"

She inclined her head and regarded him impassively. "You are right. But there are many out there who I can trust to administer the work and if I kill you, I'll have yours as well. This is the part you don't understand."

"You don't have to kill me," he whispered as she pressed the barbarian's dagger to his throat.

"But here is the issue, old man," she whispered and dragged the blade over his skin. It cut deep and he gurgled in pain and protest. "You were dead the moment you agreed to kill my sister. You merely didn't know it yet."

He fell and the blood seeped into his lungs and made him cough violently, which only increased the pain. Soon, however, everything was numb and dark and the pain slipped away.

CHAPTER TWENTY-FIVE

"And they disposed of the bodies." Micah shook her head. "They killed them all and made it look as though there was no attack at all. Where the fuck did he pull that piece of magic from? Who does he work with?"

Svana shrugged. "I do remember that you were more than willing to gut him in the past. Perhaps he has no intention of revealing all his secrets to you in case you decide to try again."

Micah smirked and her gaze slid over her guests as she sipped from her silver chalice. "Fair enough. But if you think my sister would allow me to kill him, you are crazier than she is."

"She is rather crazy."

The new leader of the underworld smiled around a mouthful of sweet pastry.

"Does that mean we need to call you the Empress of the Underworld?" Svana asked and tossed a grape into her mouth. "I admit that I like how it sounds."

"I do not." Micah shook her head with a laugh. "It's far too gauche. I chose to accept the title of Queen of the Undercouncil. After Skharr put his sword to the throat of all the survivors who refused to bend the knee," she added.

"With the rest of them dead, you'll need to do a fair amount of consolidating, I imagine."

"Not as much as you might think. Even among criminals, peace is known to be more profitable than war. A few fights have broken out but aside from that, most of the people are content to allow a new, more profitable order to arise. But with that said, I do need...ahem, bodies to join me in my endeavors. Folk I can trust and I think you are the trustworthy type, my lady."

"Me?" Svana asked and leaned closer. "I am not a criminal."

"Neither am I," Micah replied. "I am a...merchant."

"A merchant of death," the noblewoman countered smoothly. "Do not misunderstand me. I am impressed by what you are capable of but do not try to coat the truth with honey."

"No honey. I am an assassin by trade, a merchant of information, and a facilitator of illicit activities in this city. But if I happened to be interested in changing all that?"

"Why would you want that?" Svana tilted her head and took a slow sip of the honeyed wine in her goblet. "Haven't you gained all you could ever want? You are more powerful in a practical sense than the whole of the gentry in the city, except perhaps the count. The only danger lies in flaunting that power a little too much."

"Oh, but we could." Micah tugged a lock of hair that had slipped out in front of her face. "You, me, and the other gentry who were involved in this fight could find a way to make sure nothing detrimental happens in this city. We could even accept a tithe for our leadership. It would see the business here grow to heights never seen before and make Verenvan a capital of industry in the empire."

"That...is ambitious," the noblewoman admitted and a gleam of greed slid into her eyes. "Although fraught with danger."

"Danger has a way of making me feel alive," she replied.

"And what drives you to this?"

"The expectation that I could be great is the kind of thing to make a woman think hard about her prospects."

Svana tilted her head as her thoughts began to sift through the possibilities. "And Skharr?"

"I would never have thought a barbarian would reveal...me to me," Micah admitted.

"He does have his ways."

"Yes?" She leaned forward. "Do tell."

"Not too many apples!" Skharr admonished the stable hands as they led the stallion to the Mermaid's stable. "I don't want him getting too fat."

Horse snorted roughly and shook his head as he followed the boys willingly. The warrior doubted that they would listen to a word he said and Horse had an ability to persuade folk to do his bidding, even if they didn't understand him.

Especially if they didn't understand him.

When he stepped into the common room, he realized that more than a few of the patrons turned to look at him like he was something out of a bard's song.

A few of them immediately stood and left the coin they owed at the counter for the innkeeper before they hurried past the barbarian.

He decided not to ask. In all honesty, he was in the mood for a little peace and quiet after the days he'd had.

The innkeeper waved him closer and was already pouring a mug of stout for him.

"It is a pleasure to see you again, Skharr," the burly man grunted, placed the mug in front of him, and wiped the countertop with a clean rag. "Although I must say your reputation for roughing the ruffians up has brought me an enjoyable respite from their antics, even when you are not here."

"I suppose you will no longer need my services in these parts," he replied and sipped the cool, thick beer.

"Well, that group had begun to speak of you in disparaging terms before you stepped in. I think seeing you arrive might have caused them to relieve themselves in their trousers if you take my meaning. How long are you back for?"

"Only the gods know," he told him. "And even they don't know everything from my experience."

"Ah, speaking of which, I received a letter in your name. I was told to keep it until you returned but report to the sender if you did not return in a few months."

"Let's see it."

The man nodded, moved quickly into the back office, and returned with slightly flushed cheeks. "Do you want me to tell you its contents?"

"I can do that well enough," Skharr replied and took the letter from the man's hands.

"I...didn't know you could read."

Perhaps he had gone a little too far with his dumb barbarian act. The wrong folk now started to believe it. He only shook his head as he peeled the wax seal from the letter.

He inspected the contents and a broad smile crossed his face.

"I'll need three mugs of your finest ale," he said with a chuckle.

"Three?"

"Two for me and one for you."

The innkeeper laughed and immediately set to work. "It is good news, I take it?"

"The best. Master AnvilForged has finished a commission for me. I had begun to believe this day would never come."

Two mugs were placed on the counter and one more was filled. "He is the finest in Verenvan. Let us drink to fighting, food, and fucking!"

Skharr grinned and tapped his mug against the innkeeper's. "Not necessarily in that order!"

*** I feel obligated to warn you that I was in a particularly late-night commercial mental state when writing the notes below. YOU HAVE BEEN *WARNED!* ***

Thank you for not only reading this story about Skharr, but to the back and these notes as well!

I am writing these notes about six weeks after Book 04 - GodKiller came out and my mind is in the middle of Book 06, The Unrepentant.

I feel like I should jump up and down yelling into the camera for a late-night commercial. "Go! Go preorder Skharr Book six The Unrepentant right now! Don't make Horse nag you in the morning. You won't sleep right until you have Skharr DeathEater pre-ordered CLICK NOW CLICK NOWCLICKKKKKKNOOOWWWWWW!"

Ok, back to your regularly scheduled author notes. I am presently writing these notes for Book 05, The Barbarian of Theros.

The one you just finished.

Obviously.

Don't let it be said I have no empathy for those who have already forgotten the title.

I am all about empathy. Sort of. Well, not too much for

Janus...That guy is an ass. Except when he isn't. Perhaps Theros has a slander campaign against him? Even if he does... Janus is still an ass.

Stop me if you have heard this: a Dwarf, a Barbarian, and Horse go into a bar... Well, I hope your story isn't the same one as mine, because I'm talking about Skharr DeathEater... The Unrepentant!

(You should totally go pre-order it... Wait... DON'T pre-order it (is that how you do reverse psychology? I suck at it.))

Much fun aside, I can tell you a few secrets on our future plans. We have at least an additional eight (8) stories coming out in the future in Skharr's Universe.

The first two (2) are books are Skharr's book six (GO GO GO buy now!) and Book seven for Skharr titled *The Barbarian Princess*.

I'm not saying who *that* is...but you should TOTALLY go read *GodKiller* if you have not, and the hint is in that book.

It's not Skharr I promise.

Then, we have three (3) stories publishing about a wicked fighter called Axe Wed and will be arriving from the amazing talent of Aaron D. Schneider. Aaron was last seen writing an amazing alt-history World War I / Steampunk / Dark Fantasy trilogy – *World's First Wizard* that one reviewer said "Magical fantasy and re-imagined history come together in a wonderfully suspenseful adventure" and another "The setting of Witchmarked isn't one that I would normally take to (being more of a high fantasy guy myself), but I was pulled in from the get-go."

Now, Aaron has been coaxed to play in my sword & sorcery universe for three books, and I'm loving where Axe Wed is heading in his stories.

There is much ass-kicking and a bit of too much drinking. Needless to say, she has problems to overcome. Now, if I could just get him to drop me more of the story faster,

I'd *FREAKING* appreciate it.

Just saying out loud in case Aaron reads this.

Finally, LMBPN will be providing a new trilogy about a certain Paladin with an attitude.

Then, I highly suspect (and let me know in the reviews if you are game!) we will see a few more Skharr stories.

Because I'm not done with Horse yet.

Oh, and Skharr.

#UNREAL

The video game engine, not the saying "That is *SO* unreal!"

We are just playing at this time, but we have Skharr DeathEater as a rigged and rolling character in Unreal Engine to test our ability to create a storyboard. A storyboard that might accidentally look good enough to release as a graphic novel.

Cause we are cool like that. Or stupid. I guess we might be stupidly cool.

I think I might need to stop typing now. I've gone off the deep end with these notes.

You have a FANTASTIC week/weekend, and I hope to see you again at the end of book six... Skharr DeathEater – The Unrepentant!

Ad Aeternitatem,

Michael Anderle

CONNECT WITH THE AUTHOR

Connect with Michael Anderle

Website: http://lmbpn.com

Email List: http://lmbpn.com/email/

Social Media:

https://www.facebook.com/LMBPNPublishing

https://twitter.com/MichaelAnderle

https://www.instagram.com/lmbpn_publishing/

https://www.bookbub.com/authors/michael-anderle

BOOKS BY MICHAEL ANDERLE

Sign up for the LMBPN email list to be notified of new releases and special deals!

https://lmbpn.com/email/

For a complete list of books by Michael Anderle, please visit:

www.lmbpn.com/ma-books/